NO ONE CAN KNOW

Also available by Lucy Kerr

Time of Death

NO ONE CAN KNOW

A STILLWATER GENERAL MYSTERY

Lucy Kerr

CROOKED
LANE

NEW YORK

Published in the United States by Crooked Lane Books, an imprint of The Quick Brown Fox & Company LLC.

Crooked Lane Books and its logo are trademarks of The Quick Brown Fox & Company LLC.

Library of Congress Catalog-in-Publication data available upon request.

ISBN (hardcover): 978-1-68331-462-2
ISBN (ePub): 978-1-68331-463-9
ISBN (ePDF): 978-1-68331-464-6

Cover design by Melanie Sun
Book design by Jennifer Canzone

Printed in the United States.

www.crookedlanebooks.com

Crooked Lane Books
34 West 27th St., 10th Floor
New York, NY 10001

First Edition: February 2018

10 9 8 7 6 5 4 3 2 1

To Danny,
who makes everything better and
brighter, even on the darkest days.
And to my kids,
who make me the proudest
mama bear around.

ONE

Tuesday nights in an emergency room are notoriously slow. I don't know what strange combination of atmosphere, astrology, and human nature results in Tuesday graveyard shifts as quiet as their namesake, but it's held true in every ER I've ever worked. Almost nothing happens on a Tuesday night.

Almost.

But when it does, it's hard to miss.

Part of the reason an ER can swing into action so quickly is because when we're not saving someone's life, we're preparing to. We're double-checking inventory and restocking supplies, making sure that the moment the ambulance calls with an ETA and patient description, we're ready to work.

Which is how I had ended up this Tuesday night checking the cabinets in the trauma bays, counting gauze pads and suture kits and iodine wipes. At my old hospital in Chicago, this would've been a lengthy process—six trauma bays in near-constant use tended to go through a lot of gauze. Here at Stillwater General, five hours from Chicago on the banks of the Illinois River, it was fifteen minutes' work. I was more likely to find a layer of dust than an empty cabinet.

Tuesdays, I tell you.

Inventory complete, I headed back to the nurses' station, ears straining to pick up anything unusual. Aside from the seallike barks of the croupy toddler in Exam Two, all I could hear was the storm raging outside our doors. The howling winds and relentless sheets of rain were keeping all but the most critical cases home, at least until the weather cleared.

"I've had more fun watching Jell-O set." I threw myself into one of the chairs behind the nurses' station. Then I grinned. "Bet you we'll be swamped ten minutes after the rain stops."

"More like five," said Esme Vargas, our deceptively sweet-looking charge nurse. "And that's a sucker's bet."

Esme was no sucker. With her dimpled cheeks and enormous brown eyes, she'd initially reminded me of some sort of woodland creature—friendly, soft, and liable to be eaten by a predator. After our first shift together, I'd realized just how deceiving appearances could be. Esme had expertly handled a gruesome compound fracture, a stroke, and an overdose, all within minutes of each other and without losing her composure. She was efficient but not cold, cheerful but not a pushover, and those doe-like eyes missed absolutely nothing. *We make a good team*, she'd told me that night, and I'd agreed. If I'd been planning to stay in Stillwater permanently, she might have made a good friend too.

But my visit here was temporary; in a few months, I'd be back at Chicago Memorial, where a slow shift meant enough time to wolf down a protein bar for dinner while I entered a chart. On a night like this one, the spacious, tidy Stillwater ER made Chicago Memorial feel light-years away, not miles.

Esme finished her charting and swiveled to face me. "You miss it, don't you? Your old hospital?"

"Only when we're slow." Even then, I wasn't sure if I missed my old life or the adrenaline that had accompanied it. "I'm not great at sitting still."

"Be careful what you wish for, Frankie," she said dryly. "The storm will blow through soon enough, and once it does, we won't sit down until—"

She broke off at the sound of raised voices. Actually, only one *raised* voice, countered by the clear, patient reply of the admitting clerk.

The man's shouts managed to sound both agonized and petulant, a sign that didn't bode well for whoever took the case.

Esme and I exchanged glances.

"Better than Jell-O," she reminded me, the corners of her mouth twitching.

I heaved a sigh and pushed up off the counter. "Exam Three," I called to Alejandro, our unit clerk, and went out to greet my patient.

The man stood near the admitting desk, dripping a pinkish mixture of blood and rain on the freshly mopped linoleum. His nose was clearly broken, which accounted for the whine, and he clutched one shoulder with his opposite hand, the swelling evident even beneath his drenched and ratty-looking flannel shirt. "Lemme see a doctor," he demanded. "That sign says you gotta treat me, so hurry up and do it."

"We will," said Eileen, the admitting clerk. Solid and implacable as a mountain, with her cat's-eye glasses and helmet of iron-gray curls, Eileen was not cowed by mere mortals, whether they were patients or doctors. "Once we get your information, Nurse Stapleton will take you in back and get started."

The man's gaze flicked toward me, then back at Eileen. I folded my arms and waited, as if I had all the time in the world—which I did, at the moment. If this guy had come in by ambulance, the entire ER staff would have leaped into action. But anyone who could walk in, stand at the counter, and find the energy to yell at Eileen probably wasn't in immediate danger of dying.

"Sir, your name would be an excellent start," Eileen prompted.

He cursed, complained, and looked around the waiting room as if someone might provide it for him. Eileen merely blinked and kept her hands, with their shocking-pink manicure, on the keyboard.

"John," he said eventually, grimacing. "Mueller."

Eileen's smile became a little more fixed, but she coaxed him through the rest of the intake process and then gave me a nod, indicating he was clear to take back into the exam rooms.

"Do you need a wheelchair, Mr. Mueller?" I asked.

He ignored me, muttering under his breath and checking his phone.

"Mr. Mueller?" His head snapped up, and I gestured to the wheelchair. "Would you like to get in?"

"Nah." He followed me through the security doors, his movements stiff and obviously painful. When we reached the exam room, he sank onto the bed with a groan.

"You look pretty banged up," I said, fastening a plastic hospital bracelet around his trembling wrist. Besides the shoulder and the nose, a gash on his temple was still oozing blood, the laceration continuing beneath his unkempt, rain-soaked hair. "Can you tell me what happened?"

He swallowed, fidgeting so that the paper beneath him crinkled. "Hit a deer. Out in the country."

"I see." I began taking his vitals, charting his information and getting a health history. All the standard questions, but his answers ranged from sullen to evasive. John Mueller was twenty-three, with a scraggly brown beard more unkempt than fashionable. He had yet to lose his baby fat, and his jean-clad leg jounced and jittered throughout the interview.

Patients lie for all sorts of reasons. They tell me they don't drink when their breath says their liver is probably pickled. They shave years off their age and pounds off their weight. They "accidentally" fall down the stairs or "forget" how many pills they've taken. Shame, vanity, fear, pride, malice—the reasons are as varied as the lies. Over time, you learn to gauge which lies are harmless and which are dangerous, when to call a patient on it and when to let it slide.

You hone your instincts, the same way a rock climber hones their center of gravity, or you don't last long.

John Mueller, if that was really his name, was a liar. I could practically smell it on him, sour and hot like an infection. He been lying from the moment he'd stepped up to the desk. As far as I could tell, the only things he hadn't lied about were the accident—the pattern of bruising across his torso confirmed injuries from a seat belt—and his pain, which had to be considerable.

I finished the initial exam and ducked outside. Esme and Alejandro, arguing about Internet dating etiquette, broke off when they saw me.

"Three's got a dislocated shoulder," I said. "Can you let Costello know—"

"Let me know what?"

I turned. Paul Costello, the doctor who'd once proclaimed his hands God's gift to emergency medicine, stood a few feet away, scribbling on a clipboard.

"Patient in Three claims he was in a single-car MVA; no loss of consciousness or signs of concussion. Three-inch laceration on the left temple, a broken nose, and an anterior dislocation of the left shoulder."

"Claims?" Costello's eyebrows lifted.

"The injuries are consistent, but the rest of his story . . ." I shrugged. "Something's off about him."

"Off how?" demanded Costello. When I didn't answer, he rolled his eyes. "Another one of your gut feelings, Stapleton? Spare us the wisdom of your large intestine."

I didn't point out that my gut feeling had caught a murderer in this hospital a few weeks ago. Costello wasn't exactly my biggest fan. The first time we met, I'd just treated an ER patient despite the fact that I wasn't actually employed here, then publicly questioned Costello's diagnosis. When the patient was found dead, we'd each blamed the other, but it had turned out to be murder, not medical error. Whatever truce we'd called when I caught the killer had evaporated a day later, when the hospital president had hired me without Costello's input.

Rumor had it that the language he'd used upon hearing the news had made a seasoned paramedic blush.

Tonight was our first night working together since the announcement, and he'd alternated between ignoring me and criticizing my every move. Now he shoved the clipboard at

Esme and beckoned to me. "If it's all the same to you, Staple-ton, I'll stick with practicing real medicine, not voodoo. Grab fifteen hundred mil of methocarbamol and meet me in there."

He strode off toward Exam Three without another glance. Costello wasn't a big man—a head taller than me, with the compact build of a wrestler—but he never slowed down.

He never let up either.

Costello was accustomed to nurses obeying his every command; I was accustomed to doctors who respected my opinion. Our rocky start didn't look to be growing smoother any time soon.

When I opened the door to Exam Three, Costello's exam was already under way, judging from the way Mueller was yowling in pain and pleading for meds.

"You have a dislocated shoulder," Costello said as I handed Mueller the pills and a cup of water. "We need to get an X-ray, then reset your arm bone within the socket of your shoulder, and the sooner the better. How long ago was the accident?"

"I dunno." He yelped as Costello pressed lightly against his shoulder blade. "Half an hour or so. Why do you care?"

"Because," Costello said, "after about an hour, this gets much worse for you."

"Can't you pop it back in? They do it on TV all the time."

Costello waved a hand, the gesture encompassing the room. "Do you see a camera crew? This is a hospital, not a sound stage."

"I don't want an X-ray," Mueller said, chin jutting out. "Just fix my damn shoulder."

"If you've broken a bone," I said, ignoring Costello's glare, "performing the reduction could make your shoul-der worse. It could tear up your muscles or cause permanent nerve damage. Taking an X-ray will make sure we're not doing more harm than good."

His fingers twitched. No doubt the hand was already numb as bones pressed on nerves they weren't meant to.

"Just shove it back in and give me another pill," Mueller demanded through clenched and crooked teeth. He began to rock back and forth, agitation increasing. "I don't have time for this."

"And I don't do my job halfway." Costello turned to me. "X-ray for the shoulder, MRI for internal bleeding and concussion. We'll do the reduction as soon as he's out."

"Do it now," Mueller snarled. "I don't need the other crap."

Patients have every right to refuse treatment, and plenty do. But that doesn't mean we have to like it.

Costello clearly didn't, which was no surprise. Bad enough when a nurse questioned one of his orders—to have a patient do so was beyond insulting. But while arrogance was first among Costello's many flaws, indecision was not. He studied Mueller, brows drawn together in annoyance, square-tipped fingers tapping lightly on his watch. Three taps—one, two, three—and he'd made up his mind.

"Mr. Mueller, this note states we recommended an X-ray, and against my advice you are insisting on a closed reduction despite the risks we've outlined." Costello charted the note himself, signing off on it and shaking his head in disgust.

"Ready?" he asked as we got into position: me holding Mueller by the wrist, his left arm extended while my other hand braced against the front of his shoulder. Costello stood at his back, ready to manipulate the bones back into place.

"Stay still," he barked. Mueller was still agitated, leg jouncing, eyes darting around the room, body tensed for flight despite the muscle relaxant working its way through his system. Costello warned, "This is probably going to hurt."

He was right.

The good news was that an instant after Mueller's humerus bone had clunked back into place, the pain eased. Mueller took a long, ragged breath while Costello stripped off his gloves and left, saying, "Clean him up; set the nose. Get an ice pack for the shoulder. I'll come back later for the sutures."

I eased Mueller back onto the bed and went in search of an ice pack.

"I'm telling you, there's something really off about that guy," I said to Esme. We kept a freezer full of reusable cold packs beneath the counter at the nurses' station, and I tugged the door open.

"I think Costello agrees," she said, tipping her head toward the staff lounge. "You want someone to back you up in there? I can get one of the orderlies."

"He's not threatening me," I said. "He's just . . ."

". . . off," Esme finished. She understood. Every once in a while, a patient gives off a bad vibe. It's never specific, just a feeling: a shark below the waterline, a watcher in the shadows, a monster under the bed. An instinct too nebulous to act on, too insistent to ignore. No matter how dismissive Costello might be, every nurse I've worked with knew that feeling. None had ever ignored it twice. Esme frowned. "What do you want to do?"

It wasn't the lying or the agitation. Those were common. Obvious. Those were the signs even Costello noticed. I stared at the shelf full of cold packs, letting my gaze go soft and unfocused, my thoughts following suit. Whatever was bothering me about John Mueller would disappear if I looked too hard, so I tried not to look at all.

He'd been honest about his accident and his pain—the only two things he couldn't conceal. He'd barely had enough time for the meds to kick in before we'd maneuvered his arm back into place.

There. A flash of understanding like a small silvery fish in the murky waters of my brain.

Who demands drugs and then doesn't wait for them to work? Someone desperate. And in my experience, desperate people were either dangerous or in danger—or both.

"Let's call—"

Let's call security, I was about to say, but the radio squawked and crackled to life before I could finish.

"Stillwater Gen, this is Riverside Ambulance number seven five two. We are en route to your facility with a female, approximately midthirties, visible late-term pregnancy. She's the restrained driver of a vehicle involved in an MVA, unknown speed, unknown cause. Significant driver's side damage, intrusion into driver's side compartment. Patient has visible head injury and cannot maintain consciousness . . ."

I didn't wait to hear more. "Trauma One," Esme called, writing down more information while I sprinted toward the room. Behind me, I could hear Alejandro, the unit clerk, calling in the trauma team and paging to various departments. Motor vehicle accidents, or MVAs, could range from a simple fender bender to major crashes, and with a pregnant victim, we'd need all hands on deck.

I took a quick detour, poking my head into the staff lounge. "We've got another MVA incoming. Single victim, late-term pregnancy, Trauma One."

Costello, alerted by the pages sounding overhead, was already on his feet. He followed me out, peppering me with questions.

"Trauma team is on its way in," I said as we entered. Trauma rooms aren't like the usual ER exam cubes. They're designed to have every piece of equipment you might need within arm's reach, from tongue depressors to tracheotomy kits, and they've got plenty of space, because traumas tend to be crowded affairs. "The storm's going to slow them down."

"Who's on OB?" he asked as he scrubbed in.

I didn't look up from the IV bags I was hanging, two liters of saline ready to go in the minute our patient was on the table. "Garima. Alejandro paged her and called in Dr. Solano for the consult."

Even though emergency room staff is trained to work on any patient who comes through our doors, obstetrics and neonatology is a highly specialized field. We all felt better calling in an expert, and there was nobody I'd rather have on the job than Garima Karundhi, a high-school friend and star of the maternal-fetal medicine department at Stillwater. Even Costello was happy to hand over an OB case to her.

"Blood bank's sending up the O neg?" He pulled on a yellow gown, gloves, goggles—the usual assortment of protective equipment.

"Five units on its way." I laid out a series of test tubes and began labeling them for the variety of blood samples we would need to run.

He peered over my shoulder at the neat rows of supplies, no doubt looking for a mistake that wasn't there. I took his silence as approval and slipped into my own gear. Esme appeared in the doorway with the infant warmer and switched it on while a tech from radiology parked the portable CT scanner outside the door.

"Where the hell is Flight for Life?" Costello demanded as we headed for the ambulance bay. "We should be sending her to Peoria."

Esme jerked a thumb at the storm outside. "You want them to fly in that?"

Through the automatic doors, we could see the trees tossing about, the cornstalks in an adjacent field nearly flattened. The lights in the parking lot were blurred behind a curtain of rain. No wonder the helicopter team couldn't transport our patient—this weather would have endangered the entire crew.

Costello cursed under his breath, rolling his shoulders like a prize fighter warming up. "Okay, people. Our job is to stabilize her. We work fast, we work hard, we leave the baby to the OB department. I want Mom ready to go out on a chopper the minute we get a break."

Lightning crackled across the sky, and I shivered as if the wind had snuck inside. I had a feeling we wouldn't be catching many breaks tonight.

Esme's words came back to me. *Careful what you wish for.* I hadn't, of course. Nurses didn't wish for patients any more than firefighters wished for flames. But people would get sick, cars would crash, accidents would happen. When they did, I liked knowing I had the skills to make it better. To save a life. To dig in and make a difference.

There was no sign yet of the ambulance, no lights strobing across the cornfields or sirens audible amid the sounds of the storm, and the silence grew awkward as we waited.

"Did you get your apartment squared away?" Esme asked in a blatant attempt to ease the mood. This would be the first major trauma we'd dealt with since I'd started at Stillwater Gen, and like any team, we were all on edge wondering how I'd fit in.

"Finally, yeah." I'd left Chicago for Stillwater with only a few hours' notice, assuming my trip would last a few days at most. Now that a few days had turned into a months-long commitment, it hadn't made sense to let my city apartment sit empty. "A friend of a friend is going through a bad breakup, so she's subletting it. I moved my stuff into the store over the weekend."

Technically, I'd shoved everything into the office above my family's hardware store, to my sister Charlie's chagrin. There'd been no room at the family home and no sense in unpacking when I'd be leaving again soon.

"You're serious?" Costello asked. Hard to tell if it was disbelief or horror coloring his voice. Probably both. "You're really going to stick around?"

"I signed a contract, remember? Three months."

Three months—that's what I'd promised Grace Fisher, the hospital president. Time enough to help my sister get the family hardware store back on its feet; time enough for my newest niece, born prematurely, to come home from the hospital. Time enough to mend fences with all the people I'd left behind twelve years ago. I hoped so, anyway, and shoved away the whisper that said three months might not be enough time, after all.

"Doesn't mean you'll stick." He shrugged, not taking his eyes from the horizon. "Not from what I've heard."

"There." Esme pointed toward the road, where the blurred lights of the ambulance were finally visible. My pulse kicked up reflexively at the sight, my heartbeat drumming in my ears. My muscles tightened like a runner at the beginning of a race—all adrenaline and hyperawareness as if waiting for the starting gun.

Next to me, Costello was practically vibrating with eagerness, and the animosity between us fell away. Wordlessly, we tracked the ambulance's approach, knowing it was impossible to predict what awaited us when the doors slid open. It didn't stop me from running down a checklist in my mind, going over the steps we'd take as soon as the gurney rolled in. We'd need to get a monitor on her. Cut off her clothing, slap on the leads as best we could, push IV fluids, and start a ventilator, if necessary. Get a fetal monitor on her too, but the obstetrical team would handle anything related to the baby. In this moment, the mother was my only concern.

Someone brushed against my arm—Garima, mouth set in a grim line, arms wrapped around herself as if she was cold. Behind her stood a nurse I'd seen on the neonatal unit, her teddy-bear-printed scrubs lending an incongruously cheerful note. I nodded a greeting and Garima returned it, but neither of us spoke as the lights grew closer, and the sirens grew louder, and the wait twisted into awful, excruciating tension . . .

And then the ambulance was there, back doors swinging open, paramedics scrambling out, lifting down the gurney, shouting vitals and patient history as Costello barked orders and Garima demanded answers.

The victim was battered and bleeding, her face swollen beyond recognition. One of the paramedics was methodically pumping air into her lungs.

Pent-up adrenaline sizzled through my limbs. I dove into the fray, anticipation replaced by movement and instinct and speed.

In an instant, our Tuesday ER came alive, and so did I.

★　　★　　★

We burst into Trauma One, a storm of noise and motion. "One-two-three," the paramedics chanted, and our patient was on the table, the merciless overhead lamps revealing the full extent of the damage, along with her very advanced pregnancy. We swapped monitors and started fluids and oxygen, every move designed to steal a few more seconds in which to save her.

"Head looks bad," Esme warned.

"Heart's no prize either," Costello replied, but he glanced over, grimacing when he saw the shattered portion of her skull. "Get the collar off her; let's see what we're dealing with."

I glanced at the monitor, not liking the pattern of peaks and valleys. "She's in V-tach."

"What do you think, Jess? Thirty-six, thirty-seven weeks?" Garima asked her nurse as she ducked around me to hook up the fetal monitor. "Not quite full-term, anyway."

Trauma's a cross between a ballet and a battle—we all knew the moves, and any fears we'd had about teamwork evaporated as I took my place in the well-choreographed pattern. Esme assisted Costello directly, handing him instruments as he surveyed the damage to our patient's skull, while I took over artificial respiration from the paramedic.

Beside me, Garima's nurse—Jess—made a noise of distress and pressed a fist against her mouth. I followed her gaze to the silver bracelet glinting at the patient's wrist. Two painstakingly rendered bears dangled from the heavy links: one the size of a dime and the other a corn kernel.

Mama bear and baby bear.

My stomach twisted, but there was no time for sentiment. I kept going, my arms already aching from the compressions as the anesthesiologist began preparing to intubate the patient, letting a machine take over her breathing.

"Patient went over the embankment near Sutherland Road," the paramedic said. "She must've been there for at least half an hour before we arrived."

Costello scowled as he drew back the patient's eyelid and shined a penlight at her pupils. "Left side's blown," he said. "Where's the damn trauma team? Where's my neuro consult?"

In the Venn diagram of medicine, emergency and trauma overlap, but they're not the same thing. ER doctors are there to stabilize anyone who comes in the door. They're the first line of defense. Trauma teams are more specialized, working to save the most grievously injured patients. In a large hospital like Chicago Memorial, we'd had multiple trauma teams on-site around the clock. At Stillwater Gen, we didn't have the need, or the budget, for that kind of specialized support. Instead, we kept a team on call, ready to come in at a moment's notice.

"Roads are terrible," one of the paramedics said. "Unless they're driving a Humvee, you're on your own for a while."

"She doesn't have a while," Costello snarled and barked orders at everyone in sight.

I watched the monitors and called out numbers as the anesthesiologist performed the intubation, and the harsh rhythm of the ventilator joined the cacophony.

"Paul, we've got a placental abruption," Garima called over the noise.

He ignored her and kept talking to Esme, who caught my eyes and gave the barest of grimaces. Placental abruption meant bleeding that could put both mother and baby in jeopardy.

"Got a name!" cried one of the paramedics, who'd been going through a blood-spattered tote bag. He held up a driver's license. "Katherine Tibbs, age thirty-six, blood type A positive."

"Katherine," I said, adjusting the IV flow, keeping an eye on her sat levels, "you're at the hospital. We're doing everything we can to help you and your baby. Hang on, okay?"

Garima spoke again, louder this time. "I need to get the baby out." She turned to her nurse, who was breathing too quickly for my liking. "Jess, get the C-section tray."

"Not yet," Costello snapped. "I need to get the cerebral edema under control. Vargas, push forty mil of furosemide and point-two diazepam. I don't want her seizing."

"We have two patients," Garima said. "If we wait too long, we'll lose the baby."

He didn't even spare her a glance, too focused on examining Katherine's skull fracture. "Save the spaceship, save the astronaut."

Jess gasped, sweat beading along her upper lip. "She's not—"

Costello wasn't being cruel or glib. He was doing what all emergency responders do in a crisis—separating the personal from the medical, which gave him the distance he needed to work. But Jess, who had probably never encountered this degree of trauma in the neonatal unit, wouldn't see it that way.

"Keeping mom alive gives baby the best chance," I said, trying to reassure her.

"But she's . . ." Jess swayed and bobbled the tray of scalpels, nearly scattering them across the floor.

That was all it took for Garima to make the call. "Switch it up," she ordered. "Jess, you're recording. You"—she pointed to the nurse who'd been taking detailed notes of everything that happened—"take over ventilation. Frankie, with me."

"Don't move my staff," Costello began but changed his mind when he spotted Jess's slack features. "Fine. Go, Stapleton."

I swapped places, warning Garima, "I don't have a lot of OB experience."

"You're about to get some," she replied with a glance at the monitor. "Baby's heart rate is dropping."

"So's Mom's pressure," Costello muttered as he and Esme worked feverishly. "Let me get her stabilized, do a head CT to find the bleed. There might be . . ."

"Paul"—something in Garima's voice made the room go quiet—"we don't have to lose them both. It doesn't have to be that kind of night."

I watched him closely, saw the muscle in his jaw jump, saw the second his hands stilled.

"You've assisted with a C-section before," Garima said, turning to me.

I swallowed. "A few."

"Good enough." She checked with the anesthesiologist, then said with a voice tighter than piano wire, "Number ten scalpel. Retractor. Let's go."

If I wanted to, I could look back in the chart and see how quickly the procedure actually took. But no report could ever capture the strange duality of those minutes—Garima's movements swift, calm, and precise as everything around us was falling apart. The scent of blood and rain and mud mingling with disinfectant. The sound of the monitors shrieking while Costello and Esme worked to stabilize Katherine. Garima's murmured directions and my desperate attempt to follow them.

But what I remember most of all was the sense of urgency twined with a sense of inevitability—that we were working to save a life at the very instant one was being lost.

The monitors flatlined, a piercing shriek that nearly made me flinch. "Charge the paddles," Costello said to Esme. "Shock her the second they're clear."

Garima ignored him. "Here we go," she said softly. "Here we go, little boy. I've got you."

Her gloved hands cradled the infant securely, and the room stilled for an instant.

A cry. A mew, really, faint and pitiful and barely audible amid the chaos, but it was enough.

"Frankie, cut the cord," she ordered.

I did, and she stepped away, turning toward the infant warmer and hooking the baby to a tiny cannula, boosting his oxygen. Behind me, Costello shouted, "Shock her. Two hundred joules."

The defibrillator whined and chirped. "Clear," Esme called.

The monitor beeped once, then flatlined again.

"Again," Costello said. "I want to see a sinus rhythm, people."

Esme repeated the clear, voice filled with dread, but the monitor droned on.

"Stapleton, get over here." He turned back to the woman on the table, his expression fierce. "Come on, Katherine. Don't you want to meet your son? Stapleton, epinephrine syringe, one mil. Vargas, go again."

Garima waved me off, and I readied the syringe, waiting as Esme shocked her again.

I held out the syringe but kept my fingers wrapped around it as Costello reached out expectantly. His gaze snapped to mine.

"Doctor Costello." I didn't say any more. Just stood across from him, over the body of a woman who was already gone, and held my breath.

He froze, then stepped back from the table, his hands in the air like a man at gunpoint. Someone turned off the monitor.

"Time of death, ten oh-two," he said tonelessly, the infant's cries filling the air.

TWO

We'd walked up to death, battled it, and lost. In the aftermath, our routine tasks—from cleaning the body to completing paperwork—took on the feeling of a ritual, giving us a bridge back to the living.

"Rough case for Costello," Esme said in the sudden quiet of the trauma room.

"He's fine," I replied, methodically inventorying all the supplies we'd used. Gauze, IV bags, sponges, clamps. Everything needed to be recorded before we discarded it, as if we were tallying our failure.

Not a total failure. Four floors up, there was a child in the NICU who wouldn't have survived without us. We might not have saved the spaceship, but we'd made sure the astronaut landed. Tonight, that would have to be enough.

"It's not the first time he's lost a patient. Not the first time for any of us."

"Except that NICU nurse, maybe." Esme shook her head in dismay. "If I didn't know better, I'd have said she was a rookie."

Jess and Garima had left shortly after Costello called time. The baby was in shock, but the placental abruption hadn't cost him too much blood. Dr. Solano had arrived mere minutes after the delivery and insisted on transferring the baby to the neonatal intensive care unit, where they'd run a battery of specialized tests and had a team trained to care for tiny patients.

Jess had trailed behind Garima, pale and trembling as she wheeled the isolette out. I'd half expected Dr. Solano to take over for her.

"I've seen Jess working in the NICU. She never struck me as the freezing type," I said.

Esme shrugged. "Maybe it's the first time she's ever scrubbed in on that kind of trauma. Guessing it'll be her last, though. Costello's not likely to let her back in the ER unless she's a patient."

"Probably not." I glanced at the figure on the bed. We'd covered Katherine Tibbs with a sheet, but the image of her blood-streaked bracelet lodged below the surface of my thoughts like a splinter. "Why did you say it was rough for Costello? I would have thought nothing fazed him."

She glanced around as if making sure nobody would overhear. "The mom angle," she said softly. "I think it hits home for him. Stirs things up that he tries to stuff down, you know?"

I paused in the middle of gathering spare surgical clamps. "His wife."

Costello and his teenage daughter, Meg, had moved here several years ago, following the death of his wife. I didn't know the circumstances, and I hadn't felt any desire to find out, though it was likely common knowledge. Everything in

Stillwater was, after all. But sympathy was the last thing he'd want, whether it was to his face or murmured in the hallway.

"He'll be fine," I repeated as Alejandro knocked on the doorframe, shifting an ice pack from hand to hand. "Did I leave that on the counter? It's for the shoulder in Exam Three."

In the rush to care for Katherine Tibbs, I'd forgotten all about the unsettling Mr. Mueller. "Can you take it to him? I'll be in to clean him up as soon as I finish here."

"No can do," Alejandro said with a frown. "He's gone."

My skin went hot, then cold. "Gone as in dead?"

He shook his head. "Nope. Just gone. Took off while we were working on this lady, I think."

I groaned. "You're kidding me. I *lost* him? You're sure? Maybe he wandered off into another room."

Alejandro gave me a pitying look. "You really think we have that many places for a full-grown man to hide?"

"Costello's never going to let me live this down, is he?" Neither Alejandro nor Esme answered, which only confirmed it. It was one thing for a patient to discharge against medical advice; to let one slip away on my watch was another. The only thing more amateur would have been to faint at the sight of blood.

"You said he was off," Esme pointed out. "You were right about that, anyway."

Cold comfort, especially since I'd never gotten around to calling security. "Yeah, but I should have . . ."

"What? Stayed with him while the rest of us worked on Katherine Tibbs? We needed you in there, the way that NICU nurse freaked out," Esme said firmly. Then she caught sight of Eileen making her way down the hall toward us. "Exam Three did a runner."

"Expected as much. John Mueller, my Irish behind. What some people do to get out of paying a bill . . ." She shook her head, then peered over the tops of her glasses at us. "Katherine Tibbs's husband is here, along with a whole crew of people. Where's Dr. Costello?"

"I took Mueller," I said to Esme. "Your turn."

"You *lost* Mueller," she replied. "Besides, you're the one who said Costello was fine."

I sighed and shoved the clipboard at her.

The door to the staff lounge was closed. On any other night, I would have strolled right in, but this wasn't any other night. Even Esme had admitted as much, with her quiet questions about Costello and her gentle reminder about his own loss. Pride still smarting from my runaway patient, I steeled myself and knocked on the door. "Dr. Costello?"

No response. I tried again.

"Dr. Costello, Katherine Tibbs's husband is here."

Silence.

Gingerly, I opened the door. Costello sat on the edge of the ugly plaid couch, head bent, elbows braced on knees, hands loosely clasped. "Doctor—"

"I heard you the first time. They probably heard you back in Chicago."

I bit back my annoyance. "Do you want Garima to—"

Before I could finish, he shoved off the couch and brushed past me, dragging on his white doctor's coat.

I shook my head and followed him. It was almost unheard of for nurses to deliver the news of a patient's death, but considering Costello's temperament, I thought it best if someone else was close by.

He stalked down the hallway, an abrupt, graceless stride that belied the barest hint of a limp. I'd never noticed it before, but it wasn't as if we'd spent a lot of time hanging out.

Someone in an adjoining corridor was shouting. The husband, I assumed, and I quickened my pace.

"Where's my wife?" the man roared. "Why can't I see her? Why won't you people tell me anything?"

Costello stopped short before he turned the corner, tugging his white coat straight and running a hand over his shaved head. The line of his shoulders turned less aggressive, and when he started off again, his gait had smoothed out, measured and patient. By the time he rounded the corner, his transformation was complete.

"Mr. Tibbs? I'm Paul Costello, the attending physician." The contempt in his voice had given way to compassion. "I treated your wife tonight."

A whole crew, Eileen had said, and I'd assumed she meant a throng of anxious family members. Instead, Costello was speaking to a man surrounded by what could only be described as an entourage—a cluster of men in tuxedos and women in cocktail dresses, all of them wearing identical expressions of shock and dismay.

The man in front, however, with red-rimmed eyes and bow tie hanging askew, was clearly the husband.

"I want to see her," he demanded, raking his fingers through his dripping-wet hair. "You take me to her right now or so help me—"

The man next to him, similarly clad but with silver-gray hair and a florid complexion, put a hand on his shoulder, restraining him with a firm grip and a few low-pitched words. With an effort, the husband took a breath, released it, and tried again. "Please," he said, voice unsteady. "Where's Kate?"

Recognition buzzed along the nape of my neck. He looked to be about my age, with the blandly attractive features of a newscaster and the sort of build that came from semiregular workouts, not working outside. I squinted, trying to place him.

"Did you catch the husband's name?" I asked the orderly hovering at my elbow.

"Sean, maybe? Stuart?"

The pieces in my mind clicked into place. "Steven."

"That's right," the orderly agreed. "Steven Tibbs. You know him?"

"Kind of," I said. "He was a year behind me in high school." Steven Tibbs, savior of Stillwater. The boy who'd stopped a fire from destroying half the business district and saved a half a dozen lives in the process. I'd left town before it happened, but I'd heard plenty of stories about it over the years, each retelling more dramatic than the last.

A few feet away, Costello said, "Let's step into the family lounge, please. For privacy."

"I'm not going anywhere until you tell me where my wife is!" Steven shouted.

"Alejandro, clear the hallway," Costello said, not taking his eyes off Steven. Minutes later, the crowd had been ushered to the lobby, leaving only Steven and the silver-haired man.

"Mr. Tibbs," Costello began again, and Steven's entire body drooped under the weight of everything those two words contained.

Costello paused, and when he finally spoke, the words were precise and terrible. I'd witnessed this sort of scene hundreds of times, but familiarity never diminished the awfulness of it.

"Your wife was in a car accident. The storm meant Flight for Life couldn't safely transport her to the regional trauma center, so she was brought here to be stabilized. She suffered massive head trauma, as well as significant internal injuries. We did everything we could to stabilize her and maintain organ function, but in the end, her injuries were too severe and she passed away." He paused. "I am very sorry for—"

"Kate's *dead*? No." Steven looked around wildly as if he might find someone to tell him otherwise. "No! That's not possible."

"I'm very sorry for your loss," Costello said again, and only then did I notice the way his hands were balled to fists. "The baby—"

Steven, eyes wet and horrified, reared back. The other man gripped his shoulder, trying to steady him.

"Your son was delivered safely," Costello assured him. "He's upstairs in our neonatal intensive care unit. I can have a nurse take you to him right now, if you'd like." He glanced over at me, then back to Steven. "Or you can see your wife."

"You said—"

"If you wanted to say good-bye to her," Costello continued, more gently than I'd have thought him capable. "I'll make sure you're not disturbed."

Steven looked at him blankly. The other man's grip tightened on his shoulder, and with a great effort, Steven's stricken features hardened into resolve. "Yes. Please."

"The chaplain's on his way," Costello added as they made their way to the trauma room. I trailed after them, unaccustomed to feeling so helpless. "We'll send him in, if you'd like."

"No!"

Costello's eyebrows lifted, but he said nothing.

"Not right now," Steven said hoarsely. "I just . . . not now. Please." He twisted to look at the man keeping pace with me. Until that moment, my attention had been riveted on Steven and Costello, one man's loss unexpectedly illuminating the other's character. Now I studied the silver-haired man—built like an aging football player, a big man gone soft from too many hours behind a desk and too many three-martini lunches, judging from the broken capillaries in his nose and cheeks.

That was the only soft thing about him, though—his receding hairline was still immaculate despite the hour, the storm, and the situation. His rain-spattered trench coat and the tuxedo beneath were expensive without being showy. And while his blunt features were arranged into something resembling sympathy, it didn't reach his eyes.

"Go ahead," the man said as if granting permission. "I'll handle everything."

An instant later, Costello and Steven disappeared around the corner, and the stranger pulled his phone from his pocket, turning his back on all of us and keeping his voice low.

Alejandro returned. "Chaplain's here. Should I send him in?"

I shook my head. "Have him hang in the staff lounge until Steven's ready." I followed him back to the nurses' station, where Esme had started in on the reams of paperwork await-ing us.

"I'll wrap up the charting for the Tibbs case," she offered. "You make sure we've documented everything on the shoul-der patient, make sure Costello signs off on it."

"Ugh," I said but sat down at the other computer and pulled up John Mueller's chart. "Is Costello always so kind during notifications?"

Alejandro shrugged. "More than he is to us, sure. But this time . . . he's practically human."

It hit home, as Esme had said—and with the force of an F5 tornado.

Before I could ask more, the silver-haired stranger returned, looking annoyed. He pointed at me. "You there. Nurse. The short one."

I pasted on a smile while Esme stifled a laugh. At five two, I've heard all the short jokes, even the "clever" ones, and they're never as funny as the teller thinks. But this wasn't a joke; it was a summons, and I bristled at it. "Frankie Staple-ton. Can I help you, sir?"

"Call security down here and make sure that no one from the press gets in. Nobody on staff should be commenting on the matter, either on or off the record. I want to talk to some-one in hospital administration and the public relations depart-ment. Get them out of bed, if you have to. Mr. Tibbs will need to make a statement, and I'm thinking the lobby would be best unless you've got a decently sized meeting room. Get the custodial staff to set up an area just inside the front doors to corral the press, maybe put up a podium, and make sure the lighting—"

"The press?" I asked, not bothering to hide my skepticism. Turning back to my computer, I added, "The only press we have in town is the *Standard*, and I guarantee the editor won't be coming down to ask for a statement tonight."

The editor of the *Stillwater Journal-Standard* was my uncle Marshall, and he was asleep by nine on the dot every night. The only story that could get him out of bed between the hours of nine PM and four AM was a presidential assassination, as he frequently reminded us.

The man stared at me like I was a not-very-bright toddler. "Every newspaper in the state, not to mention the major networks, will be covering this story. The first wave will be here within hours, so it's essential that we get ahead of this. Control the narrative."

"The narrative," I snapped, swiveling to face him, "is that a man just lost his wife and a baby lost his mother. The last thing we need to do is call a press conference. Let Steven grieve privately."

"Mr. Tibbs doesn't have the luxury of grieving privately," the man replied. "We are three weeks out from Election Day, and as a public figure, this is more than a human interest story—it's national news."

"A public figure?" I echoed. "*Steven?*"

"Mr. Tibbs is running for Congress," the man said. "The nineteenth district?"

"'Tibbs for a Stronger Tomorrow,'" Esme added from her side of the nurses' station, and he gifted her with a smile.

I stared at both of them, trying to wrap my head around the idea of Steven as a congressman. Sure, he'd been a local hero, but had he really managed to parlay that into a national political career?

I tried to remember the details—I'd already left for college, but according to my mother's breathless recounting, Steven had been working at his father's convenience store. It was the kind of place that stocked chips and beer, magazines and nail polish, ice cream from a chest freezer and wine from a box. The kind of place you stopped in when you ran out of milk or dishwasher detergent midweek. He'd gone in early and discovered a fire raging through the building—the wood-frame building, surrounded by the rest of the wood-framed buildings that made up Stillwater's quaintly charming and optimistically named business district. Not only had he alerted the fire department, he'd also braved the flames to warn the residents of the second-floor apartments. Without his quick thinking, the mayor had proclaimed, the entire downtown would have burnt to the ground, along with a number of senior citizens and the historical society's archives.

When I tried to remember teenaged Steven, the only impression I could call up was an average kid—not particularly popular, smart, or athletic. He'd been amiable but not particularly memorable. Then again, my own interests in high school had been focused on two things: Noah MacLean and getting out of Stillwater. Steven had barely registered in my peripheral vision back then—and now his very personal tragedy was playing out directly in front of me.

"I take it we don't have your vote," the silver-haired man said dryly. "Yet."

"Yes. I mean, no. I mean . . . I don't live here. I'm . . . Congress? Of the United States?" I pinched the bridge of my nose, trying to focus. "Who are you, exactly?"

"Ted Sullivan. His campaign manager," he said. "As I said, this story is about to make the national news. So. Podium.

Lights. Cordons. Security." He ticked the items off on his fingers and was gearing up to rattle off more directions when he realized neither Esme nor I were scurrying to obey. His expression darkened. "Are you two deaf or just incompetent?" He snapped his fingers at Alejandro. "You there. Get me someone who actually knows what's going on around here."

Tragedy or not, arranging press conferences wasn't my job. "You're the manager," I shot back. "Manage it yourself. We're working, and you need to wait in the lobby."

I nodded to Alejandro, who took a sputtering Ted Sullivan by the arm and guided him forcefully into the lobby.

"Steven Tibbs is running for Congress?" I asked Esme.

She nodded. "Haven't you noticed the eight zillion yard signs in town?"

Between working at the hospital, helping at Stapleton and Sons Hardware, and keeping my niece Riley out of trouble, I hadn't exactly had time to catch up on local politics.

"Is that moron with the shoulder ready for his sutures?" Costello asked, returning to the nurses' station.

Wordlessly, Esme slipped away from the desk.

I stood. If Costello was going to lord this over me, I'd rather not be sitting. "He left."

"AMA? Figures." He shook his head in disgust. "Where's the form?"

Typically when someone leaves the hospital against medical advice, they have to fill out a liability waiver. I have no idea if they actually hold up in court, but hospitals—and hospital lawyers—love documentation.

"No form," I said and dragged in a breath. "He took off while—"

"He left? He—" Costello made a choked sound, but it wasn't anger. It was laughter. "He snuck off? On the great Frankie Stapleton's watch? Aren't you supposed to be the observant one? That's what Fisher told me when she hired you. 'Good instincts and a sharp eye,' she said."

"Mueller took off while we were working on Katherine Tibbs," I said hotly. "Would you have preferred I left before the C-section, or after?"

"I would've preferred you stayed in Chicago," he said with a snort, "but since you seem determined to stick around, I'd rather keep an eye on you. Less dangerous that way."

I blinked.

"Be good if *you* could keep an eye on your patients, though," he added over his shoulder as he walked away. "Even the morons."

Esme reappeared an instant later. "That went better than I expected."

"Yeah." But I had a feeling it wasn't done. Costello would file this away, ammunition for a later battle. The knowledge I'd handed that ammunition to him only deepened the blow to my pride.

Esme must have realized where my thoughts were going. She elbowed me, saying, "Storm's about blown itself out. Better brace yourself for the aftermath."

She was right. Over the next hour, fresh cases flooded the ER. I admitted a broken hip from the county nursing home, wrapped a sprained ankle, and handled a pediatric trifecta—double ear infection, pinkeye, and strep. My least acute case, a factory worker with a wrenched back, took the most time. Due to the opioid addiction crisis, treating soft-tissue injuries was no longer as simple as requesting a prescription from the doctor on duty. There were forms to fill out and databases to check. I could have complained about jumping through so many hoops, but I'd dealt with enough overdoses to know that paperwork was preferable to a body bag. Meanwhile, a subdued Esme took Steven upstairs to the NICU and supervised the transfer of Katherine Tibbs's body to the morgue.

I might have been busier, but she'd had the tougher jobs by far.

"I'm grabbing dinner upstairs," I told her once we'd hit another lull. Dinner was a misnomer, but in twelve years, I hadn't figured out what else to call a meal eaten at four in the morning. "Call the NICU if things pick up."

"Sounds good. How's Rowan doing?"

"Fantastic. Putting on weight, breathing strong." I was veering into braggy-aunt territory and didn't mind a bit. "She's a fighter."

Rowan was a Stapleton girl, after all. How could my tiny niece be anything else?

I checked my cell: three calls from my other niece, eight-year-old Riley, each a breathless report on some crucial detail of her day that couldn't keep until morning; one from my soon-to-be tenant; and the last from my ex-fiancé, Peter Lee.

No matter what people say, nobody ever stays friends after a breakup—especially if the breakup involves the return of a diamond ring. But since my return to Stillwater, Peter had continued to stay in touch. Nothing stalker-like, just a friendly voice mail every few days, leaving me baffled, a little suspicious, and a lot guilty, which is why I had yet to return any of his calls.

Peter, a pediatric surgeon at Chicago Memorial, had been the one to call off our wedding. He'd been convinced that I didn't actually want to get married, and he'd been absolutely right. I was most assuredly not the marrying type, as evidenced by not one, not two, but *three* failed engagements. I was grateful to Peter, not only for recognizing what I wouldn't admit to myself and saving both of us from a terrible mistake, but for handling the fallout. Less than twenty-four hours after we'd ended our engagement, I'd come home to Stillwater, leaving him to explain the situation to our friends and coworkers.

I'd call him tomorrow, I decided. Definitely.

Probably.

Maybe.

Ignoring my snickering conscience, I used my freshly minted hospital ID to buzz into the maternity ward, then headed for the neonatal ICU. My steps slowed as I caught sight of Steven Tibbs through the glass door. He sat in the far corner, gloved and gowned, cheek pressed against the incubator where his newborn son lay.

The moment was so raw, so private, that I nearly turned around. But this brief visit was my only chance to visit Rowan before my shift ended, and after witnessing such a tragedy, I needed to see her, to remind myself that sometimes we got a happy ending.

Steven didn't look up as I entered. No doubt the enormity of his loss would blind him to everything else, at least for a while. If Ted Sullivan was right, this might be Steven's last opportunity to mourn privately. I had no desire to intrude.

Rowan lay sleeping inside her clear plastic box, monitor leads trailing from her feet and chest, hair peeking out from her knitted cap, one tiny fist raised above her head. The temptation to wake her was irresistible, and I was just reaching for the isolette door when Donna, her nurse, walked over.

"Rule number one," Donna murmur-scolded. "Never wake a sleeping baby."

"You wake them all the time," I whispered. "I've seen you do it."

"It's my job. You're the auntie." She grinned. "You wake that baby before her next feeding, and I'll make sure you're paged for every single diaper change until discharge."

I sank into the plush rocking chair next to the isolette. "How's she doing tonight?"

"Good," she said and gave me a quick rundown of Rowan's vitals. "Doctor Solano thinks she'll be home before Thanksgiving."

"Charlie can't wait."

"I've heard," she replied. "Frequently."

Generally speaking, my sister was considered the level-headed one in the family—but Rowan's early arrival had rendered her short-tempered and panicky. She'd settled down in the last week or so, but it didn't take much to set off her mama bear instincts.

Mama bear, I thought and glanced over at Steven, still glued to his son's bedside.

Donna followed my gaze. "So sad, isn't it?"

"It's terrible," I said. "How's the baby?"

"A miracle, really. He's shocky, of course, and we've started him on steroids to boost his lungs, but he's doing pretty well. Dr. Solano's concerned about internal injuries, but nothing has showed up on the scans." She paused. "Not yet, anyway."

I knew what the pause meant. It meant that it was early days, that anything could go wrong, that there were miles to go.

She shook her head. "Poor little guy."

"How's Jess?"

Donna tipped her head toward the back of the NICU. A wall of windows revealed the nurses' station on the other side. Jess was seated with her back to us, shoulders hunched, her body rigid. Every so often, she'd turn her head a few degrees, but aside from that, she sat, motionless and solitary.

"What's she doing?" I wondered.

"Dr. Solano assigned her to a low-intervention baby for the rest of the shift," Donna said. "When she's not with him, she just sits there, watching the monitors."

I glanced up at the discreet black-domed security cameras overhead. "Does she typically take it this hard?"

"She's soft-hearted," Donna said, defensiveness creeping into her voice, "but I've never seen her like this before, and I've worked with her for three years. We have tough deliveries all the time, but not trauma patients. Not like this. It must have been a nightmare."

Some cases did, in fact, give you nightmares. Every nurse had a few patients who haunted their sleep, sometimes for years. For me, it wasn't the patients I'd lost, but the ones I'd questioned: What if I'd done something differently? What if I'd done *more*?

I doubted I'd dream of Katherine Tibbs. But I was one hundred percent certain Jess would.

I studied Rowan more carefully than usual, as if my scrutiny could keep her safe. More than once, my younger sister, Charlie, had accused me of being an adrenaline junkie, but parenthood—taking responsibility for a tiny life, loving it despite all the risks—was more adventure than I wanted to take on. How on earth did Charlie, a control freak since before she could spell, manage so much uncertainty and fear?

Donna went to check on other patients, leaving me with a stern warning not to wake Rowan. I spent a few minutes surreptitiously reaching into the isolette, tracing the shell of her ear and her tiny fingers, humming half-remembered lullabies. As much as I tried to push the memory away, I thought of the bracelet on Katherine Tibbs's wrist, with its two bloodstained charms.

On impulse, I made my way over to Steven, still bent over his son's isolette.

"Mister—" I broke off. It felt too strange to call him Mr. Tibbs. "Steven."

He didn't look up. His skin was waxen, misery etched into his features. "What now?"

"I wanted to tell you how sorry I am for your loss. I was on the team that treated your wife and son tonight."

"It's not right," he said, turning to face me. "None of it. That doctor—the one who told me about Kate—he said there was nothing they could do. That the head injury . . ."

"It's true. It was a miracle she held on as long as she did, but that's what saved your son's life."

"This should never have happened," he said. "Kate was a wonderful woman. So dedicated. So giving."

I nodded.

"She would have been a wonderful mother too. I don't understand why . . ."

All I could do was shake my head, but Steven didn't see me, his gaze fixed on his son.

"None of that matters, though, not now. But I swear I'm going to make her proud. I'm going to do everything in my power to make the world the best possible place I can for our child. For everyone's children."

His voice grew stronger, less tentative, as if he was gaining confidence as he spoke. He should be holding the baby, I thought. No doubt the doctor had warned against it, as a precaution, but I couldn't help thinking that's what Steven needed—not proclamations, but the chance to bond with the only surviving member of his family. To take comfort and give it in equal measure.

"What's his name?" I asked.

"Trey," he said, with the faintest of smiles. "Technically, it's Steven Jefferson Tibbs the third, but Kate thought that was too much name for a baby, so we were going to call him Trey, just as a nickname."

I tended to agree with Kate. "That's sweet."

He turned, studying me more closely. "Have we met?"

I shifted under his scrutiny. "Stillwater High. I was a year ahead of you. Frankie Stapleton?"

"Frankie, of course." He trapped my hand between his, pumping my arm like we were at a campaign rally. "It's been . . ."

"A long time," I said, gently escaping his grip. "I wish it were under better circumstances."

"Thank you." He swallowed hard. "You're sure Trey's okay? You trust the doctor?"

I pointed to Rowan's isolette. "See that little girl? That's my niece, and I am trusting Dr. Solano with her life. Trey's getting the best possible care, Steven."

He took a deep breath, returned his gaze to his son.

"I need to get back downstairs, but if you need anything, let me know."

He nodded, acknowledging my words. But words, no matter how well-intentioned or wise, can only do so much. As I let myself out of the NICU, Steven sagged against the isolette, grief swallowing him up again.

THREE

Garima's office door was open a crack, so I nudged it wide and stuck my head in. She sat at her desk, expression shifting from annoyance to relief when she realized it was me.

"It's after four," I said, leaning against the doorframe. "You should head home."

"Just finishing up my report." She took off her glasses, pinched the bridge of her nose. "I haven't had a case like that since my residency. I hope I never do again."

"You kept it from being a million times worse. Imagine if Steven had lost both of them."

"I know, but I wish . . ." She shook her head, knowing as well as I did how fragile wishes were—they tended to shrivel under the bright lights of an operating suite. "How are you holding up?"

"We all lose patients." I waved off her sympathy, but it was too late; melancholy rolled back in like a fog. I forced myself to gather it up, that tangle of sadness and regret and might-have-been, and tucked it away. Early in my career, I'd learned that there was no room on the ER floor for lingering emotions. They would only trip me up, put more lives at

risk, and leave me unfocused at a critical moment. Compartmentalization was a survival skill I'd had to master, for my
patients' sake as well as my own. "It's part of the job."

She tipped her head, as if hearing something beneath my
words. "That doesn't mean it's easy."

"True." I paused, then forced a lightness I didn't yet feel.
"So Steven Tibbs, huh? Congress? How'd that happen?"

Garima and I had been classmates, but while I had left
for college and never really returned, she'd come back after
medical school to work at Stillwater Gen and take care of
her parents. "Exactly how you'd expect. The town sent him
off to college as a golden boy. When he came back from law
school, the powers that be got him a job with the district
attorney's office. He's been on a path to politics ever since."
She stretched and glanced at the clock above her desk. "Are
you headed back to the ER?"

"Yeah, I don't want to give Costello another reason to
yell." I filled her in on the disappearing John Mueller. "I feel
like an idiot."

"Don't let him get to you," she ordered.

Easier said than done. I'd known from the get-go that
Mueller was shady; I should have called security the first time
I stepped out of the room. Nothing good had ever come from
ignoring my instincts.

Garima stood and followed me into the hallway. "Let's
have dinner this week. We can celebrate now that you're offi-
cially on staff."

"I'd love to. Let me check with my mom, find a night that
works."

She smirked. "When was the last time you checked with
your mom for permission? Twelfth grade?"

"Tenth, more likely."

"Ah, yes. Once you and Noah were together, there was no stopping you." She shook her head. "How is it, moving back home?"

Normally I would've launched into a complaint, but something about tonight, the reminder that families could be wrenched apart in a moment, kept me from being too flip. "It's an adjustment."

"Charlie said you're sharing a room with Riley?" She didn't bother to hide her laughter. "She must be in heaven. If ever a kid had a case of hero worship . . ."

"It's only because she doesn't know me," I said. "Riley's sweet, but I've been living on my own for twelve years. It feels weird to have a roommate—especially one who's not allowed to see PG-13 movies. And then there's my mom . . ."

Garima winced in understanding. "You could move out."

"I just moved in," I said as we rounded the corner to the main hallway. "And it's not like I'm rolling in money—Charlie's not paying me for my shifts at the store, I'm only here part-time, and my new sublet barely covers the rent."

"Not ideal," she agreed. "Give me some time to think. I'll have a plan by our dinner date."

"I'm glad someone will."

She looked past me. "Speaking of dates . . ."

I followed her gaze and spotted a familiar figure leaning against the counter of the nurses' station. My heart tripped briefly, then steadied. "Nope."

She grinned. "Really? Considering the last time I saw you two together, I would have said a date was definitely in the cards."

"The last time you saw us together was the last time I saw him."

Him, of course, being Noah MacLean. High school boyfriend, ex-fiancé number one, current sheriff's deputy. Our last meeting had been in one of the exam rooms downstairs, shortly after I'd helped capture the person who'd framed me for murder. Since then, it was as if Noah had vanished off the face of the earth. Which, I reminded myself, was his right and not something that bothered me in the slightest.

I shrugged, the very picture of nonchalance. "No dates, no cards. We're friends."

"I see," Garima said in the tone of one who neither saw nor believed. "Officer MacLean," she called as she set off for the desk. "Looking for someone? Frankie, maybe?"

He said something over his shoulder to another officer standing nearby, then headed straight for us. His steps were deliberate, tension coiled in every muscle. It might have been twelve years, but I could spot the signs of his temper as clearly as I could a storm front. Whoever Noah was looking for would do well to take cover.

"Wish I was," he said when he reached us. "Is Steven Tibbs around?"

"He's in the NICU," Garima replied, shifting from friendly to official in the span of a breath. "Can't you give him a few hours peace? The man lost his wife tonight."

The other officer, an older man with ribbons on his uniform and the lumbering gait of a lifelong cop, joined us with his hand outstretched.

"Sheriff Michael Flint. One of you the doctor who delivered that baby?"

Garima introduced herself. "I'd prefer you wait until tomorrow to talk to Mr. Tibbs, Sheriff. He and his son have endured enough this evening."

The sheriff dipped his chin in acknowledgment, ran a hand over his closely cropped dun-colored hair. "I agree, ma'am. Fact is, it's already morning, and the sooner we put this to rest, the better. Mr. Tibbs is holding a press conference in a few hours, and I'd like the first questions he answers to be ours, not some yahoo reporter's. All things considered, it's a sensitive situation, especially this close to the election."

"Talk about an October surprise," I muttered. "Since when has Stillwater politics gotten so dirty?"

The sheriff surveyed me blandly. "Not saying it has, Miss . . ."

"Stapleton. Frankie Stapleton—I'm an ER nurse here."

"Are you, now?" He glanced at Noah, speculation gleaming in his eyes. "Good to finally meet you, Miss Stapleton. Heard you were quite a help with the Clem Jensen case. You work on Mrs. Tibbs tonight?"

"Yes, sir."

"You and I will chat later, then. Might as well let that that bald doctor know too. In the meantime, we're going to need to talk to Mr. Tibbs. Considering the circumstances, I'm not inclined to wait around."

"Circumstances?" Ice pooled at the base of my spine, a sign that our bad night was about to get worse.

Noah and the sheriff exchanged glances.

"Might as well," Sheriff Flint said, hitching up his utility belt. "Word'll get out soon enough."

Despite the empty hallway, Noah spoke so quietly we had to lean in to catch the words. "Katherine Tibbs didn't crash on her own. Someone sent her car over that embankment."

"Someone hit her?" I said. "How do you know?"

Noah scowled. "Skid marks."

"She could have swerved to avoid a deer," Garima protested. "It's the season. Or maybe she lost control in the storm."

"Two sets of skid marks," he insisted. "Plus strange paint on her car."

"Was it deliberate?" I asked. The words felt frozen, unlike my racing thoughts.

"We don't know that yet," the sheriff cautioned. "Could have been an accident and the other car fled the scene. Could have been road rage. Could have been that she was targeted. Lots of questions, which is why we want to talk to Mr. Tibbs."

Garima started to protest, but I cut her off.

"You think he did it," I said flatly. Garima's head whipped around to contradict me, and I shrugged. ER nurses, particularly those in big-city ERs, spend a lot of time around cops. "You guys always look at the husband. It's the number one rule of police work."

"Top three, anyway," he said with a wry grin.

Garima shook her head. "I saw him minutes after he left the ER. Minutes. He was devastated. Totally in shock. There's no way he killed his wife—this has utterly destroyed him."

"I'm not saying he did it. But we have to question him, and I'd rather do it now, get an honest reaction—assuming you can get one from a politician." His mouth quirked, but there was a hard edge to the humor.

"It wasn't Steven." Noah must have heard something in my voice, because his smile faded and his brow lowered.

Sheriff Flint studied me. "Is that so, Miss Stapleton?"

"What time was the accident?"

Noah answered without having to look at the notebook I always teased him about. "The nine-one-one call came in about eight forty-five; ambulance got to the crash site a little after nine. By the time they extracted her and brought her in, it was around nine thirty. As for how long between the accident and when the call came in, we don't know. Probably no more than half an hour."

That fit with what the paramedics had said. It fit with my own suspicions too. "Any other crashes reported around then?"

"None that I know of." Noah's eyes, green as the deep woods, met mine. "Spill, Frankie."

"We had an MVA come in about half an hour before Katherine Tibbs arrived," I said. "He said he hit a deer, but . . ."

"But you're wondering if he was lying." Noah bared his teeth, the smile of a predator about to hunt.

"Oh, I'm not wondering." The heat of my anger drove out the frozen feeling. "He's your driver, I'm sure of it."

Noah shifted, his hand drifting to his gun. "Then let's go see him."

"We can't," I said, and next to me, Garima sagged with understanding. "Your guy ran off, right about the time Katherine Tibbs was flatlining."

FOUR

"Let me get this straight," Costello said as Noah's team turned Exam Three into a crime scene. "The moron with the shoulder killed our pregnant head trauma? And then walked out?"

"We won't know until we find him," Noah said, "but it's an awfully big coincidence."

"He gave us fake information," I warned. "Eileen and I both pegged him as shady from the minute he got here."

But I hadn't done anything about it. I'd known John Mueller—or whatever his name was—had lied, and yet I'd done nothing except patch him up and turn my back. My good intentions had been swallowed in the chaos of Katherine Tibbs's arrival.

Chaos, however, was no excuse. How many times had I claimed to thrive on chaos, that my love of the ER was rooted its unpredictability and frenetic pace? I'd prided myself on being able to manage it, to ride it like a wave. Now I was caught up in it, tumbling below the surface.

Chaos had bested me, and Katherine Tibbs's killer had escaped.

"We're dusting for prints," Noah said, watching me closely. "Between that and the security tapes, we'll figure out who he is."

"I should have called you." I pressed a hand to my stomach, trying to quell the pitching, yawing sensation.

"Why didn't you?" Sheriff Flint asked me. His tone was gentle, but the question cut deeply nevertheless. "Seems to me that you'd want to keep a close eye on anyone comes in here under false pretenses. Criminal element aside, it's a poor way to do business, letting people run out on their bill."

"We're here to save lives, not worry about nickels and dimes," Costello cut in. Despite the fact that he was shorter than the sheriff by several inches, it felt as if he was looming over the older man. "You want us to try it the other way when one of your officers comes in?"

Sheriff Flint chuckled. "No, Doctor, I don't. All I'm saying is—"

"I don't care what you're saying," Costello replied. "My staff did exactly what they were trained to do. Now it's your turn."

"That's why we're here," Noah said. The atmosphere had turned so frigid I half expected our breath to turn visible. "Is there anything else you can tell us about this John Mueller?"

I shook my head. "I did the exam, we popped his shoulder back into place, and then Katherine Tibbs came in. I never saw him again."

"What about Katherine Tibbs? Did she say anything when she came in? Did you notice anything unusual about her?" Noah asked.

"I noticed the four-inch dent in her skull," Costello said. "Everything else was secondary."

Noah's gaze turned to me, and I nodded agreement. "She never regained consciousness."

"What about Mr. Tibbs?" Noah asked Costello. "How did he seem?"

"Like a man who'd just lost his wife," Costello snapped. "You're asking if he was faking? He wasn't."

"In your opinion," Noah countered.

"It's my ER," Costello said. "Nobody else's matters."

Steven's press conference began just as our shift was finishing. I watched it in the staff lounge, coat zipped and backpack over my shoulder, desperate to leave but unable to look away. Steven stood in front of the cameras, blinking at the staccato bursts of camera flashes. Ted Sullivan positioned himself nearby, somber and supportive, shaking his head in a photogenic display of disbelief.

Even in a fresh suit, Steven looked gray and rumpled, his hands gripping the podium as if to keep from trembling. His brief statement, read from a single sheet of paper, echoed his earlier words to me.

"Kate, as anyone who knew her will attest, was as dedicated to her family as she was to making the world a better place. We are waiting to learn more about her senseless death, but I believe I owe it to her, and to our son, Trey, to continue working for a stronger tomorrow. Kate fought for families, and so will I. We will be suspending our campaign for the next several days as we lay her to rest, but in her honor, we will carry that fight all the way to the ballot box and then, with your help, to Washington. Thank you."

Voice breaking, he stepped away. Ted Sullivan took over without missing a beat, asking the press to respect Steven's privacy and direct all questions to him for the next few days.

When, as the sheriff had predicted, someone asked a question about rumors of a homicide, Ted shut them down with practiced efficiency and a vote of confidence in the police. There was no sign of the shock and distress we'd seen with Steven.

The show was over—or another one was beginning, perhaps. Either way, I'd had enough. A few feet away, Costello was watching as well, the set of his mouth flat and unimpressed.

The temptation to leave without saying anything was strong, but my conscience wouldn't allow it. I turned and faced him straight on.

"Thanks," I said, and his expression turned quizzical. I clarified. "For earlier. With the sheriff. Sticking up for me."

My words felt clumsy, as if I'd forgotten how to string them together in any coherent order. Then again, Costello and I hadn't had much practice speaking nicely to each other.

He waved the words away like he was swatting at flies. "Stapleton, if you screw up, I'm more than happy to point it out. But God Himself doesn't get to come in here and question my staff."

"Do you think I screwed up?"

"You did what I told you to do." Threaded through his irritation and his certainty was the very faintest note of doubt. Impossible to say if he was questioning my actions or his own. "We needed to keep Mom alive until the baby was out, and we sure as hell couldn't have pulled it off with that ditz from the NICU. Would you feel better if we'd caught the driver but lost the baby?"

"No, but—"

"But nothing," he said. "Quit wringing your hands like a newbie. You did your job; let your boyfriend do his."

"Noah isn't my boyfriend. I mean, we used to—"

"Don't care," Costello said and turned back to the television, where Ted Sullivan was fielding questions about rumors that Katherine's death was intentional.

"Do you think it was political?" I asked. "Someone trying to intimidate Steven or affect the election?"

"Don't care," he repeated. "We did what we could, and now we move on."

"Mmn-hmn," I said noncommittally.

He glared at me, clearly not buying my act. "If you're going to play detective again, save it until you're back in Chicago. Once was enough."

"Don't you think it's suspicious? Don't you want to find out what happened?"

"What does it matter?" Costello looked tired. I'd had the impression he thrived on the manic energy of the ER, but now he seemed deflated, as if the night's events had taken too much out of him. He scrawled a signature over the last of his paperwork, then dropped the pile in front of me with an air of finality. "She's gone. The cops will find who did it, or they won't. Either way, it's got nothing to do with us."

I wished I felt the same.

*   *   *

The storm had left debris everywhere. My drive home took me past a nonstop parade of downed tree limbs, roofing shingles scattered like confetti, front yards turned to swamps. No doubt Charlie was already planning a poststorm cleanup sale at our family's hardware store. She'd have a sign in the window by lunch.

Our house seemed to have escaped the damage, though the flowers remaining in my mom's garden were sorry, bedraggled looking things. I trudged up the front steps, overcome by a wave of exhaustion. Visions of my bed—the twin-sized lower bunk in the room I shared with Riley—danced before my eyes, a welcome antidote to the chaos of last night.

The visions shattered before I even crossed the threshold.

"Riley Grace," my mother called from the kitchen, "for the last time, get down here and eat your breakfast. We are too busy for you to be sick."

A groan floated down the stairs as my brother-in-law, Matt, dashed past me, adjusting his tie and throwing on a tweed sport coat. He was in full professor mode—all he lacked was a meerschaum pipe. "Briefcase, briefcase, briefcase," he muttered, peering around the room.

I spotted the battered leather case poking out from beneath the couch and handed it over. "Riley's sick? She was fine last night."

He grimaced, then shouted up the stairs, "Riley, get a move on. I'm late for school, and you're about to be."

"I don't feel good," she moaned piteously from the second floor.

I poked my head into the kitchen, shuddering as always at the wall-to-wall chicken-themed decor. My mother heaved a sigh of relief.

"Francesca, go handle Riley. Your sister is already at the store, and I promised to stop by and work the counter while she visited Rowan."

"Good morning to you too," I said, and she swatted at me with a bright-yellow dish towel.

"Go. Consider this payback for all the times I needed a bullhorn to get you out of bed." She must not have heard about Katherine Tibbs's death yet, or she'd be reenacting the Spanish Inquisition. The surge of relief nearly made me light-headed. I wasn't in any condition to dodge questions or defend myself. No matter what Costello said, guilt was gnawing away at the lining of my stomach.

"Do we still have that thing? Might be handy."

She ignored me and continued packing a lunch. "Once you've woken Riley, you can clean up the mess your cat left on the back porch."

"It's not my cat!" I wasn't convinced the creature *was* a cat, not entirely. The scrawny orange-and-white beast appeared to be on its sixth or seventh life. It came around periodically, usually sporting some new injury, and would deign to eat a dish of leftovers—but only when my mom cooked. When I had dinner duty, the offering went untouched. I tried not to take it personally.

"You feed it, you own it. That thing is bringing you presents now."

Rather than argue, I headed to the second floor of our saltbox Cape Cod. Matt shouted a farewell and escaped, muttering about the futility of early classes for freshmen and new parents.

Riley lay on the top bunk in our shared purple room, still clad in pajamas, a curtain of red hair covering her face.

"Let's go, kiddo. Time to get up." I looked longingly at my own bed, the narrow bottom bunk with its bright violet comforter and matching pillows. It beckoned to me, promising dreamless sleep and a chance to forget about Katherine Tibbs, at least for a few hours.

"I'm sick," Riley said.

"Good thing I'm a nurse," I replied, boosting myself onto the ladder for a better look. "Let's do a quick exam."

"No exam," she said, rolling away. "I'm sick. I should stay home."

"Tell me your symptoms."

"I have a fever. A *bad* one. And my tummy hurts. And . . ." She coughed, piteously. "My throat hurts. And my ears."

"That sounds terrible," I said. "We can skip the exam, I think."

"Really?" She sat up, my diagnosis giving her a boost. "No school?"

Her forehead was cool, and her eyes seemed clear enough. True, her color wasn't great—her cheeks were wan beneath her freckles, and dark smudges marred the skin under her eyes—but that wasn't enough to qualify for a sick day at the Stapletons'.

"No school," I agreed cheerfully. "We should run you over to the hospital right now, admit you to the pediatric ward."

"What's that?"

"The kids' department. I mean, there's a lot of babies there, so you won't get a ton of rest. But you can have all the applesauce you want."

"I hate applesauce."

"Bummer," I said. "It's good for a sore throat, and it's easy on the stomach. They'll probably want to start you on some antibiotics. They might even give you a shot."

Riley's eyes went wide. "I don't want a shot."

I shrugged, too tired to feel more than a smidgen of guilt for instilling a fear of needles in a child. Sure, it would make some poor pediatric nurse's life a misery come vaccination time, but desperate times called for desperate measures. "Sorry. An illness this severe that comes on this quickly—we can't mess around."

Riley considered, watching me through narrowed eyes. "Maybe I'm just hungry."

"Could be," I agreed. "A drink might help that sore throat too."

"Maybe."

"Tell you what," I said. "Let's get ready and see how you're feeling. If you decide you're up for school, I will walk you over. If not, we'll call the doctor and see what she says."

"Why can't I stay here with you?" she pleaded. "We could play soccer. I've been practicing my penalty kicks a *lot*."

"Can't wait to see 'em," I said. "After school."

With a sigh, she clambered out of bed. "You didn't come home at *all* last night."

"Nope. Remember how we talked about what a twelve is? I go in at seven at night, and I come home at seven in the morning."

"But when do you sleep?"

"As soon as possible."

She nodded blearily and trudged downstairs. "Did you help all the sick people last night?"

"I tried," I said, deliberately vague. "I got to see Rowan for a little while."

"That's not fair," she muttered as we entered the kitchen.

"Your eggs are getting cold, young lady," my mom said. Riley thumped down in her chair and began methodically shoveling in scrambled eggs.

"Francesca. Outside, please." My mother didn't wait, just marched to the back door, held it open, and waited, foot tapping a supremely annoyed beat.

"I've been home for fifteen minutes," I began when we were both standing on the back deck. "What could I possibly—?"

"*That*," she said, "was waiting for me last night when I came home."

I followed the line of her finger to a small motionless lump on the doormat.

"Oh."

"'Oh,' indeed."

"It's a chipmunk."

"It *was* a chipmunk," she clarified. "Now it is a corpse."

"On the plus side, he can't eat your tulip bulbs anymore."

"This is your doing." She folded her arms and fixed me with a glare. "You've been feeding that cat, and now my back porch looks like a drop-off taxidermy service."

"First of all, nobody taxidermies rodents. At least I hope not. Second of all, the cat is scrawny. He's practically starving. I don't see the harm in giving him a bite to eat every once in a while."

"Once in a while," she scoffed before growing serious. "You can't feed a wild animal, Francesca. He'll lose his instincts. And he'll never be tame, you know. Some things aren't meant for domesticity."

She was probably right about that last bit—the mangy orange-and-white tabby showed no signs of warming up to me despite the late-night feedings. The most I'd gotten for my efforts was a swipe across the shins and an assortment of dead vermin. But I wasn't looking for a pet any more than he was looking for an owner. That was a little more permanence than either of us was ready for.

"Looks like his instincts are spot on, Mom." I nudged the chipmunk with my toe, wrinkling my nose.

"Get rid of that thing," she ordered, "and stop feeding the other one."

Rather than argue, I pivoted. "What's wrong with Riley? She looks like she barely slept—and since when does she fake sick?"

Mom shook her head. "I don't know what's gotten into her. She was even more of a handful than usual last night."

"Is there a problem at school? Is somebody pushing her around?"

"Can you imagine someone pushing that child around?" She pursed her lips, considering. "It's always hard when a new baby comes along. You certainly weren't a fan of Charlotte."

"I was two!"

"Nearly three. You covered her head in stamps and tried to give her to the mailman." She frowned. "Riley's had eight years as an only child. It's a big adjustment, especially considering all the changes around here."

Changes like me moving in, just as her parents started spending all their spare time at the hospital. Not that Riley had complained about our living arrangement. If anything, she seemed delighted, sticking to me like a burr whenever I was home, schooling me in soccer, keeping me up half the night with her endless musings on superhero rankings, Christmas lists, or ice cream flavors. It was like having a constantly hungry, perpetually chatty shadow.

Bunk bed aside, it was pretty awesome.

"She idolizes you," my mother said.

"She doesn't even know me." Which was my own fault. For the first part of Riley's life, I'd barely made it home for

Christmas each year. For twelve years, I'd stayed away so I didn't have to hear about how I'd disappointed everyone by turning my back on the family hardware store or endure well-meaning questions about why I couldn't seem to find a nice guy and settle down, when settling down felt like suffocation.

"As far as Riley's concerned, you are her exciting, adventurous aunt from the city, who makes everything fun. You caught a murderer, introduced her to sausage biscuits, taught her how to shuffle cards, and always give her seconds of dessert. Most importantly, you have never, ever told her how lucky she is to have a baby sister."

"I had one," I said with a shrug. "Charlie turned out okay, I guess, but . . ."

"Exactly," my mother said. "Which makes you the perfect person to figure out what's eating Riley."

It didn't seem quite fair—if I was the fun aunt, how come I had to have the tough conversations? I heaved a sigh. "Fine. I'll handle it."

"Thank you," she replied. I reached for the door, and she blocked my path. "But first, handle that chipmunk."

★　　★　　★

After a twelve-hour shift, nothing feels better than your head hitting the pillow.

And nothing feels worse than someone waking you up a mere two hours later. It's just long enough that your body has moved into deep sleep, but not long enough to actually feel rested.

"You didn't tell me Steven Tibbs's wife died!" My mother's voice was an octave higher than usual and less than a foot away. I rolled over, giving her my back, and pulled the comforter over my head.

She tugged it away. "Why didn't you say something this morning? I had to hear it from Helen Barker, of all people, smug as you please that she'd gotten the news first. You know I don't allow television in the mornings, Francesca, but if this is how you're going to behave I might have to reconsider."

"Can we talk about this later? Like, in five hours? Or never?"

"Helen said you were there when they brought Kate in." She sat on the edge of the bed as if readying herself for a long chat.

"I was, but I can't tell you anything about it. There are privacy laws—which you well know—and I'm not going to risk my job because you want to one-up Helen Barker."

"There's no need to be snippy," she grumbled. "It's so awful. Poor Steven. He and Kate were such a sweet couple."

"You knew them?" Of course she did. What my mother didn't know about Stillwater, or couldn't find out, wasn't worth knowing.

"I'm voting for him, aren't I?" Her gaze sharpened. "If you really want to know more about Steven, you should talk to Marshall."

But I knew Steven. Everyone knew Steven. It was his wife who'd been run off the road, whose lungs I had pumped air into. Whose death I'd witnessed. "What was Katherine like?"

"Kate," she said absently, tucking a wisp of silver-white hair back into its neat twist.

"Kate," I echoed. The nickname made her seem more real, somehow. Less a patient, more a person. "Did you know her well?"

"Mostly by reputation. She wasn't local, you know. She and Steven married while he was in law school, and when he moved home to take the job with the district attorney's office, she got a job as a case worker at Children and Family Services."

"Tough job," I said. I'd spent plenty of time with social workers in the ER—we frequently called them in for cases of suspected abuse. Greenstick fractures, where a child's bone breaks from being bent or twisted, cigarette burns, a thumb-shaped bruise . . . and those times when your sixth sense prickled, the ice in your gut and the hairs on your nape telling you that the usual ER philosophy—treat 'em and street 'em—didn't apply. When keeping a child safe meant keeping them away from their parents.

"One of the toughest," my mom said. "You treated her."

It wasn't a question, which meant I wasn't breaking confidentiality. "I tried to."

Her hand brushed over my shoulder, and she paused for a moment, watching me closely. "Helen said there was another driver. He was in the ER too, but he escaped before the police could arrest him."

That was a generous description of events; it made it sound like I hadn't screwed up at all. Had Noah planted that story, or was it one of my coworkers, trying to shield me? "Mom, come on."

"I'm just asking!"

"Well, you're asking the wrong person. Talk to the police."

"Aren't you and the MacLean boy talking again? I thought he might have mentioned something to you. A name? Helen didn't seem to know."

"I didn't get a name." Not a real one, at least. "When would Noah have talked to me?"

"Well, you saw him at the hospital. I assumed . . ."

Now I was fully awake. "Do you have actual spies around town, or have you upgraded to surveillance equipment? Drones, maybe?"

"So you did speak to him," she crowed. "What did he say about Kate's murder?"

"First of all, we don't know that it's murder," I said. "It could've been an accident, considering how bad the storm was, and the driver freaked out and fled the scene. Second, even *if* Noah knew something, I'm the last person he'd share it with."

"I thought you two . . ."

I cut her off. "Third, I'm going back to sleep. Wake me up when it's time to get Riley, please."

I retreated beneath the covers, and with a huff, my mother left. But the damage was done. Soon enough, my mom would find out that I'd been the one to let Kate's killer escape; soon enough the whole town would find out. I would be the juiciest news on the grapevine. Even worse, it would be true, unlike half the gossip that flooded Stillwater regularly. My mistake, and I might as well own it.

And if I owned it, I should fix it.

For a long time I lay staring at the wall, wondering if the grapevine was right about something else too. Social workers tended to make a lot of enemies. So did politicians. Was it possible Kate Tibbs's accident was actually murder?

★　　★　　★

"Feeling better?" I asked when I picked Riley up from school. The two-story redbrick building hadn't changed since I'd been a student there. A barely suppressed shudder ran through me at the sight. Even the playground was the same—old-fashioned metal equipment and wood chips that left splinters embedded in your knees and palms. My hands stung at the memory.

She nodded glumly. Her color was better, but she'd lost her typical bounce. Even her pigtails seemed subdued.

"Does the lunchroom still smell like hot dogs?" I asked.

Riley made a face. "And bleach. Who was your teacher when you went here?"

"Mrs. Lundstrom," I said. "She was pretty mean. Is your teacher nice?"

"I guess. She's teaching us about fossils. Fossils are cool."

She dribbled a soccer ball as we walked, feet scuffing through the still-sodden leaves. She glanced over at me, taking in my fleece jacket and scrubs.

"Do you have to work again tonight?"

"Yeah. Another twelve."

"But I have a soccer game."

I winced. I hadn't thought to check Charlie's meticulously color-coded family calendar before signing up for shifts. Coordinating schedules was a new experience for me. "I'm really sorry, Riley. I'll try to catch the next one, okay?"

"Yeah, sure." She kicked the ball a little too hard. It shot away, and she scrambled after it, propelled by barely concealed hurt.

When I caught up to her, she asked, "Why do you have to wear those clothes?"

"My scrubs?" I plucked at the blue poly-cotton shirt. "They show patients I'm a nurse. Plus, I get pretty dirty at work, and I'd rather keep my regular clothes clean, you know? They're comfy too. Like pajamas."

"But you look like everyone else," she said. "That's boring."

Avoiding boredom was Riley's mantra, in life as well as fashion. Today she was sporting purple-and-white-striped leggings under a pair of blue shorts, in deference to the chilly air, and a neon-green T-shirt that said, "You snooze, you lose," beneath a red zip-front hoodie. She looked like a cross between a rainbow and a tornado, but somehow she managed to pull it off.

"I'm sorry I have to miss your game," I said again. "You're going to be awesome. Maybe your dad can record it, and you can give me the play-by-play tomorrow after school."

She shrugged. "I guess. If you're not working."

"I'm off for a while now. Almost a week."

"Really? Could we do something fun this weekend?"

I started to say yes but caught myself. "I'm supposed to help at the store."

The soccer ball shot into a nearby hedge. "You're *always* helping at the store."

"Only for the weekend," I said quickly, alarmed by the sheen of tears in her eyes. "Maybe we can have a movie night. Or bake cookies. Or we could get your Halloween costume. That would be fun, right?"

She considered this as she dug the soccer ball out from the shrubbery. "I guess. Mom says you have to do something with all the junk you brought home."

"It's not junk," I said. "And I did do something with it. I put it in the office."

"Yeah, but Mom told Grandma it's in the way." She slipped her hand into mine. "You should bring it home and unpack. Then it wouldn't be in the way, and you'd be all moved in."

"Riley, there's barely room for *me* in Grandma's house. Besides, I'm only going to be here a few months. I'd have to turn around and pack it all up again."

It would have been more practical to put everything in storage, but as my mother had pointed out, it was silly to spend money on a storage unit when the space above the store was free, in both senses of the word.

"I guess." Riley's face darkened. "Are you sure you have to work tonight?"

I tugged her pigtails, remembering only too well that feeling of powerlessness. "It's not fair, is it?"

She leaned into me, smelling of pencil shavings and sunshine. "When will you be back?"

"In the morning, just like today. We'll do something fun this weekend, okay? You and me. In fact, that's your assignment while I'm at work tonight. Come up with an adventure for us."

"Sausage biscuits?" she said hopefully.

"Excellent start," I assured her. "But why stop there?"

FIVE

Despite Steven's plea for privacy, television news vans had taken over the hospital parking lot, and a gaggle of reporters crowded the main entrance. Rather than fight my way through, I headed for the emergency room doors. Jess Chapman seemed to have the same idea. Keeping her head down and her coat collar up, she scurried through the rows of cars.

"Jess! Hold up!"

She started at the sound of her name, her shoulders easing as she spotted me. As I drew closer, she forced a smile.

"How are you doing?" I asked.

"Good. How are you?" The reply was rote and stiff, meant to discourage real conversation. It would've been the easiest thing in the world to follow suit and leave her to handle the lingering effects of a tough case on her own. But easy didn't mean right. More senior nurses had helped me through my toughest traumas; it was only fitting that I pay those lessons forward.

"I'm hanging in there," I said. "It always takes me a few days to bounce back after a case like last night."

She blinked at my admission but didn't respond. Her hands worried the strap of her tote bag as we continued walking. Rather than spook her by making eye contact, I hitched my backpack more securely over my shoulder and kept my gaze fixed on the building ahead of us.

"I used to think it was a sign of weakness, letting a patient's death get to me," I said. "The first time it happened, I threw up in the staff lounge. I figured if I wanted to be a good nurse, I had to toughen up. Turn off my feelings."

Her voice was hoarse, barely audible. "I can't."

"Good," I replied firmly. She glanced over at me, eyebrows lifted in a question. "I was wrong. We're not meant to be robots, Jess. If you don't care about your patients, you're in the wrong line of work."

"But . . ." She brushed a wisp of pink-streaked blonde hair from her eyes.

"Last night was rough. Every single person in that room took it hard, not just you." I paused and took a deep breath. "I treated the other driver. The one who hit Kate Tibbs."

She stumbled. "What?"

I recounted John Mueller's arrival and escape. "If I had called security, they might have been able to detain him long enough for the police to arrest him. I didn't, and he got away, and we don't even know his real name."

She shook her head, ponytail swinging emphatically. "You don't know—"

"That he was the driver?" I finished for her. "I'd bet my nursing license on it. I let him get away, Jess, and that's on me. Nobody else."

"It's not the same. You left him to save Kate's baby. Everyone worked to save her baby, except me. I just . . ." She waved her hands, the gesture sheer frustration and helplessness. "I choked."

"True." A bitter pill, but I was in no mood for sugarcoating. She'd simply have to swallow it and move on, same as I would. "Next time, you won't."

"How do you know?"

"Because next time—and there's always a next time, whether it comes in a month or five years from now—you'll take a beat, you'll remember last night, and you'll tell yourself, 'Never again.'" I shrugged as the doors to the ER lobby slid open. "And then you'll get to work."

"Never again." Her expression shifted from distress to resolve, and she gave a short, sharp nod. "Never. Again. Thanks, Frankie."

She headed toward the main elevators while Alejandro buzzed me through the ER security doors. The clock above the nurses' station showed I was cutting it close, so I dashed to the lounge, stopping short when I saw the entire night shift assembled.

"Nice of you to join us, Stapleton," Costello muttered as I edged my way into the room.

"Nice of you to be so welcoming," I said sweetly. Apparently last night's truce had an expiration date. He snorted and went back to studying a batch of test results. Esme, standing near the coffeemaker, waved hello.

"Did I miss an e-mail?" I asked as she scooted over to give me a scant few inches of wall. We normally began shift change clustered around the nurses' station for a quick overview before assigning patients and reviewing their charts with the outgoing nurse. Despite the crowded lounge and late notice, this felt much more serious.

Before Esme could reply, the chatter in the room diminished from a hum to silence.

The source of the interruption was instantly clear. Grace Fisher, the hospital president, was making her way into the room, cool and elegant in a sage-green wool suit that made me acutely aware of every single wrinkle in my scrubs.

"We'll start at seven on the dot," she said in a clear carrying voice. "Everyone can relax until then."

Despite her words, the tension in the room thickened. Hospital administration rarely visited the overnight shift. At Chicago Memorial, we didn't see upper management unless something was very wrong—or unless you were engaged to a hotshot surgeon. Since I no longer fit the second category, I could only assume there was trouble on the horizon.

"Sale announcement?" Esme asked out of the corner of her mouth.

Consolidation was the name of the game in health care these days, and with the dearth of medical facilities in the area, Stillwater Gen looked like an excellent opportunity for big health care corporations looking to get bigger. But I'd seen enough hospital reorgs to know that the staff rarely came out ahead.

"I haven't heard anything," I replied. It seemed unlikely that the hospital could have been sold without my mother and her silver-haired intelligence network hearing about it. Before I could say anything more, Grace Fisher approached me.

"I understand you had quite an evening, Frankie."

"Yes, ma'am," I said, wishing I hadn't worn my hair in pigtails. Effective for keeping the short, wild curls out of my face when dealing with patients, but next to Grace's cool polish, I felt like a ragamuffin.

"Rest assured that if the police feel any need to discuss matters with you further, hospital counsel—and the board—will support you fully."

"Thank you, ma'am."

She nodded. "You're settling in well otherwise? You and Dr. Costello have managed to iron out your differences?"

Nearby, Costello choked on his coffee.

She gave him a thin smile. "I'll take that as a yes. Let's begin, shall we?"

She strode to the front of the room, the crowd parting before her.

"As many of you know, we treated a high-profile patient last night. Katherine Tibbs was the wife of Steven Tibbs, an assistant district attorney and local resident who is running for Congress. While the team was unable to save Mrs. Tibbs, we were able to safely deliver her son, who is currently admitted to the NICU."

A brief sympathetic murmur swelled, then ebbed as Grace continued. "Considering how close we are to Election Day, this has become a national news story, as you can tell from the media presence outside. However, it is also a very personal tragedy. The board and I expect that every member of the staff will maintain a strict No Comment policy when dealing with the press, even about matters not directly related to the Tibbs family. I will also reiterate that maintaining confidentiality is an expectation of all our staff, and violations relating to *any* of our patients will result in immediate dismissal and possible legal action."

From behind me, someone said, "I heard it wasn't an accident."

The murmurs rose again, more persistent this time, but Grace pressed on. "The police are investigating the crash, and it is our intention to cooperate fully. Hospital counsel is sending out an e-mail detailing how privacy laws are applied during criminal inquiries, but if you have further questions, please contact them at any time. Our goal, as always, is to deliver the best possible care to our patients and to maintain the sterling reputation of Stillwater General. Thank you, and have a good shift."

I sighed and filed out with the rest of the staff, eager to avoid any more conversations with Grace Fisher.

As we dispersed, I caught sight of Meg Costello in her purple hospital volunteer blazer. It never failed to amaze me that someone as perpetually cranky and bullheaded as Paul Costello could have raised such a sweet kid. Painfully shy, with clear hazel eyes and round cheeks, she was the kind of girl who, in ten years, would have finally come into her own. She'd be happy, confident, and stylish. For now, she was enduring adolescence with a heartbreaking stoicism.

"Hey, Meg! How are you?"

"I'm good," she said, so quietly I had to strain to hear the words. "How are you?"

"I'm good, thanks."

"My dad said you went home."

"Just for a quick trip." No doubt Costello would have preferred I stay in Chicago—and he hadn't limited his commentary to the ER. "That reminds me, though . . ."

I dug through my backpack, shoving past expired sun block, a paperback novel, a spare pair of sunglasses, and a protein bar. "Here you go. I picked these up while I was in town."

Meg's mouth made a perfect O as she took the stack of exhibit brochures from me. "You went to the Art Institute?"

The way she said the words, color rising in her cheeks, eyes sparkling, made it sound like Riley when she talked about Disney World.

"Not really," I confessed. "You can get these without going into the museum itself. Have you been there?"

"A few times," she said, tucking her hair behind her ear. "When my dad has a conference in Chicago, sometimes he lets me come with him, and we stop in. It's never long enough, though. I could spend days there and still not see everything."

Meg's hands, I noted, were covered in ink stains. They looked almost like bruises, black fading to blue, dotted with flecks of other colors, remnants of her passion for drawing.

"There's one in there for the school too," I said. "Junior year is when you start looking at colleges, isn't it?"

She stared at the floor, enthusiasm fading like a balloon losing its air. "Yeah."

"How's the graphic novel going?"

She nudged at her glasses. "Okay, I guess. I don't really have time for it lately."

"Why not?" I kept my voice light but fought a sinking feeling in my chest.

"School and stuff. Physics is kind of tough this semester, and so is precalculus. I'm trying to make first chair in band too—I play French horn, and I don't practice enough. Plus, I need more service hours. That's why I'm here tonight."

For her college application, no doubt. To Harvard, the school her father insisted would be the best place to study medicine even though Meg had as much interest in medicine as I did in accounting.

"Doesn't seem like that leaves much time for fun."

She jerked a shoulder, the gesture an echo of her father. "There'll be time for fun later."

The words sounded like her father's too, and my skepticism must have shown, because she added hurriedly, "Besides, what could I do for fun around here? My options are basically to drink at somebody's house or drink at some creepy old abandoned farm."

"Henderson's," I said fondly, and her eyes widened in recognition—and surprise. Henderson's Dairy, long-abandoned, had been the site of legendary high school parties when I was Meg's age. It probably *was* pretty creepy—the place had been falling down when I was in school, and it seemed unlikely that anyone had bothered to fix it up since then. But I had very fond memories of it nevertheless.

"You partied there?" Meg asked, equal parts awe and dismay in her voice.

"A few times," I hedged, suddenly worried she might take my stories as an example—or worse, permission. "You're right to skip the parties, but . . . there's got to be something you could do that isn't just school and volunteering."

"Drawing," she said softly. "I like drawing."

The impulse to push her toward something more social was so strong, I literally bit my tongue. It was like my mother had taken control of my body.

When the urge had passed, I bumped her shoulder and smiled. "Hey, if drawing's what makes you happy, go for it."

Costello caught sight of us and frowned.

I tipped my head in his direction. "No matter what anyone says."

"Meg," Costello called, striding toward us. "What are you doing here? Your shift ended at seven."

"I thought I'd say good night," she replied, staring at her feet.

"Good night," he said and brushed a kiss over the top of her head.

"Daaaad," she said, flushing and twisting away.

"Get that homework done, and I'll see you tomorrow morning. And be good for Aunt Lori tonight." When she'd left, he turned to me. "Something you wanted to say, Stapleton?"

"She's a nice kid," I said.

"She got it from her mother," he assured me.

The night dragged despite the steady stream of patients. The police had left, and the cleaning crew had restored both Exam Three and Trauma One to their usual spotless states. Tragedy had been tidied away as if it had never occurred so we could start fresh with the next one.

"Reporters still out front?" I asked one of the paramedics as he wheeled in a possible carbon monoxide poisoning.

"A few," he replied.

"I wish they'd leave," Esme said, directing him to an exam room. "It feels like we're being watched."

"They'll go away soon," I said, attaching the oxygen mask to our patient and bringing up the chart. "Gotta chase the next big story."

I'd seen it a million times. A reporter in a black wool overcoat, clutching a microphone, somberly intoning words like "tragedy" and "devastation," urging the viewer to trust in their sincerity. Seconds after the camera switched off, they were moving on without a thought for the people who had to pick up the pieces while they chased ratings. They trained a spotlight on people's darkest moments, beaming them out for the world to see, claiming it was their duty, but they never seemed particularly interested in helping repair the damage.

"What if this *is* the next big story?" Esme asked when I returned to the desk. She leaned in, lowered her voice to a whisper. "I heard from a friend of mine on dispatch that the nine-one-one call was weird."

I paused in the middle of labeling test tubes for blood work. "Weird how?"

"The first call was fine—some couple that came across the crash site and called it in right away. But there was a second call that came in when they were already on their way to the scene. A guy, who told them that a car had gone over the embankment and a woman was trapped inside."

"So?"

"So," she said triumphantly. "How would the caller have known it was a woman unless he'd seen her up close? It must have been your patient."

I tried to picture it. The shriek of metal as Kate's car tore through the guardrail and tumbled into the water below. The cold. The rain. Kate, drifting in and out of consciousness as the pressure from her head wound built. Had she called out for help? Had the driver tried to reach her, or had he left her bleeding and alone as the darkness closed in around her?

I swallowed against the hot bilious rush of anger. "Can they trace the nine-one-one call?"

"They did," she said. "It came from the pay phone in the lobby. *Our* lobby. A few minutes before nine."

"Why would Mueller call nine-one-one in the first place?"

"Maybe it was a genuine accident," Esme said. "He panicked, drove off, and then felt guilty about it."

"So he left her there for half an hour? He couldn't have known about the earlier call. If he had called right after the accident, we could have had another fifteen minutes."

Esme looked queasy at the realization.

Fifteen minutes was an eternity when it came to traumas. Those fifteen minutes could have saved Kate Tibbs's life.

"He must have been planning to take off all along," Esme said. "That's why he gave us fake information. He knew they'd bring Kate here, but he needed to get fixed up first, so he gave himself a head start."

"Awfully risky," I said. "What if we'd been swamped? He could have been here for hours before we treated him."

Esme shook her head. "Didn't you see? We have billboards now on all the major highways, with live estimates of the wait time. He would have known he'd have time, especially since they had to extract Kate from the car."

Mueller had known it was a woman trapped in the car. That would have been a hard detail to make out on a back road during a nighttime storm. Hard to imagine Mueller, with his dislocated shoulder, climbing down a slippery embankment to check on his victim, then climbing up again and abandoning her.

He knew he'd hit a woman because he knew who he'd hit. He'd targeted Kate Tibbs.

"I don't understand," Esme continued, bringing my thoughts back to the present. "I want some sort of explanation, even if it's horrible. There has to be a reason, right? It can't be that the universe is just that cruel?" She tapped the newspaper resting on the nurses' station. "Look at them. Don't they seem happy?"

A photo from a recent campaign rally dominated the front page: Steven in a navy suit, an adorably pregnant Kate at his side in a powder-blue maternity dress. Her long brown hair was pulled back at the sides, leaving the back to cascade down her shoulders. The silver charm bracelet glinted at her wrist, and Steven's arm circled her waist. The perfect happy family.

The article not only detailed their hopes for the election but gave a brief summary of Kate's own accomplishments—twelve years at the Department of Children and Family Services, the last ten in Stillwater, a commitment to justice for children and helping families. Coworkers described her as a tireless fighter for her young charges.

Twelve years was a long time to fight, I mused. A hint of strain was evident in the photograph, a slight shadow around her eyes. Twelve years of fighting for kids was likely to make you some enemies too. Unlike Chicago, where it was easy for a caseworker to keep their personal life private, Kate Tibbs would have been highly visible even when she wasn't working. I wondered how she'd felt about Steven's rise to prominence, if she'd felt uncomfortable with so much attention. In the article, it said that she planned to leave DCFS if her husband's bid for Congress was successful and begin working with other nonprofits to promote child welfare and strong families. A reprieve from the job, if not from the spotlight.

The question was, had Kate's own enemies come after her, or was Steven the true target?

"Frankie, Exam Five won't let me examine him," Esme said, returning sooner than I expected.

I frowned. Esme didn't seem like the type to let a patient ruffle her. "Tell him he can either let you work, or he can leave. Bring an orderly in if you think he won't believe you."

"No, he's fine with an exam. But he only wants *you*."

I looked up from the paper. "What?"

"He's asking for you. Specifically."

"What's his name?"

She glanced up at the board where we listed the patients. "Art Gundersen."

"I don't know anyone named Art Gundersen."

She shrugged. "Well, he knows you."

"Why are we standing around, people?" Costello asked, passing through.

"Frankie has an admirer," Esme said. "He won't let anyone else examine him."

Costello's eyebrows lifted. "Is that so?"

"I have no idea who it is," I replied, heat rising in my cheeks. "Esme can handle it. Tell him I'm on break or something."

"I did. He said he'd wait."

"Does he seem like a perv?" Costello asked Esme.

"No," she said immediately. "He's really polite. He keeps saying he'd prefer Frankie, and he'll wait until she's available."

"Fan club, not stalker." Costello propped an elbow on the counter, black humor lighting his eyes. "Take an orderly with, if you're worried, but let's get him gone."

"But . . ."

"Go," he ordered. "Save the soap opera for after your shift."

The radio crackled. "Stillwater General, this is Riverside four-forty-one. We're en route with the victim of an MVA resulting from a police chase; patient is a member of law enforcement, presenting with minor injuries, including back pain and possible concussion. We are transporting per department protocol. ETA five minutes."

A whooshing noise sounded in my ears as the blood rushed from my head, and I reached for the counter to steady myself. Not Noah, I told myself. It wouldn't be Noah, if for no other reason than sheer stubbornness—he'd never let his quarry escape.

"Guess your admirer will have to wait," Costello said, taking no notice of my reaction to the call. "Go prep Exam Three. Vargas, finish discharging the gastro case in Two—bland diet, lots of fluids, call his physician in the morning."

For once, I was happy to follow Costello's orders. I began prepping the room—test tubes for blood work, a suture tray, and for good measure, an ice pack.

A few minutes later, the ambulance pulled up. "Rig's here," Costello called, passing by my door. I hurried out after him and waited, outwardly calm but inwardly quaking as the back of the ambulance swung open and a figure emerged.

Not Noah. My gut had been right this time. The guy climbing down stiffly from the ambulance did look familiar, but half the department had shown up at Stapleton and Sons during the Clem Jensen case. This officer barely looked old enough to shave, let alone carry a weapon. He winced and waved off the paramedic, who was trying to keep a straight face as they walked in.

Costello took one look at the baby-faced deputy, who had a nasty cut above his right eyebrow and a hangdog expression, and snickered. "Call me when you're ready for sutures, Stapleton."

"I've got him," I told the paramedic, who was reciting the deputy's vitals as we walked toward the exam room. "What's your name, Deputy?"

"Travis Anderson, ma'am," he replied.

"Great. I'm Frankie." I ushered him into the room and shut the door, leaving Costello still chuckling outside. "What happened, Deputy Anderson?"

"Call me Travis, ma'am." He adjusted his hat and practically stood at attention, despite his furious blush and the blood trickling down the side of his face. "At approximately ten-oh-two, I was surveilling a residence when I noticed a figure approaching on foot who proceeded to gain access to the residence in question. After identifying myself . . ."

"I don't need the official report, Travis. Just a recap."

"Yes, ma'am." His posture relaxed slightly. "I knocked on the front door, but he went out the back and ran off. I chased after him, but he managed to reach a car he'd stashed the next block over. So I ran back to my vehicle and began a pursuit."

"Did you catch him?"

"No, ma'am." He stared down at his feet, his voice lowered to a mumble. "There was an unexpected obstruction. I swerved."

"Roll back your sleeve," I said, and he obeyed. I fitted the blood pressure cuff around his arm and prompted, "You swerved. To avoid the obstruction, I take it?"

"Yes, ma'am," he sighed as the cuff released with a hiss.

"And hit something else?"

"Yes, ma'am."

"Quit calling me 'ma'am,'" I snapped. He flinched, and I gentled my tone while I continued the exam. "What *was* the obstruction?"

Woeful as a basset hound, he said, "A raccoon."

I pressed my lips together to keep from laughing. "And that's when you crashed?"

"Yes, ma'am. Into a telephone pole."

"In your squad car?"

"Undercover unit," he said with a faint note of pride. Then his shoulders slumped. "It's county property, you know."

"Oh, I know." It would be a long time before young Deputy Anderson lived this one down. "Well, Travis, the good news is you're not too banged up. How's your neck? Any whiplash, you think?"

"I'm fine," he insisted. "But I really need to get back to the station and file a report. There's special forms, you know, when you damage county property."

"I'm sure there are." I began cleaning the cut above his eyebrow. "This isn't deep, but it'll probably leave a scar unless we suture it. And Dr. Costello will want to examine you before you're released, maybe do a CT scan to check for concussion. You'll be here for a little while yet."

"I'm fine," he said again. "Honest, I feel great."

Great was probably overstating the case, but I could only imagine his embarrassment. No doubt he was hoping that the sooner he recovered, the sooner the rest of the officers would forget the incident.

"How many years have you been with the department, Travis?"

"A year," he said and then amended, "maybe a little less. Ten months."

Still a rookie, then. I felt a rush of sympathy for him. The new guy always had something to prove; even with a decade's worth of experience, I felt the same every time I walked in to Stillwater Gen. Now I wondered if we had something else in common. If we'd both let John Mueller slip away.

"Ready for those sutures?" Costello said from the doorway.

Travis paled, and I patted his hand. "We'll numb the cut before he starts. All you'll feel is a pinch."

Sewing someone's skin back together takes less time than you'd expect, but there's still prep work to be done. As Costello scrubbed in and I finished prepping the suture tray, I mulled over Travis's story. It was possible he'd been staking out a house completely unrelated to the Tibbs case, but I doubted it. Which meant I felt only the slightest twinge of guilt when I asked, "Whose place were you staking out?"

"Ma'am?" He started to turn toward me, but the sight of Costello holding a needle and thread stopped him from moving. "It's part of an ongoing investigation."

"John Mueller, right?"

"Miller," he corrected me woozily as Costello began stitching the cut closed. "I'm not supposed to talk about it."

"I understand," I said. "We have rules about confidentiality too. I'm just trying to make sure I have the right information for our files since we treated your suspect the other day. You know how important it is to get those reports right."

Costello snorted but didn't stop suturing.

"So," I prompted. "You were keeping an eye on John Miller?"

"Josh," corrected a familiar voice. "Josh Miller. Anderson, I see you've met Frankie Stapleton. She's more trouble than you're ready for, son."

"Hey!" I whirled around to scowl at Noah, who was leaning against the doorway and scowling right back. "I am with a patient."

"And I am checking on one of my men," he returned. "A raccoon, Anderson?"

"I'm sorry, sir." Travis turned and Costello tugged sharply at the suture thread, causing him to yelp.

"Stay still," he ordered. "Unless you want an eyebrow piercing."

Noah stepped inside and shut the door behind him. "Dispatch said Miller was on foot?"

"Yes, sir. He had the car parked a block over, on Jefferson. I followed him as far as Roosevelt when the . . . um . . ."

"The obstruction," I prompted, and he nodded, then winced.

"Stay still," Costello muttered while I filed away the intersection of Jefferson and Roosevelt. The south side of town, not far from where Noah grew up.

"The obstruction appeared," Travis continued doggedly. "Were the other units able to apprehend him?"

"Not yet," Noah said. Travis twisted to face him, flushing with distress.

"I'm really—"

"Out." Costello straightened and pointed to the door. "Now."

I didn't think he meant Travis.

"I need to speak with my officer," Noah said evenly.

Costello didn't spare him a glance, merely bent closer to inspect the neat line of stitches. "In five minutes—assuming you people will *let me work*—you can serve him high tea for all I care. Right now, leave."

Noah didn't move.

"Stapleton, call security."

"Come on," I said, tugging off my latex gloves and catching Noah by the sleeve. "I'll find you some coffee."

"That guy is a piece of work," he fumed as we headed toward the staff lounge.

"Costello? You should see him on a bad day." I spoke lightly, trying to ease the tension. The lounge was empty, and I gestured to the ancient plaid couch. "But he's fast. You'll be back in there before the coffee cools."

Luckily, there was still some left in the pot. I filled a Styrofoam cup and handed it over. "Black, right?"

He took a cautious sip and grimaced. "This is terrible coffee."

"Better than the cafeteria," I said, and he chuckled. "So Josh Miller? Sounds a lot like John Mueller."

Noah sobered instantly. "Not your concern."

"A little late for that," I said. "Was it the fingerprints on the payphone?"

He shook his head. "How'd you hear about that?"

I simply propped my chin in my hands and smiled.

"I don't know why I'm surprised," he muttered. "Yes, we got it from the prints, then matched an old mug shot to the security footage. He's a small-time dealer looking to move up in the world."

"What's his connection to Kate Tibbs?"

"You are familiar with the concept of confidentiality, aren't you? Despite the fact you just weaseled information out of a police officer?"

"I didn't weasel anything," I said. "I was distracting him while Costello put in sutures so he didn't pass out and hit his head again."

"I'm not discussing Josh Miller," Noah said, settling back against the couch. "And unlike young Anderson, I know how to handle you, so don't bother."

"He is really young, Noah. He keeps calling me 'ma'am.'"

"And yet he lives?" The frown lines etched into his forehead eased slightly.

I grinned. "We've come to an understanding."

Someone had left the day's paper on the table, and I studied the front page article Esme had pointed out earlier. "This says Steven was at a fundraiser last night. Does that mean his alibi checks out?"

"It does," he said. "Which we assumed would be the case."

"Wonder why Kate didn't go with him," I mused.

"According to Steven, she didn't feel up to a night of schmoozing."

I'd done those nights of schmoozing and hated them—it was hard to imagine how much worse they'd be at eight months pregnant, the endless rounds of smiles and handshakes and fake cheer. I stifled a shudder and turned my attention back to the article.

"Have you looked into the other candidate? Norris Mackie?"

Noah's eyebrows lifted. "Frankie."

"What? I'm just curious."

"One, I've already told you too much. No more. Two, it says right in the article that Mackie was *also* at a fundraiser."

"He could have hired someone," I said. "Politicians never do their own dirty work."

"And three," he continued, "you are never 'just' curious. You're never 'just' anything."

"I'm not! You looked at Steven, so checking out his rival seems like a logical next step."

"Some people," he said mildly, "would be insulted at the suggestion that they were not capable of running an investigation."

"You're more than capable." I tossed the paper onto the scarred table, frustration giving voice to an ugly truth. "But I'm the one who patched up Miller. I'm the one who should have called security. He escaped on my watch, and that makes me responsible."

He leaned forward, caught my hand in his. "Miller is responsible for his actions. Not you. You think Travis is to blame for Kate's death, since Miller gave him the slip tonight?"

"No, but—"

"This isn't on you. It was never on you, so let it go."

Before I could explain how very unlikely that was, the lounge door swung open.

"I hate to interrupt your coffee klatch, but I'm finished with Babyface," Costello said. "Get him down to imaging, then take care of your fan club in Exam Five."

"Fan club?" Noah asked.

"It's nothing." I set off for Travis's room again, chagrined.

"You're sure?" He followed me in. "Because the phrase 'fan club' definitely sounds like something. Something I'd like to hear more about."

I helped Travis into a wheelchair, ignoring both his protests and Noah's ribbing. "All I'm saying is, maybe it wouldn't hurt to check Mackie's alibi."

"There's no need," Noah said as I maneuvered the wheelchair out. "We know who did it."

"And why," Travis chimed in. "Revenge."

Next to me, Noah ground his teeth.

"For what?" I asked. "Hold on. Kate was a social worker. Did she take Miller's kid?"

Noah sighed. "Miller has a five-year-old daughter. Kate had been the caseworker of record for years, but after his last arrest, she finally convinced the judge to grant custody to an aunt up north."

"You think Miller killed her to get even." Murder, then. My mother was right. And yet it felt wrong. If Miller wanted Kate dead, he had no reason to call 9-1-1. He would have wanted to give himself as much time to escape as possible, so why call attention to the crash? "So that's it? Revenge, open and shut?"

"Not that open and shut," Noah said as we continued down the maze of corridors. "We still have to find him. He's dropped off the radar—not even his customers know where he is."

I dropped off Travis with the imaging technician, then led Noah back toward the ER. "That's why Travis was staking out his house. You were hoping he'd come back."

"We have people watching his usual hangouts. The house was one of them."

"He should have known you were keeping an eye out. Why would he risk going back to his house?"

"Josh Miller is not known for his towering intellect," Noah pointed out. "We're assuming there was something there he didn't want us to find."

"You've already searched it, haven't you?" I took his silence and the faint curve at the corner of his mouth as assent. "He would have known you'd toss the place and were watching—and yet he came back anyway. That's a desperate man."

"Killers are," he said. "Murder is rarely someone's first choice, unless they're a sociopath, and I don't believe Josh Miller is a sociopath."

No, I didn't think so either. A sociopath wouldn't have called in Kate's accident. A sociopath would have been pleased by what he'd done. He would have manipulated me, tried to get me on his side. All Josh Miller had wanted was a shoulder reduction and narcotics.

Which brought us right back to desperate, a thought that didn't strike me as reassuring.

"Why are you telling me all of this?" I asked, coming to a sudden stop. "You didn't even want to give me Miller's real name. One slip from Travis, and you're practically looping me into the investigation."

"Hardly," he said. "Fact is, we're releasing Miller's name and picture tomorrow morning, announcing him as a person of interest in the investigation and asking for the public's help in locating him. So while I'd rather you didn't shout it from the top of the water tower, I'm not overly concerned if the word gets out early."

"Why wait until morning?" I asked. "Wouldn't it be better to get the word out as soon as possible?"

Noah grimaced. "That's Ted Sullivan's call. He felt hitting the morning news would maximize our exposure; he didn't want the story to get lost overnight. The sheriff agreed."

Ted's approach somehow managed to be both savvy and smarmy. Every move he made was to maximize exposure, to increase Steven's appeal by serving up a man's private tragedy as public spectacle.

"You're absolutely sure it's not about the election?" I asked again.

"Frankie," he said tiredly, "I am never sure about anything until I get a signed confession. Sometimes not even then. But right now, I have what Steven would call a preponderance of evidence that Josh Miller is our guy. So while I am never sure, I'm almost certain. And I'm not inclined to wait."

Who could blame him? I'd waited, and Miller had escaped.

Stress and exhaustion roughened his voice. I studied him, noting the stubble along his jaw, the tension etched around his eyes and mouth. He always took his work seriously, but a case like this, high-pressure, high-profile, would only spur him to work harder—not because he wanted the attention, but because he wanted the attention over as soon as possible. "The reporters must be driving you nuts."

"They're everywhere," he said, leaning against the wall. "Like crows on carrion. My phone's ringing every five minutes from people wanting updates. State police, governor's office, state's attorney, district attorney. It never ends."

"How are you supposed to chase down leads if you're on the phone all the time? You hate the phone." He used to, at least. Some girls stayed up all night talking to their boyfriend on the phone, but I'd preferred sneaking out of the house. I'd meet up with Noah a few blocks away, and he would drive while we talked. In warm weather, we'd go to the quarry and swim in the moonlight. Once the weather turned, we'd go to Henderson's, build a campfire in one of the abandoned worker cottages, and talk for hours.

Sometimes we didn't talk too.

"I know what you're doing," he said, poking me in the shoulder. "We have plenty of people investigating. Trained people. Official people. I do not need your help to find Josh Miller."

"You're asking the public for help. How am I different?"

"We're asking the public to notify us if they see him. We are not asking them to actively seek him out, which is exactly what you're planning." I started to protest, but he cut me off, the set of his mouth flat and unamused. "Do not tell me otherwise, because you are a terrible liar."

I paused, regrouped. "I was helpful with the Clem Jensen case."

"Investigating Clem's death nearly got you killed. So the answer is no. Do not help. Do not ask around. Do not do anything that might bring you into this investigation. You do your job, and I'll do mine."

"I have been! I was doing my job when I pumped air into Kate Tibbs's lungs as they were shutting down. I was doing my job when I helped bring that baby into the world." I'd been doing my job when Josh Miller came in too. Whether victim or killer, it's my duty to treat my patients to the best of my ability. But letting Miller escape was my *failure*, no matter what Noah said, and I needed to make amends. "I've been a part of this from the beginning. I'm not quitting now."

"Nobody's asking you to quit. But your work ends at the hospital doors. Mine is just starting, and I can't focus if I'm busy worrying about you."

The sentiment caught me off guard, and my temper softened. "You don't need to worry about me."

"Maybe not." His mouth quirked, caught between amusement and irritation. "But I do."

I stepped closer, touched by the admission, until he added, "This is too important to let you interfere."

Stung, I turned away, saying, "Esme will bring the discharge papers for Travis once he's back from imaging. It should only be a few minutes."

"Frankie . . ."

"Are you Francesca?" asked an older man, slowly approaching. "Francesca Stapleton?"

A hospital bracelet circled his wrist, and I pasted on my best nurse smile. "That's me. How can I help you?"

"I've been waiting for you. Art Gundersen." He hooked his thumbs into his suspenders. "I've been in that room down the hall."

Exam Five. I should've known. "Thank you for waiting, Mr. Gundersen. Let's go back in, and I'll fix you up."

"Frankie," Noah said.

"We're done here," I told him and began escorting Art back to his room.

"Busy night," Art said, glancing over his shoulder at Noah as if sensing the tension. "Your mother didn't say . . ."

"My mother?" My gaze snapped toward him, then flashed to his left hand—no ring—and mortification began to roar in my ears like a fast-approaching train.

"Yes," he said, his voice echoing down the corridor. "Lila suggested I come in and see you."

Behind me, Noah snickered.

I stiffened my spine and lowered my voice, as I ushered Art down the hall and back into the exam room. "What brings you in tonight?"

"Oh, nothing terrible." He settled onto the bed, cheerful as if he'd only been here a few minutes. "A bit of a cold, but your mother said I should get it checked out before it turned into something more serious. She recommended I see you, nobody else, and said that you'd make sure I got the proper care."

"Did she?" I managed through gritted teeth. "So thoughtful, my mother."

Art agreed, and I logged in to read his chart on the computer terminal.

Art, it seemed, was sixty-three and widowed. Closer to my mom's age than mine, in fact. Clearly, my single status was bothering her more than she'd let on.

I started taking his vitals. "Did you get the pneumonia vaccine this year, Art?"

"No, not the flu shot either. Those things will make you sick."

"Actually, they won't. The virus in the vaccine is dead, so it's impossible to contract the illness from the shot."

"Huh. My daughter"—he paused to cough—"she's a bit younger than you, and she told me otherwise."

I kept my voice breezy despite the black mood overtaking me. Compartmentalization worked as well for annoying ex-fiancés and interfering mothers as it did for work stress. "Ah, well. You can set her straight. Show her dad still knows best."

"Might as well go ahead and get it now since I'm here." He winked. "Promise you'll be gentle."

"Breathe in," I said, stethoscope in place. There was a crackling in his lungs that confirmed my suspicions—it was too late for the vaccine. Art had contracted pneumonia. "Breathe out. Good."

I logged the results as Art said, "Your mother's told me a lot about you."

"I'm sure she has."

"Family's important. It's nice you've moved back. Shows your priorities are in the right place."

"I'm not that nice," I assured him. "I'm only here temporarily."

His bushy eyebrows lifted. "That's not what Lila said."

"She's . . . biased." Delusional, actually, if she thought I was here for longer than my initial commitment. Considering she was trying to use the ER as a matchmaking service, delusional seemed generous. "Dr. Costello will be with you shortly."

I escaped into the hallway, ready to flag down Costello, but there was no need.

"Hear you made a love connection with Exam Five," he said as he caught sight of me.

"Pneumonia," I said shortly. "Pulse eighty-two, temp ninety-seven point eight, phlegmy cough and crackling in the left lung."

"And a broken heart," Esme chimed in, giggling.

I rounded on her. "Really? We need to do this now?"

She shrugged, phone tucked between her ear and shoulder. "Your guy wasn't exactly subtle."

Neither was my mom. "He's not my guy."

"Night's young, Stapleton," Costello said and went to examine Art.

I fixed Esme with a glare. "What else have we got?"

"We're quiet right now. The deputies left a few minutes ago. Is it true you and Noah MacLean used to be engaged?"

I ignored the twinge behind my sternum. "Six or seven lifetimes ago, yes."

Right after high school, actually, in a burst of hormone-fueled dreams. By the time I'd graduated from nursing school, the dream had turned to ashes. I couldn't bear the idea of living in Stillwater for the rest of my life, and Noah couldn't live with himself if he left. Twelve years later, the memory of what we'd said to each other still scalded despite our efforts to move past it.

"That's gotta be awkward, right? Seeing him here?"

Awkward wasn't quite the word. There wasn't a single word that summed up the tangle of emotions I felt every time Noah and I crossed paths, but the current frontrunner was annoyance. "It's fine. All part of the job. For both of us."

Do your job, Noah had ordered, and I would.

My free time, however, was my own.

SIX

Some nights, the ER never slows down and there's barely enough time to use the restroom. But for the second night in a row, I was able to grab a few minutes with Rowan in the NICU. Charlie would appreciate the report, and I relished a few minutes away from the staff teasing me about Art. My mother had a lot to answer for.

In the NICU, Rowan was wide awake. Donna was holding her and swaying gently as she crooned a lullaby. "You all have a night owl on your hands," she said. "She's been wide awake for the last hour or so."

"Charlie will be thrilled," I said, rolling my eyes. My sister had always been, in true Benjamin Franklin fashion, an early-to-bed, early-to-rise kind of girl. Riley too seemed incapable of sleeping past six thirty—except for today's episode. "Can I hold her?"

Rowan felt like a cloud, soft and nearly weightless. I walked in a small circle, mindful of the monitor leads still attached to her foot. A few feet away, Jess was checking on Trey, whispering to him as she bent over the isolette.

"How's he doing?" I called softly, and she jumped, pressing a hand against her heart. "Sorry, didn't mean to startle you."

She waved it off, returning her attention to the baby. "He's doing great. A little trouble maintaining his body temp, so we're still running some tests, but he's very lucky, all things considered."

"Are they going to step him down to the regular nursery or straight to discharge?"

Her hands fumbled on the tiny knit cap. "I don't know. I hope they'll keep him here."

"I heard Dr. Solano saying they want him here until discharge, no matter how fast he bounces back," Donna put in. "For security reasons."

"Really?" Funny how Noah hadn't mentioned that. Were they worried Miller might come after Trey? If so, a locked and monitored ward like the NICU was the best place for him, no matter what his medical status.

Donna shrugged and moved to another isolette. "It's nice for him to have that kind of attention, poor little mite. And I'm sure it gives his father some peace of mind."

True. I let Rowan grab tightly to my finger, worked her little arms up and down like she was lifting weights. "Look how strong you're getting, little buddy! Keep it up, and you'll be home before you know it. You'll even get your own room, unlike me."

"You don't have your own room?" Donna asked, chuckling. "Are you sharing with Lila?"

"Riley," I said. "The big sister. She's sweet, but I thought I'd outgrown roommates."

"I shared a room when I was a kid," Jess said, glancing up from the isolette. "Four of us in a room smaller than the family lounge."

"How'd you manage that?" I asked.

She reached in through the porthole, brushed a thumb over Trey's foot. "Being together wasn't so bad. Eventually we split up, but . . . I hadn't minded it, really. We survived."

"So did my boys," Donna said, giving me a mock frown. "Builds character, if you ask me."

"Yeah, yeah. I know. And Riley's cute." I tapped Rowan's button nose, and she regarded me seriously. "Runs in the family, I guess."

Trey squeaked, and Jess cooed softly to him.

"Has Steven been in tonight?" I asked. "How's he holding up?"

"I was with the twins," Jess said stiffly, nodding at a pair of isolettes across the room. "I didn't see him."

Typically NICU nurses stayed with one or two patients until discharge. The most critical cases might require constant one-on-one care; as the baby improved, her nurse might take on a second, less-acute case. If Jess was assigned to the twins across the room, visiting with Trey was more social than medical. Perhaps keeping an unofficial eye on him was her way of making up for last night.

"Steven was here during day shift," Donna said. "Someone said he stepped out for a bit to make arrangements for the funeral on Monday." She shook her head. "Imagine, burying your wife while your baby's in here."

Jess turned away, blinking rapidly.

"Anyway," Donna continued after a moment, "once that was done, he came in and didn't leave until after dinner. That manager of his was here too, though they wouldn't let him in since his phone was glued to his ear. Someone told me he sat right out on the bench in the hall, and every time he needed something, he'd wave through the glass, and Steven would have to run out and talk to him."

So much for suspending the campaign. But all I said was, "Election Day's coming, I guess."

Donna sniffed. "You'd think he'd care more about his family than a stupid election."

"For some people, work is a refuge from the rest of their life. Maybe Steven feels that way." I certainly had, plenty of times. "Maybe he thinks that winning the election will help him get justice for Kate."

"Someone said it was intentional," Donna whispered as Jess scowled. "Can you believe it? Who on earth would have done such a thing?"

"The police ID'd the driver," I said and filled them in on Josh Miller and tomorrow's announcement.

Both women looked at me blankly. Finally, Donna said, "It doesn't make sense. Why would anyone want to hurt that poor woman?"

"She was a social worker," I pointed out. "She'd taken kids away from their families."

"For their own good," Jess said hotly. "She didn't do it on a whim."

"Of course not." No doubt, the NICU had seen plenty of babies born addicted to drugs; it was only natural they'd want the best for their patients. "But Miller probably didn't appreciate it; the police think he was holding a grudge."

"I suppose," Jess said, the words heavy with doubt. With a final glance at Trey, she crossed back over to the twins.

"Did you know her?" I asked. "Kate, I mean."

"Me?" She looked startled, busied herself with checking monitor leads. "I think she might have been in here for a case once or twice. Donna?"

Donna nodded agreement. "Do the police think they'll find the guy? He could be halfway across the country by now."

I hadn't mentioned that he'd been spotted last night. Josh's name might be public knowledge in a few hours, but Noah would want most of the case details kept quiet. "They seem pretty determined."

Noah's determination came from someplace more ingrained than the job. He'd had a lousy home life growing up. After he'd practically raised his younger siblings, his family obligations had kept him in Stillwater when all he'd wanted was to escape. Of course he'd want to do right by a woman who had tried to protect kids going through the same things he had. Whether he'd known Kate personally or only by reputation, I didn't doubt that finding her killer meant more than he'd admitted to me or anyone else.

I gave Rowan a kiss on the head and handed her over to Donna. "Time for me to get back."

On my way out, I paused to look at Trey dozing in his isolette. Technically he was younger than Rowan, but he'd had the benefit of more time in utero. Despite the trauma of the accident, he looked downright plump next to Rowan, with his bald head and rounded cheeks.

I wondered if he looked like his mother, if he'd grow up comforted in the knowledge they shared a nose, a dimple, or a chin. If he'd carry some mannerism of Kate's within him, surprising everyone when it emerged. It was heartbreaking that he would never know his mother and she would never know him. Never see the person she'd carried inside her for so many months.

I'd lost my father young, but at least I had memories of us. Moments I could call up when I was feeling particularly lost. Trey would have none of those, and the knowledge made me want to cry for a family I hadn't known until twenty-four hours ago, a family shattered before they even began.

Noah wasn't the only one who was taking this case personally.

SEVEN

In the ER, we take our humor anywhere we can find it. Unfortunately, my colleagues had found plenty in my mom's matchmaking attempts. By the time I'd finished my shift, they'd taken to paging me as Nurse Gundersen, changing my name on the whiteboard that listed our cases, and working it in to every conversation. The only upside was that it meant everyone was talking about my social life instead of my failure to contain Josh Miller.

Even so, I was not inclined to go straight home after my shift. I hadn't decided what I would say to my mother, but odds were good that it wouldn't be appropriate for Riley's ears. Instead, I headed for Stapleton and Sons, our family's hardware store.

"Morning," Charlie called from the back counter as I pushed open the front door, bell jingling overhead. When she realized it was just me, not a customer, she turned her attention back to the man in paint-spattered jeans and an old sweat shirt.

The store looked like it always had, though Charlie's window displays were more inviting than anything my father had ever done. Inside, the aisles were still narrow, the shelves crowded with a hodgepodge of tools and building supplies. The wide, dark wooden floorboards creaked beneath my feet, the sound familiar and comforting. As I made my way to the back of the main room, I breathed deeply, filling my lungs with the smell of sawdust and machine oil and varnish, as heady and evocative as it had been when I was a child.

I boosted myself onto one of the stools at the long oak counter, propping my chin in my hands and half listening to their conversation about paint quantities and color-matching. My feet barely brushed the floor, same as always.

When they'd finished, the contractor—it was always a contractor, this early on a weekday morning—glanced over at me. "This the sister everyone's talking about, Charlie?"

"What gave it away?" she deadpanned, holding up her long russet braid. Charlie usually kept her hair neatly tied back, while I had long ago given up any attempt to control the unruly curls, chopping it to chin length whenever I lost patience. But the color was unequivocally, unmistakably Stapleton red.

He tugged on the brim of his battered cap. "Nice work."

I paused. "Thank you? I think?"

He raised his Styrofoam coffee cup in what was either a farewell or a toast, telling Charlie he'd be back for the paint the next morning.

"What was *that* about?" I asked when the bell over the door jangled as he left.

"You're notorious now," she said. "Clem Jensen was a handyman. You caught his killer. People appreciate what you did for him."

I'd caught Clem's killer in this very store and nearly lost my life in the process. "And that's good for business?"

"Every little bit helps," she replied. "Why do you think you get so much traffic during your shifts? Everyone wants to get a look at you."

"Notorious," I muttered. "Glad it's working out so well for you."

"I work with what I've got," she said, unperturbed by my sarcasm. "Aren't you supposed to be helping Mom with Riley?"

"I needed a cooling-off period," I said, filling her in on Art Gundersen.

By the time I finished, her shoulders were shaking with laughter.

"It's not funny."

"Not to *you*, maybe." She wiped her eyes and began sorting through paperwork, readying the stacks of special orders so she could pull inventory. Judging from the way she checked and rechecked the pile, worry lines carving a vee between her eyebrows, she'd been hoping for more. My newfound notoriety didn't seem to be helping as much as she'd hoped. "How was Rowan last night?"

"Good," I said. "That reminds me, did you see Steven Tibbs when you were visiting yesterday?"

It was what I'd been wanting to ask since I walked in. I needed some background on the man whose tragedy I'd been swept into.

She nodded absently, scrutinizing the order in front of her. "We didn't talk much, though. I was trying to give him some privacy. Rowan's really getting the hang of eating."

"She'll be home before you know it. What's the deal with Steven running for Congress? Does he have a shot at winning?"

"Probably. You know how everyone here feels about him. The man can do no wrong in this town."

"True. It's strange to think of someone we went to school with as a Congressman," I said. "Attending the State of the Union. Making laws."

Charlie shrugged. "Not that strange. He was on student council, wasn't he?"

Steven had been a year behind me at Stillwater High, so it's not as if I'd paid much attention to his budding political career, even back then. Once I'd graduated, I hadn't given Stillwater High, or its denizens, another thought. "Lobbying for a better hot lunch isn't quite the same thing as the federal government."

"Probably not," she admitted. "I'm not sure trotting out the story about the fire is going to do him much good in Washington either, but he's definitely making good use of it here. Works it into half his speeches, which is ironic considering it's only half true."

I gaped at her. "What are you talking about? We could have lost the store if he hadn't come in early that day."

She made a small noise of irritation, waved her hand like she was brushing away a fly. "Sure, but he wasn't coming in early. He was coming back late."

This was the first I'd ever heard of it. "Coming back from where? What are you talking about?"

She shrugged. "The story is that Steven came in early to get a head start on inventory, to help out his dad, right? So he got here at some crazy hour, like . . . four in the morning."

"That makes sense," I pointed out. "The store is open late." Steven's parents had sold the store and moved to Florida sometime in the last decade, but the store was still here and was still the only place aside from restaurants and bars that stayed open past eight.

"Sure," Charlie said, "but Steven came back closer to midnight, not four. And he didn't stay long enough to do much inventory."

"Then what was he doing? And actually, how do you know this?"

She gave me a sly smile. "You aren't the only one who used to hang out upstairs in the wee small hours, you know."

I opened my mouth, eyebrows shooting to the ceiling, and closed it again. I had no good response except to ask who, exactly, Charlie had been "hanging out" with at midnight, and that felt a little too much like a nagging older sister for comfort.

Charlie flipped her braid over her shoulder, the gesture verging on smug. "Anyway, I was upstairs, and I heard Steven—and some girl I didn't know, which probably meant she was from some other town—go into the store. They were trying to be sneaky, I think, but they actually ended up making more noise than they would have walking in like they owned the place."

"Which Steven did, sort of," I said.

"Exactly. They didn't stay long, maybe ten minutes, and left with a bunch of glass bottles."

"Booze," I said. "Steven was stealing from his dad?"

"Probably. I was too far away to see exactly what they were, but why sneak into a convenience store to steal diet soda?" She shrugged. "I assume it wasn't the first time he'd done it, which is probably why he wanted to be the one to do inventory. One missing bottle isn't a big deal, but if the count was way off . . ."

"And you didn't say anything?"

"I wasn't supposed to be here, remember? I couldn't rat him out without getting myself in trouble."

"Were you here when the fire started?" I asked, frowning.

She shook her head. "You know how early Mom gets up. I was tucked in bed by two. It's not as if he's lying. He really did spot the fire; those people never would have gotten out without him raising the alarm. I could have been one of them if I hadn't gone home. But every time I hear him tell that stupid story, I can't help rolling my eyes a bit."

"So it's safe to say you're not on board the Tibbs Train," I said lightly.

"I don't know," she said, sounding nettled. "He's fine, I guess. Saves the city, locks up bad guys, has excellent teeth."

"I've never noticed Steven's teeth."

"That's because they're flawless," she shot back. "You only notice when things need rescuing."

"Hey!" Her words cut a little too close to the bone. "I think what you mean to say is, 'You're far too busy working, helping out with the kids, and covering shifts at the store to brush up on local elections, dearest Frankie.'"

"Sorry," she said, holding up a hand. "Honestly? I've got my hands full with Rowan and the store. Politics and ancient history are the last things I'm worried about."

"Rowan's doing better. So is the store."

"I know. But . . . winter is always tight. We can't afford to have our sales drop off."

"That's why I'm here: I'll draw customers in with my notoriety and charm."

She laughed despite herself.

"We'll think of something," I promised, yawning midway through the words.

"Coffee?" she asked.

I shook my head. "Sleep."

"I don't know why you agreed to work nights." She poured herself a fresh cup. A faded picture of Riley was printed on the side, along with her name in blocky, kindergarten writing. I had a similar mug in my cabinet at home, but the image was fresh and clear, the inside pristine. Nobody wants their coffee served with a heaping spoonful of guilt.

Now that I knew what I'd been missing, I felt even worse.

"That's the job they offered," I said, more sharply than I intended. With an effort, I lightened my words. "The good news is, I'm off for a while. Once I get about six hours of sleep, I can do whatever you need."

"Great," she said. "You can start with cleaning up the office."

"The office is fine."

"It's overflowing with crap," Charlie said. "Most of which is yours."

"First of all, it's not crap. It is my home, packed into boxes, because I am very kindly staying in town to help you. Second, it's only for a few months. What's the harm?"

"It's a fire hazard," she retorted. "I can barely move in there, it's so crowded."

"If I can share a room for three months," I pointed out, "you can maneuver around some boxes. What's the point in rearranging everything when I'm going to schlepp it all home soon enough."

"Right. You'll go *home*." She put a nasty twist to the word, like one of our teenage fights.

Ah. "You knew this was temporary, Charlie. I can put my life on hold for a little while, but I can't abandon it."

"I know that," she snapped, "but do you have to be so eager to leave?"

"I'm not leaving!"

"You will, though. In three months, as you keep reminding us at every turn, you'll be off to a new adventure. Or back to your old one, I guess. And when you go, you'll break Riley's heart. She worships you, Frankie. You'd have to be blind not to see it."

"She'll be happy to get her room back," I protested.

She turned away as the door opened again. "Keep telling yourself that. In three months, you might even believe it."

"Morning, Charlie!" called a cheery voice, rough and reedy at the same time.

"Hi, Uncle Marshall," we replied in unison. A moment later, he popped into sight, wearing his newsman's uniform: windowpane-check shirt, knit tie, brown felt porkpie hat. I'd known him my entire life, and the only time I'd seen him without that hat was at my father's funeral.

"Frankie too! It's my lucky day." His smile faded as he caught sight of our faces. "What's wrong?"

"Nothing," Charlie said, brimming with false cheer.

"Don't lie to an old man," he chided her and turned to me. "Frankie, your mother's wondering where you've gotten to."

Funny how being faced with my father's oldest friend made me feel like I was ten again. Marshall Davis wasn't technically our uncle, but he'd been a constant presence in our lives, even after my dad's death more than twenty years ago. Now he was nearly seventy, the editor of the local paper, and happy to play the curmudgeon when it suited him.

"I was at work," I said.

He raised a bushy eyebrow. "The desk clerk told your mother you'd left quite a while ago."

"She *called* them?" I buried my face in my hands. "I'm never going to live this down."

Charlie grinned at my mortification. No doubt she viewed it as cosmic retribution for our fight. "Slow news day, Uncle Marshall?"

"With the Tibbs case in our backyard?" he scoffed. "Hardly. Police named their suspect, now we've got a manhunt on our hands. Half the town wants to tell me their crackpot theories about Josh Miller, and the other half wants me to give them the scoop. Why would I do that when they can read about it for a dollar tomorrow?"

I managed to keep myself from pointing out that most of his readers could get the same information online. Somehow, the *Stillwater Journal-Standard* had managed to stay in print all these years, operating out of an office above the local dance studio. *Tutus and News*, Uncle Marshall called it. And even though he looked a lot older now, with his narrow build slightly stooped and blue eyes surrounded with wrinkles after a lifetime of squinting at copy, it was obvious there was nothing he'd rather do.

"Everyone's talking about it," he continued and fixed me with a stern look. "Except the people I want to hear from. Word is, you were there. Worked on Kate Tibbs *and* Josh Miller. Talked to Steven."

"No comment," I said, holding up a hand. "The hospital administration was very clear about not talking to the press."

"I'm family!" he protested.

"Family with a steno pad in his coat pocket." I gestured to the notebook peeking out. "No. Comment."

"Fine, fine." He shoved the notebook away, but his eyes never left my face. "You're as bad as the MacLean boy."

"Don't badger Noah," I ordered. "He's got enough on his plate."

"I'm exercising my First Amendment rights!"

"We were just talking about the election," Charlie said in an attempt at distraction. "Do you think the accident will change anything?"

"Hardly an accident," Uncle Marshall replied. "Not from what I'm hearing."

"Noah didn't tell you that," I said.

"I have sources other than your deputy," he said with asperity. "Also, they just wrapped the press conference."

"He's not *my* deputy," I replied, but Charlie waved me off.

"Are they close to catching the guy?" she asked.

"They'll find him," Uncle Marshall replied. "When they do, we'll know exactly what his motive was."

"You don't think it's revenge?" Open and shut, Noah had said, but some part of me continued to resist the idea.

"Could be." Uncle Marshall settled at the counter with a groan, cast a longing look at the coffeepot. "Interesting that they've been looking at the campaign, though. Makes me think not all the conspiracy theories people are nattering on about are as half-baked as they sound."

"Steven has an alibi," I said. "So does his skeevy campaign manager. Noah cleared them almost immediately."

"True enough. But there's more than one campaign running, isn't there?"

"Norris Mackie?" I said. "He was at a fundraiser that night too. What's his story?"

Charlie set a mug of coffee in front of Uncle Marshall, and he sipped ruminatively before saying, "Mackie's a long-standing incumbent—he's been in office since you two were kids. You should know your representatives, girls." When I didn't take the bait, he continued. "Mackie's known as some-one who toes the party line but doesn't rock the boat. Looks after his district."

"So he's popular?" I asked.

Marshall shrugged. "As popular as a politician can be—which is to say, not particularly. This is the first time in a long while he's had to run a real campaign, and based on what I'm hearing, it might be his last."

"Steven has a real shot, huh?" I tried to envision Steven in Washington, Ted Sullivan at his shoulder whispering and guiding. Steven's name was on the ballot, but who had the real power there?

"That's what the polls say, though they get it wrong more often than not," he replied. "Ask the same person the same question three different ways, you'll get three different answers."

"What does your gut say?" Charlie asked with a grin. Uncle Marshall's "gut" was legendary. As a kid, I'd scoffed, but these days I relied on my own enough to respect his.

He removed his hat and settled it on the counter like a judge with a gavel. "Steven Tibbs will be in DC come January."

"I don't get it," I said as Charlie skirted the counter and headed toward the paint machine. "If people are happy with Mackie, how could Steven beat him?"

"Fresh blood," Charlie said as she measured out pigment. "Mackie's ancient. He's been in office forever, and people want someone fresh, someone with the energy to get stuff done."

Uncle Marshall bristled at the assessment but didn't dis-agree. "Steven's got that rare combination of new ideas in a familiar face. He'll shake things up—but not too much."

"I thought you said you didn't care about the election," I said to Charlie.

"I don't," she called back over the rumbling of the paint shaker. "But it's all anyone can talk about these days—other than you."

"It's hard to defeat an incumbent," I said to Uncle Marshall, who nodded.

"Mackie's built up quite a war chest, but he's out of practice," he said. "Tibbs has more energy to visit nursing homes and kiss babies. The better his numbers look, the more his backers shell out. Television ads don't come cheap, you know—and neither does an operative like Ted Sullivan."

"What's the deal with that guy?" I asked. "If he's such a big deal, why is he here? This is a small district in rural Illinois. I'd think he'd be working on some campaign in Chicago or New York. Someplace big."

"Rumor is that Steven has some donors with deep pockets, and they wanted to protect their investment. Mackie's a tough old bird, and he's not going down without a fight. Sullivan's a bulldog, a bruiser. He'll do all the dirty fighting, and Steven's halo won't wind up tarnished."

Asking the question made me feel calculating and cold, but I did it anyway. "Will Kate's death help Steven's numbers?"

"Hard to say," Marshall replied. "He'll gain some points out of sympathy, probably. But it's one thing to elect a family man, and it's another to send a grieving single father to Washington, especially if he was voted in with the idea he'd get a lot done."

"So he's more electable if he has a wife to take care of the house and the baby? That's pretty sexist," grumbled Charlie as she started mixing the next can of paint.

"That's politics," Marshall replied with a shrug.

"Mackie couldn't possibly say that," I argued. "People would be horrified. They'd think he was using Kate's death against Steven—it would totally backfire."

"He won't say it himself," Marshall said. "He's been in the game too long to make that kind of mistake. But mark my words, there'll be murmurs soon enough masquerading as concern. Rumors you can't trace back to a source. If they catch on quickly, it could turn the tide—the election's only a few weeks away, after all."

"Is Mackie that desperate to hang onto his seat?"

Marshall's eyebrows lifted. "Desperate enough to start rumors? Or kill his opponent's pregnant wife?"

"Everybody knows who did it," Charlie said. "That Miller guy."

"In my experience, what 'everyone knows' is usually wrong," Marshall retorted.

We fell silent, mulling over his words.

"Mackie could have hired him," Charlie suggested, revealing a cynical streak I hadn't realized she possessed.

Unease stirred. Josh Miller—a not-very-bright career criminal with a sizeable grudge—would have made the perfect patsy. Noah's open-and-shut case creaked a little wider every time I thought about it.

"Quite a risk for Norris, even assuming Miller got away clean," Uncle Marshall said. "Not something he's known for."

Charlie, however, wasn't giving up. "He might have figured that Steven would be so devastated he'd drop out, or maybe he'd hoped Steven would take it as a warning. Maybe he thought Steven would be in the car too. Wasn't Kate supposed to go to the fundraiser?"

"A double murder? That seems extreme, doesn't it? This is Stillwater, not Chicago," I said.

"How could I forget?" she retorted. "It's all you talk about. People are people, no matter where you go. I'll bet you a milkshake that Steven Tibbs and Norris Mackie care as much about this election as any Chicago politician."

Maybe she was right. Maybe it was time for me to look a little more closely at the opposition.

*   *   *

Charlie left for the hospital, and Uncle Marshall took over the register while I went home. My temper had cooled during my visit to the store—or perhaps it had found a new target. Either way, a confrontation with my mother over her meddling could wait until after I'd slept.

"Francesca, where have you been?" Mom called as I walked in, dropping my bag on the floor and toeing off my shoes. "Your cat has been—"

I brushed past her and started up the stairs. She trailed after me, still complaining about the cat, all the way to the second floor and down the hallway to my room.

"Honestly, Francesca, what on earth is the matter with you? You haven't said two words since you got home."

I turned to face her, bracing my hand on the doorframe. "You want two words? Fine. *Art. Gundersen.*"

She opened her mouth to reply, caught sight of my face, and closed it again.

I nodded, shut the door, and went to bed.

EIGHT

I woke to an unexpectedly silent house. No chatter from the kitchen, no squeaking floorboards or clatter of dishes. Just sweet, sweet silence. I rolled out of bed and padded to the closet, throwing on a clean pair of jeans and a favorite flannel shirt, worn soft and thin. It smelled of the same fabric softener my mother had used when I was a kid, artificial but comforting. Rubbing the grit from my eyes, I went downstairs and hunted in the fridge for a snack, coming up with an apple when what I was really craving was something deep-fried and deeply unhealthy. A faint crackle and hum emanated from the counter, next to the phone. When I checked, I found a police radio scanner plugged in and turned down low. I rolled my eyes and switched it off. No wonder my mom was always up on the latest gossip.

In the living room, the grandfather clock chimed, jolting me out of my skin and out the door, apple in hand. Time to pick up Riley.

I expected the usual greeting when I got to the school—Riley, giddy with freedom, racing across the playground, arms outstretched with her backpack bouncing.

Instead, she trudged toward me, eyes downcast, shoulders slumped.

"Hey, kiddo. What's wrong?"

She shrugged, tracing an arc in the wood chips with the toe of her shoe, then held out an envelope.

I frowned and took it from her, skimming the note inside. "You fell asleep during a social studies movie?"

"I didn't mean to. The room was dark, and the movie was so boring, Aunt Frankie. I couldn't help it." She staggered, as if the sheer weight of her boredom was toppling her.

I'd felt the same way as a kid. Charlie had always been the conscientious one. I'd felt like I was stuck in a twelve-year prison sentence. I hated to see Riley feeling the same way—but even though school had never seemed to be her favorite, this was a new low. Combined with her sickbed routine yesterday, I was starting to suspect there was more to the story.

"Do you have a best friend?"

"I have two," she said. "Jasper and Janie."

"Are they twins?" Instead of turning for home, we went the other direction toward the hardware store.

"Nope," she said as if it should be obvious. "Janie's my *soccer* best friend. Jasper is my *school* best friend."

"Ah, got it." I'd forgotten about the intricacies of school friendships and alliances, but nothing in her reply suggested that was the source of the trouble. "Did you learn more about fossils today?"

"A little."

When she didn't elaborate, I tried again, desperate enough to go with a fail-safe. "How was the soccer game last night?"

"Okay." She yawned, gave another shrug.

Now I was starting to worry. Riley was a chatterbox most days, but even when she was feeling grumpy, the chance to give me the play-by-play of her soccer skills never failed to engage her.

Except now.

She looked wan, her eyes dull instead of their usual sparkling green. But she wasn't flushed, and when I felt her forehead, I couldn't detect any sign of a fever.

"What time did you go to sleep last night?"

"I dunno," she said, gaze sliding away.

Charlie kept Riley on a strict eight o'clock bedtime. As I knew only too well, however, bedtime was not the same as in bed, fast asleep. I'd mastered that nuance during my teen years; I'd hoped every day since that my mother never found out.

"Sleep's pretty important," I said offhandedly, not wanting to come across as a nag. Nagging was Charlie's job. "I took a giant nap today, and I feel a zillion percent better."

"I am too old for naps," Riley said firmly.

"We'll revisit this conversation when you're in college, kiddo. In the meantime, no staying up past bedtime, okay? Otherwise, you won't have energy to do fun stuff with me."

She watched me for a moment, suspicion plain on her features. No doubt she was thinking of all the times she'd been promised something fun—some reward for enduring a week of school or a particularly boring visit with aged relatives or a long, dull day at the store—only to discover that her idea of fun was not the same as Charlie and Matt's. I'd been there enough times myself, and I vowed not to disappoint.

"First up," I said. "Let's talk Halloween. We should carve pumpkins, don't you think?"

She nodded eagerly, and I felt the tiniest bit smug. I'd timed my distraction well—downtown Stillwater was brimming with autumn charm, every window decked out in black and orange in preparation for Halloween, jack-o'-lanterns grinning toothily.

We stopped to inspect each one on our way to the store—we'd be late, but it seemed like a small price to pay when Riley was reverting to her usual garrulous self. She dragged me from pumpkin to pumpkin, critiquing them and planning out her own carving session. ("Zombie pumpkins, Aunt Frankie! It'll be awesome!") Two blocks away from Stapleton and Sons, the sign on a white brick building made me pause. Curious, I peered in the darkened window, cupping my hands around my eyes to make out what was inside.

After my conversation with Uncle Marshall, Congressman Mackie—and his local office—were irresistible.

With the lights off, I could barely see row after row of tables crammed with phones, binders, and office supplies. The walls were plastered with posters and maps, and along the back of the room, a long red banner proclaimed: "NORRIS MACKIE: FIGHTING FOR YOU."

Despite the deserted appearance, I reached for the door handle.

"Have you been waiting long?" A young woman who couldn't have been more than a year or two out of college raced across the street, holding up a white paper bag from the town diner. "I'm so sorry! I was just getting a late lunch."

"Is the office closed?"

She beamed. "The Congressman's door is always open to his constituents."

Rather than admit I wasn't a constituent, I told Riley to check out a few more pumpkins, then followed the woman inside. Phone banks and campaign posters aside, it was decorated in generic office chic: industrial-gray carpet, air tinged with the scent of burned coffee, and the faint buzz overhead from the fluorescent lights as they flickered on.

"Are you interested in volunteering?" Her voice was nearly breathless with delight. "Or did you need a yard sign?"

I shifted, hitching my backpack over my shoulder. What *was* I doing here? The entire sheriff's department was hunting Josh Miller. Even if there was more to it than simple revenge, and Norris Mackie was involved, it seemed unlikely that he'd leave evidence between the brochures and the bumper stickers. Like Uncle Marshall, I believed in my gut—but gut reactions were no good if you didn't have something to react to, and I needed something more solid than town gossip or mere conjecture.

"I wanted to learn a little more about the Congressman," I said, leaving out the reason for my newfound political interest. After all, politicians excelled at that sort of evasion. I was simply speaking their language.

"You're undecided." She sagged a bit, then forced herself to recover. If she was going to have any future in politics, the girl needed to practice her poker face. A lot. "Well, let's get you some literature. I think you'll be really impressed at all the Congressman's accomplish—"

"Amanda, is that you?" a voice rumbled from the rear of the building. I hadn't noticed the darkened corridor to the back, light pooling outside the open door.

"Yes, sir," she said. "I've got a constituent here who wants to meet you."

Again I stayed silent, fighting the urge to flee. I'd wanted to know more about Mackie, hadn't I? This was my chance to find out about him firsthand.

Something—a chair, hopefully—emitted a long, piercing squeak. A moment later, Mackie himself appeared.

He didn't look like my idea of a cutthroat politician. He'd been tall, once, though now he hunched over slightly, shoulders held stiff and arms rigid at his side. When he caught sight of me, he pasted on a smile and smoothed his disheveled gray hair. He was jowly as a brindle bulldog, his skin pale as whey, with a belly that spoke of one too many campaign barbecues. I couldn't help but marvel at the difference between the man in front of me and the robust, ruddy-cheeked Norris Mackie of the campaign poster just behind him. Either it had been taken several campaigns ago, or someone on staff was a wizard at Photoshop.

"Norris Mackie," he said in a voice that tried and failed to boom.

"Nice to meet you," I said. "I'm sorry to interrupt your work."

"Not at all." He waved away my apology. "My time is yours."

"I assumed you were closed. You know, since the campaigns are both suspended."

"Terrible, terrible tragedy," he said after a moment's hesitation. He scratched his jaw and considered me. "We're taking a break from the campaign, out of respect for Mrs. Tibbs. But representing the people of the nineteenth district isn't something I suspend for anything, Miss . . ."

Rather than give him my name, I said, "That's very noble—especially so close to the election. It's a pretty tight race, isn't it?"

"I have faith in my voters," he said. "I've still got work to do, and I believe they'll send me back to DC to finish it."

Amanda pressed a glossy brochure into my hand. "As you can see, the Congressman has laid out an ambitious plan for his next term, but we believe it's entirely feasible, considering his long and successful track record."

I studied the paper. "I'm surprised you're not in your Springfield office," I said. "Seems like it would be easier to get work done away from all the hubbub."

"I like to stay connected with my constituents," he said smoothly. "Keep an ear to the ground."

More likely, I suspected, he wanted to make sure Steven wasn't getting all the press coverage. If the cameras were in Stillwater, he should be too. My temper stirred, and I found myself wanting more than a mere introduction—I wanted answers.

"Funny that you and Mr. Tibbs were both at fundraisers that night."

Amanda ran a nervous hand over her ponytail.

"Necessary evil," he said with a chuckle, then sobered. "Shame to think that if Mrs. Tibbs had gone with her husband, she might not have had that accident."

Conversely, if Steven had been in the car with Kate, they might both be dead. Had that been someone's goal all along?

"Is there a particular issue you're interested in hearing about?" Amanda asked, stepping forward a shade too eagerly. "The Congressman's views on the tax code? The upcoming farm bill? Environmental regulations?"

She sounded increasingly desperate, but I smiled at Mackie, trying to turn up the charm. "Are they boring? Fundraisers,

I mean? Is it mostly a lot of people in tuxes asking you for favors?"

"It can be," he said. "More often it's a chance for me to share a meal with people who care deeply about a cause. I find—"

"You don't ever sneak out?" I pressed. "I'd *totally* be tempted to sneak out."

Dryly, he replied, "That would defeat the point of meeting all those voters, wouldn't it?"

"So you always stay until the bitter end? Like Tuesday night? Terrible storm, long drive home—you didn't leave early?"

Mackie and Amanda exchanged narrowed glances. Before either of them could speak, the door opened.

"Aunt Frankie," Riley called, "come on! Mom's going to be mad if we're late, and we are almost late."

"Frankie," said Amanda. "I didn't catch your last name. Are you a constituent? Or a reporter?"

"She's not a reporter," Riley said. "She's a nurse. She works at the hospital."

"Ah," Mackie said. "And who might you be, little lady?"

Rather than let Riley shake hands with a potential murderer—which would result in *my* murder, courtesy of Charlie—I drew her behind me.

"I'm a citizen," I said firmly. "Is there a problem with me asking about your campaign events?"

"You can ask." Mackie's voice was stern, but sweat beaded along his hairline. Amanda watched him closely, biting her lip. "I've already made my statement about the tragedy, and I don't intend to speak further on it."

Beside me, Riley squirmed with impatience.

"I won't take any more of your time," I said. "Thanks for the brochure."

"Don't forget to vote," Amanda called after us as we made our escape.

"Who are they?" Riley asked me when we were out on the sidewalk. "They looked kind of mad."

"They did, didn't they?" I'd pushed too hard, asked too many questions. While Mackie hadn't given me a real answer, the evasion was an answer of its own: he was hiding something.

Twice now, my instincts had been correct—first Josh Miller, now Norris Mackie. I'd learned my lesson about ignoring my gut. *Never again*, I promised myself, the same way I'd instructed Jess. Now I needed to find the connection between my two instincts and bring the proof to Noah.

Riley tugged on my sleeve, bringing me back to myself. "I said, 'Why'd you go in there?'"

"I made a bet with your mom. About grown-up stuff." Before she could ask, I added, "Boring stuff."

"Who won?"

I sighed. "Your mom. I owe her a milkshake."

NINE

Happily, my sister was nowhere in sight when we arrived at the store. Matt hailed us from aisle four, where he was restocking the bins of fasteners.

"Charlie's at the hospital," he said after he'd recovered from Riley's tackle-hug. "She wondered if you could handle some of the paperwork, place the orders."

As a teenager, if there was anything I liked less than working behind the counter of Stapleton and Sons, it was working in the office. Tallying accounts, placing orders, arguing with vendors . . . it had never been my strong suit. Even charting was my least favorite aspect of nursing. But I could see the value in it, which helped keep my butt in the chair long enough to do the work. If doing a stint upstairs would help me get a better sense of what Charlie was facing, I could probably manage that too.

I poured myself a cup of coffee from the pot behind the counter and headed up the narrow wooden steps to the office.

The apartment above the store had served many functions over the last century—family home, bachelor pad, storage space. A tiny kitchenette sat unused in one corner and both of the bedrooms were now filled with file cabinets and spare stock, while the bathroom's shower stall served as a catchall for various broken pieces of furniture. My boxes and bags added to the jumble, creating towers and pathways reminiscent of a reality show about hoarding. I could barely see the pale-yellow walls.

Our old dining table sat in the center of the living room, the aging computer surrounded by stacks of paper spilling out of trays and file folders—though knowing Charlie, each one was meticulously labeled.

I dumped my backpack on the floor and took a closer look.

I was wrong.

The files were color-coded. *And* labeled.

A sticky note was attached to the monitor, the precise lettering looking more like a cipher than a letter.

F—

Nudge 30+
Spec/Rec Ord
R FRACTIONS!!!

—C

I scowled. Pester past-due accounts, place and bill the special orders, do the same for our monthly recurring ones, and help with math homework.

Naturally, she'd leave the dirty work to me.

Then again, only a few weeks ago, Charlie had nearly bitten my head off when she realized I'd peeked at the store's accounts. Asking me to work with them now was a sign of progress.

Really, really boring progress. A half-eaten tray of sandwich cookies sat on the kitchen counter. I scooped up a handful, scowled at the note again, and dove in.

I found a surprising number of past-due accounts. Not enough to put us into the black, but definitely enough to staunch the bleeding, at least for this month. Getting regular accounts to pay up was a tricky business. Too nice, and they took advantage of you. Too tough, and they'd go elsewhere. From what I could tell, Charlie was tilting too far toward nice. If she'd struck a balance, it wasn't a comfortable one.

Letting me loose on those accounts was almost guaranteed to upset things.

Maybe that was the point—she wanted me to play bad cop to her good cop. It was a canny move, actually, and since my visit to Mackie had left me tired of double-speak and evasion, I was more than happy to oblige.

The office door creaked open while I was on my third call. Riley, correctly interpreting my tone, tiptoed into the room, stuck a cookie in her mouth and took one in each hand, then curled up on the couch. I waved, smiled, and continued to make calls.

By the time I was done, she'd fallen asleep, crumbs trailing down her shirt. I stood, rolling my neck to work out the kinks, and covered her with a ratty old blanket. She stirred but didn't wake.

"You used to do that when you were little," my mother said from the doorway. "You and Charlotte would take opposite ends of the couch, or the bed in the spare room. You'd always say you weren't tired, and five minutes later . . ."

The memory of the scratchy mustard-colored upholstery was vivid on my cheek.

"Should I take off her shoes?" I whispered.

"Leave them," my mom replied. "She needs the sleep."

Judging from Riley's slow, deep breaths—unbroken by her usual snores—Mom was right.

Probably for the best, considering. I pinned my mother with a glare.

"Art Gundersen?"

"He's a nice man," she protested.

"You think he's so great, you date him."

She flushed, and the guilt struck me immediately. After my father's death, my mom had never found anyone else. He was irreplaceable, she'd said whenever anyone broached the subject. Besides, she'd often point out, with me, Charlie, and the store, her hands were plenty full.

I was about to apologize, but she continued, "Lots of women think he's quite a catch."

"Are any of them under fifty?"

"Well," she said, seemingly unruffled, "it's not as if you've had much success with men your own age. Have you returned even one of Peter's calls? I'd thought perhaps you and the MacLean boy would try to make a go of things again, but he hasn't come around in weeks. I thought someone older might be a . . ." She paused, searching for the words. "A steadying influence."

"I don't *need* a steadying influence."

Her expression made it clear she disagreed. "I want you to be happy, Francesca."

I am happy, I nearly said, but then I considered the words more carefully. Was I really? Sleeping on the bottom bunk, working a temporary job, and harassing contractors to pay their bills?

I wasn't *un*happy, but that wasn't quite the same thing. It wasn't just my current situation—I'd been not-unhappy in Chicago too. Usually that meant it was time for a change—to indulge my wanderlust, to throw a dart at a map and find a new city, a new view. But the energy that typically fizzed in my veins at the prospect of starting over didn't fizz when I considered it now. Rather than figure out what *that* meant, I said, "I don't need a guy to be happy. You're happy, right?"

Her hesitation was so slight, I barely caught it. "Of course."

"Well, there you go. I'm following your lead."

She twisted the single strand of pearls around her neck, sputtering, but I cut her off. "Quit sending people to the hospital. Those beds are for genuine emergencies."

"Art was genuinely sick," she pointed out.

"I am a professional," I ground out. "When I'm on duty, one hundred percent of my attention needs to be on helping people. On saving their lives. It's not a place to meet guys. No more, Mom."

She bowed her head.

"Promise."

"I promise," she said. She sounded exactly like Riley swearing to do her homework after "a few more minutes" of soccer. She lifted her head, an unrepentant glint in her eyes. "Speaking of the hospital, why didn't you tell me you'd treated Josh Miller?"

I bit my lip. "Where did you hear that?"

"You know what this town is like. News travels faster than you'd like—especially bad news."

"I was hoping to be the exception," I mumbled.

She put two fingers beneath my chin and gently forced me to meet her eyes. "Francesca, nobody blames you. You couldn't have known what he'd done."

The shame rose up again, a hot choking pressure. "I let him get away."

"You treated a patient, and then you treated another one, exactly as you were supposed to. If you were in charge of deciding who was worthy of help and who wasn't, you'd be God—and I think we can both agree you are not the Almighty."

"But—"

"But nothing," she said firmly. "Of course people are talking. That's what they do, and they'll talk until there's a new story to replace this one. Since when has Stillwater gossip ever bothered you?"

This was different than the usual gossip, though. This was my career. People would hear this story and think I was a bad nurse, and when I had so little else in my life that was stable, undermining that identity would leave me with nothing but rubble.

For all her flaws, my mother was a perceptive woman. Her expression softened for a moment, her mouth drawing down and her forehead creasing with concern. Then the moment passed, and her face turned cool and practical. "Enough wallowing," she said. "If you don't like the topic, change the conversation."

"How? Kate Tibbs is all anyone's talking about."

"You're a smart girl, Francesca. Show some initiative and figure it out." She paused and brushed a microscopic piece of lint from her jade-green sweater. "Josh Miller can't hide forever, after all."

I goggled at her. "Wait. You know him?"

"I know *of* him," she corrected, pretending to look over a sheaf of bills. "Which is more than enough. He lives over on the south side of town, you know. The whole area's gone downhill."

"What do you mean?" The southern edge of Stillwater had already been pretty far downhill when I was living here. One would think it didn't have much further to go. Noah had grown up there, but sometime in the last twelve years, he'd moved and left that part of his dark damaged past behind. I hoped so, anyway.

"Drugs," she said. "That neighborhood has always been rough, but people used to be able to make a life there. Now people move out as soon as they can, and nobody moves in—or if they do, they bring trouble with them. The city's tried to clean it up, but it never works."

"Noah said Josh was a dealer." I reached for my phone and googled Josh Miller's address.

Mom watched over my shoulder, frowning. "Francesca, you're not thinking of going over there, are you?"

"You're the one who said to show initiative."

"I meant you should offer to help Noah. You two might reconnect! I certainly did *not* mean you should go skulking around terrible neighborhoods. The police have already searched his house. They've canvassed the neighborhood. What makes you think you'd find something they've missed?"

Truly, my mother's intelligence network was a marvel.

"I don't know." There was no logical reason to go over to Josh's place, but I couldn't resist. It was like a sore tooth that you couldn't stop poking at—fruitless, painful, and impossible to stop until the cavity was fixed. "I want to understand it, I guess. Because we couldn't save Kate, and now that little boy is going to grow up without a mother."

"So you'll give him justice instead?" I couldn't tell if her pity was directed at me or Trey. She tapped the pile of paperwork and sighed. "Did you finish calling the past-due accounts?"

"Taken care of," I said firmly. "*Really* taken care of."

"Good girl," she said and made a shooing motion. "Go on, then, if you're so set on it. You've only got an hour or so of daylight."

TEN

My mother's parting words made perfect sense as I parked down the block from Josh Miller's house. This was *not* a neighborhood I wanted to hang out in past sunset. Between the neglected houses, with their weed-choked yards and dangerously sagging rooflines, and the snarling dogs, straining at their chains as I emerged from the car, I had enough sense to cross the street briskly, radiating "don't mess with me" as hard as I could.

Ill-tempered dogs aside, I was alone on the street—no sidewalks, only the crumbling shoulder of the pavement. I'd been in these kinds of neighborhoods before when I was out with an ambulance crew. The kinds of places where it was best to mind your own business. To see little, say less, and stay inside.

When Noah had lived here, only a few streets over, this area might have been rough, but it still felt like a neighborhood. On any given day, you'd see people working on their cars or drinking with their buddies after a hard day, kids racing their bikes or playing ball in the street. It didn't have this oppressive silence, and I shivered despite my fleece jacket and down vest.

There was no car in Miller's driveway, and the yellow caution tape around the door fluttered in the wind. The police had given up the stakeout method, it seemed. In the rapidly encroaching dusk, the small, squat house felt abandoned. I picked my way up the wooden front steps, boards dangerously springy beneath my feet, and knocked. The door sounded unexpectedly solid, and the shiny new dead bolt was a contrast to the rest of the aging house. Miller took his security seriously.

No answer. The blinds were drawn, but I craned my neck, trying to peer through a gap where some of the slats had broken off. The interior was dim, but I caught a flickering of light and movement, heard voices raised in argument. Josh might be missing, but it sounded like someone else was home.

I knocked again and waited for a response that didn't come. Rather than try a third time, I circled around to the back door.

The kitchen, based on what I could see through the uncurtained window, was several decades out of date. Crookedly hung cabinets, peeling countertops, a sink filled with dishes, and a rickety table covered with pizza boxes.

As I raised a fist to knock, a voice behind me said, "Nobody's in there."

I jumped, spinning around to find the source of the voice. A tiny old woman in multiple cardigans—all beige—and a knitted hat that was probably white once upon a time stood in the yard next door.

"Are you sure?" I asked. "I can hear someone."

"Television," she said. "He's got one of those big screen models with lots of speakers. Makes the windows rattle, and he never turns it off, neither."

She broke off, overtaken by a coughing spell, bracing her hand on the side of the house.

"That's quite a cough," I said lightly. "Why don't we get you a drink of water?"

She straightened as much as she could and waved me off. "I'll be fine. Had it for years."

"Have you seen a doctor?"

She snorted. "Don't have one. Don't need one. What are you looking for, missy? You're not his usual type."

"Josh Miller's type?"

"Who else?" She stumped across the lawn toward me, her shuffling steps obviously painful. "Like a train station in here, people always coming and going, music playing, television blasting."

Now that she'd said "television," I could pick out the announcers' voices, commercial jingles, a swell of dramatic music that made me think Josh favored reality television. "Does he live here alone?"

"Had his little girl with him for a while. She was tiny thing. Sweet, mostly. State took her away, I heard, and I'm glad of it. This is no place for a child."

"Where's her mother?"

"Ran off when the baby was still in diapers. Haven't seen her in years. Good riddance, I say." Another racking cough, and the knitted hat slipped over her eyes. She pushed it back with a quick, irritated shove.

"Have you seen Josh recently?"

"Not since the ruckus with the police," she said. "What do you want with him? Same as all the others?"

"I doubt it." I peered in the windows again. "Was there ever anyone who came by that surprised you? Somebody else that wasn't his usual type?" Someone like Norris Mackie—or more likely Amanda, the too-cheerful assistant.

"Not that I recall. I've got better things to than sit and watch the parade all day, you know."

"I'm sure you do," I said, though I would have bet she didn't miss much of the activity. Of course, if Miller really was working with someone else, they'd probably tried to be a little more discreet. "Did you talk to the police when they were here?"

"Sure did. Told them he was a menace, told them to hunt him down and hold on to him this time. Not that they will. They never do. They arrest him, and in a few days he's back, worse than before."

"At least you get a little break while he's gone," I offered, hoping to placate her.

"You'd think so. Not this time, though. Those officers were here till nearly one AM. And what happens nearly two hours later, just as I'm finally falling back asleep? An almighty crash, that's what, some fool knocking over the garbage can." She was so disgusted she nearly spat.

"Are you sure it wasn't raccoons?" I asked.

Her eyebrows lifted so high, they disappeared under her hat. "You ever met a raccoon that put the bin back when they were done eating?"

I looked—sure enough, the large black trash bin was standing upright, the lid fastened shut. No self-respecting raccoon would have done such a thing. "Someone was here? In the house?"

Could Josh have really been so stupid as to return once the police had left?

The woman gave me a speculative look. "Told you he blasted that television. You think the raccoons let themselves in and turned the volume down?"

I eyed her right back. She might look like she was a few pencils short of a box, but she was as keen an observer as my own mother. Adrenaline made my fingertips tingle, but I kept my tone easy. "I don't suppose you happened to catch a look at them, did you?"

"That's my house," she said, pointing to the tired-looking cottage next door. Run down, certainly, but it didn't have the air of neglect so many here did. The drive was swept clean and while the lawn was patchy, weeds hadn't yet overtaken it. A single window box, filled with faded plastic tulips, hung from the nearest window. "My bedroom's on the other side. Can't see anything from there."

I tried to mask my disappointment. "I understand."

"So I had to watch from the kitchen," she added triumphantly. "Kept the light off so he wouldn't notice."

"He?"

"Couldn't see his face 'cause he wore one of those hooded sweat shirts. But he moved like the Miller boy, sure enough. Kinda boneless and slouchy, which makes sense as he doesn't have much of a spine."

"Did you call the police?"

"They'd only just been here. What was the sense in calling them back?" She scowled. "I didn't know he was connected to that terrible crash either. If they'd said something, I would have known. But they don't *tell* you anything. It's just question, question, question." She squinted at me. "A lot like you."

"I wish I knew enough to tell you something," I said honestly.

"You don't seem like the police," she said as another coughing fit overtook her. While we were talking, the sun had slipped below the horizon. Time for me to go.

"I'm not," I assured her, helping her over the grass to her back porch. "But you should call them if Josh comes back again. In fact, it wouldn't hurt to call them today, let them know what you saw. They'd appreciate it."

"Lot of good that'll do," she grumbled, but I didn't miss the way her eyes lit up at the prospect. I'd seen it plenty of times with geriatric patients—they were so often overlooked, dismissed, or forgotten that the prospect of being useful was like catnip.

"In the meantime," I said, putting on my most no-nonsense nursing voice. "Get that cough checked out."

ELEVEN

"Charlotte wants to speak to you," my mother said when I came downstairs Thursday morning. "She's popping over to the store for a bit this morning, so she'll see you then."

"That sounds ominous," I said, ruffling Riley's hair. "Feeling better today?"

Her mouth was too full of toast to answer, but she nodded eagerly. I breathed a sigh of relief. There'd been no battles about going to school today, no faking sick. We'd played soccer last night after a brief battle with fractions, and she'd helped me set out food for the cat. He seemed to like her even more than me, going so far as to leap onto the porch railing while we were outside, though he hissed when she offered him a piece of chicken. By the time I'd come upstairs for the night, she'd merely lifted her head, greeted me with a drowsy hello, and gone right back to sleep.

"Wait a minute. Why is she coming back? I'm working the counter this morning."

"She's going to cover the wholesale orders, and then you can take over," Mom said, busying herself with the breakfast dishes.

"I can handle the wholesale accounts," I said, helping myself to a handful of cereal straight from the box. "I've done it before, you know. Like, since I was old enough to see over the counter."

"She wants to handle them herself." Mom held up a soapy spatula, warding off my protests. "I'm not getting in the middle of you two. I'll take Riley to school; you can go over to the store and sort this out with your sister when she comes in."

I sulked into my coffee, pride stung. My so-called notoriety was useful, it seemed. So was my willingness to play hardball with deadbeat customers. But I couldn't be trusted behind the counter? I checked my watch. Charlie would still be at the hospital. If I hurried, I could catch her there, settle this, and make it back to the store in time to handle the wholesale customers myself.

Traffic jams were rare in Stillwater, but farm equipment could have the same effect on a morning commute. I found myself stuck behind an ancient combine, tacking another ten minutes onto my drive to the hospital.

"You just missed her!" exclaimed Rachel, one of the daytime NICU nurses. "In fact, she said she was heading over to meet you at the store. You two must have gotten your wires crossed."

"Must have," I said grimly.

Rachel brought me up to speed on Rowan's progress (excellent, with further remarks on her charm and intelligence, naturally). It was impossible to stay angry when faced with such a tiny perfect human. I kissed her good-bye and turned to leave.

The motion must have caught Steven's attention. A moment later, he'd joined me at Rowan's isolette, waggling his fingers at her. She stared at him through the Plexiglas, unblinking as an owl.

"I saw Charlie this morning," he said, straightening. "Rowan's a little beauty."

"Thanks," I replied. "How's Trey doing?"

He gave a halfhearted smile. "Good. He's healthy. I keep reminding myself of that, of how lucky I am. But . . ."

He broke off, fighting for composure.

"But you don't feel lucky."

"I never thought it would be like this," he said, wandering back over to a dozing Trey. I followed, torn between sympathy and awkwardness. "I never planned for it. I thought Kate would be here. We were supposed to do this together."

"It must be so hard," I murmured.

Offering condolences to a grieving stranger was a regular part of my job. It wasn't easy, exactly, but I'd had plenty of opportunities to practice. Dealing with the pain of someone I knew, however, was harder. My own emotions refused to be neatly tucked away, and somehow the typical words of comfort felt insufficient and trite. Instead, I fell back on unvarnished truth. "It's so awful, Steven. It completely sucks."

His bark of laughter startled Trey awake, tiny arms flinging wide. He began to wail, a thin, angry sound that Steven shushed quickly.

"That's exactly the word," he said once the baby settled, "but nobody says it. They're too polite."

"I'm never polite," I assured him. "But I am so, so sorry. Do they have any leads on Miller's whereabouts?"

He grimaced. "There's a lot of places he could hide, people he could go to for help. People with their own grudges."

"Because of Kate's job?"

"And mine," he said. "Prosecutors have plenty of enemies, and so do politicians."

Enemies like Norris Mackie, I almost said but caught myself.

"I'm sure Noah's doing everything he can," I said. "The entire department is."

Steven's mouth twisted. "Never expected I'd need a favor from Noah MacLean, of all people."

The bitterness in his tone surprised me. The two hadn't crossed paths much in high school, and I'd always assumed prosecutors and cops got along well. "It's not a favor. It's his job, and he's very good at it. Once they find him, he'll go away for a long time."

Steven didn't seem convinced. "All they have is a phone call and conjecture, Frankie. It's circumstantial at best. I'd get laughed out of court if I tried to make a case with that."

I thought about Miller returning to his house despite the manhunt, so desperate to recover something that he'd risk capture twice. "They'll find proof. I'm sure of it."

He shook his head. "I'm not. But sometimes the universe dispenses its own justice. Guys who live the kind of life Josh Miller does . . . they tend not to live very long."

My palms went clammy at the threat beneath his words. "You cannot interfere, Steven. You have to let the police do their job, and you take care of Trey. That's all that matters now, okay? Focus on Trey."

For a moment, he didn't seem to hear me. Then he let out a shuddery breath and nodded, slowly, like a patient coming out of anesthesia. "You're right," he said. "Absolutely. Trey."

Suddenly, my presence seemed intrusive, not comforting. "Charlie's waiting for me at the store," I said, backing away.

"Wait. Would you consider coming to the funeral? It's on Monday."

I started to protest, but he continued, "You helped save my son's life. You were with Kate when . . ." He stopped, then started again. "It would mean a lot to me."

It's a privilege when a patient's family asks you to attend services. They feel a connection to you, and they're willing to share a deeply private moment with someone who was, not long ago, a perfect stranger.

"I'd be honored," I said quietly.

Just then, someone tapped on the NICU glass. Ted Sullivan, the campaign manager, was pointing to his phone and gesticulating. Steven sighed and withdrew his hand from the isolette.

"Great news," Ted said as we emerged into the waiting area. "New poll out of Gallup. We're up twelve points."

Steven blinked as if someone had aimed a spotlight directly into his eyes, then grinned. "Twelve? What's the margin of error?"

Charlie was right. He did have perfect teeth.

Too caught up in discussing optics and resources, neither man noticed when I slipped away.

TWELVE

Some stores greet customers with a smile and a good-natured "How can I help you?"

Those stores are not run by my sister.

Then again, I wasn't a customer.

Charlie was speaking to someone just out of my sight line when I walked in, but she broke off the instant she spotted me. "I cannot *believe* you took Riley into Mackie's office."

"I was—"

"Actually," she continued, "I can believe it. I should have expected it."

"I was going to—" I began again and then froze. Noah was standing at the counter, arms folded, looking like he wanted to smirk but was too annoyed—or too smart—to try. I tried to smooth my hair down, then gave up. It was only Noah. I hadn't broken any laws recently. No need to be nervous. "Hey, there."

"Hey, yourself," he said. "Taking an interest in local politics?"

I tossed my backpack onto the counter. "I didn't plan on bringing Riley in. She was supposed to hang out and look at the jack-o'-lanterns. I guess she got bored."

"Gee," Charlie sniped. "Who could have predicted that Riley, who can't sit still for five minutes and thinks you hung the moon, might have decided to follow you? Oh, wait. Me. I could, along with anyone else who had two brain cells to rub together. You shouldn't have left her alone to begin with."

"She was two blocks from the store," I pointed out, my own irritation rising to meet Charlie's. "She walks to the diner by herself all the time and you've never complained."

"No, because it's my call to make. What were you doing in Mackie's office, anyway?"

"I just wanted to get a look at him."

"Because you're suddenly interested in politics?" she said with a wave of her hand. "Spare me. You think he's got something to do with Kate Tibbs's death, and you decided this was the perfect time to check out your suspect."

I ducked my head, abashed and half-afraid of what I'd see on Noah's face.

"Did you even consider that maybe it isn't appropriate to bring an eight-year-old into a murder investigation? Or that possibly you should not be investigating a murder to begin with?"

"I'm sorry! It wasn't my intention to go in, you know. It just sort of . . . happened. I was looking in the window, and one of the staffers came out of nowhere and invited me in." I paused. "I wouldn't have taken her in there deliberately."

"Of course you wouldn't. You don't do deliberate, right? Or responsible, for that matter."

"Hey!" I snapped, temper breaking free. "What do you think—"

Something in my face must have warned Noah that violence was imminent. He stepped between us, saying, "Coffee. I could use a refill. Anybody else?"

"I'll get it." Charlie snatched the mug from his hand and stalked back, as he must have known she would.

"I'll take one too," I called sweetly.

"Why are you baiting her?" Noah scolded.

"I'm the big sister. It's my *responsibility*." With an effort, I brushed away the lash of Charlie's words and focused on Noah. "You didn't come here to play referee. What's up?"

"Well, I am an officer of the peace. Also, I wanted to talk to you."

"Everybody does today," I muttered, boosting myself onto the counter. "You're here in an official capacity, I assume?"

"Wondered if you'd had any developments in the Tibbs case," he said. "Since, you know, you seem to be working it."

"What's she done now?" Charlie reappeared with a single cup of coffee. She handed it to Noah, then turned to me. "You want to play girl detective, I can't stop you. But do it while Riley's around and you'll be headed back to Chicago earlier than you think."

There were times I could push Charlie, could bait her just for the fun of seeing her blow up, but this clearly wasn't one of them. "Got it."

"Good." She turned to Noah. "I take it she's in trouble with you too?"

"No, but it's still early in the day." A smile tugged at the corner of his mouth. "Give her some time to warm up."

The bell above the door jangled, and we turned in unison to greet the customer.

"Toilet plungers?" the man asked desperately.

"Aisle seven, right over here." Charlie led him through the store, calling over her shoulder, "Take this outside, you two. Some of us are trying to run a business here."

Noah shepherded me onto the back porch. "You went to Josh Miller's house."

"Who told you that?"

"Heard it from a neighbor," he said. "She mentioned a little bitty redhead came by last night, peeking in the windows."

"Bitty?" I said, straightening my back to gain an inch. "That could be a lot of people."

"'Looked like Little Orphan Annie,' she said." He rubbed a lock of my hair between finger and thumb. "As eyewitnesses go, she seemed pretty reliable."

"Hold on," I said, folding my arms. "You were at Miller's place again this morning? What were you looking for?"

He stared past me, lips moving slightly. He was counting to ten, I realized after a moment. Possibly one hundred. Finally he said, "Not your concern."

"The neighbor said Josh came back. At least, she thinks it was Josh. Something's keeping him here, Noah. I bet if you rounded up some of his associates, or even the customers, one of them would know . . ."

I trailed off. Noah's face had darkened during my recitation, eyebrows drawing together, muscle in his jaw jumping. Now he took a step toward me, authority and anger mingling in the movement. I eased back, but the distance between us narrowed.

"Stop," he said quietly. "Just stop."

So I did. I closed my mouth, forced myself to breathe normally, and tried to focus on what he said next, instead of his nearness or the way he smelled like coffee and clean cotton.

"Do you think I haven't been out tracking down anyone connected with Josh Miller's so-called business? I'm not a rookie like Anderson. I've been doing this job for eight years. We're running down every angle you've thought of and some you haven't. So while I appreciate that you are on a mission to help, you need to leave Josh Miller alone." He leaned in closer, his breath warm against my cheek, his words rumbling in my ear. "I will *not* ask nicely next time."

"This is you asking nicely?" Noah wasn't the only one with a temper, and I felt mine spark. I drilled a finger into his chest, harder than strictly necessary. "Because I didn't hear you say please. Not even once."

The corner of his mouth twitched. "Please, Frankie."

"Please what?"

"Please leave this alone." He met my eyes squarely. "Or hand to God, I will slap a pair of cuffs on you and stick you in the back of my squad car."

I stuck my chin out. "Liar."

"I'll let Charlie watch."

"That's just *mean*."

"I'll let your mom visit you in the holding cell."

"You're being unreasonable."

"Hang out with Riley," he ordered. "Have fun. Let her spend a couple of days basking in your undivided attention, and *stay out of my way*."

"Or you'll arrest me?" I snorted.

"Try it and see." There was no humor in his smile now, only surety. "I'm not messing around this time."

He wasn't. It might have been twelve years, but I could still read Noah. Whatever was happening with the case, he didn't want me involved—and not simply because of macho posturing.

"What is it?" I asked softly. "I'm not being nosy. You're worried."

Not merely determined, or driven, or outraged by Kate's death. He was *worried*.

Which worried me.

Before he could answer, my phone rang. He stepped away from me as if he'd been caught stealing.

"Noah, what's going on?"

He gestured to my coat pocket. "You going to get that? Might be the hospital."

I pulled out the phone. *Peter*.

"It's not," I said as he craned his neck to get a better look at the display.

"The surgeon, right? You sure you don't want to pick up?"

"Positive." I sent the call to voice mail, but the damage was done. Noah retreated behind his cop face: unreachable, unreadable, and infuriating. Any connection, any sense of familiarity or warmth, had disappeared. He was looking at me as if I was any other citizen, and the sting of it turned my words waspish. "Thanks so much for your concern."

He nodded, unfazed. "I need to be getting back to the station. Good talk, Frankie."

And with that, he jogged down the rear steps, leaving me fuming on the porch.

"That sounds like it went well," Charlie said as I stalked inside.

"You heard us?"

"No. But I heard the door when you slammed it, and you're stomping around loud enough to knock over displays." She watched me pace in front of the counter. "Do you want to talk about it?"

"No."

"Good, because I'm supposed to be at the hospital by now. Can I trust you not to break anything while I'm gone?"

"No guarantees," I said. "He might come back."

★   ★   ★

I'd turned my anger into cleaning energy, dusting shelves, rearranging displays, and filling inventory. I also answered the same questions—"How does it feel to be back?" "How long are you staying?"—approximately a billion times. If everyone who'd come in to catch a glimpse of me had spent ten bucks, Stapleton and Sons would have been set for life.

By the time Charlie and Riley returned, I was helping a woman with an unfortunate bowl haircut decide on the perfect grout for her bathroom retiling project. "It looked so easy on the Internet!" she'd exclaimed when she walked in. Riley settled in at the counter with her homework. When the woman left, she gave a world-weary shake of her head.

"Pinterest fail?" she asked knowingly.

"Don't knock 'em," Charlie muttered. "Internet DIY is going to send you to college." She turned her attention to me. "Are you ready to talk about what Noah wanted?"

"Nothing," I said, and she snorted. "Just to chat."

"Noah doesn't chat," Charlie said. "He definitely doesn't want to 'just chat' with you."

"Why not?" asked Riley. "What does he want to do with Aunt Frankie?"

"Nothing." *Wring my neck.* "Noah's busy, honey. That's all. He's busy with police stuff, so he doesn't have time for anything else."

Charlie faked a coughing fit to cover her laughter. "Finish restocking," she croaked, pointing at me. "Riley, you sweep. Let's get out of here in time to have dinner before it's dark."

THIRTEEN

"You need to take care of the office this morning," Charlie told me over breakfast. "I can't move for all those boxes."

"It's not that bad," I said, waving her off. "All you need to do is sort of . . . shove them out of the way."

"I've tried," she said dourly, "and nearly set off an avalanche. At least shift the bulk of it away from the file cabinets, will you? I have a system."

Of course she did.

"I could help," Riley said. She pulled back her sleeve and flexed her skinny little arm. "I'm strong."

I whistled. "Look at those muscles, kiddo!"

"You have school," Charlie cut in. "Which you're not ready for, so get on upstairs." After Riley had stomped off, still flexing, she added, "Remember, we have the funeral this afternoon."

As if I could forget. "You're sure you can take the time off?"

"Half the town will be at the church," she said. "It's not as if we're going to be overrun with customers, but Mom said she'd cover the store."

"Since when does she pass up the chance for gossip?" I asked through a mouthful of cereal, but Charlie was already heading out the door.

Charlie left for the hospital; I dropped Riley off to school and then drove over to the store.

"Did Charlotte ask you to organize those boxes?" Mom asked as I came in. "It's going to require a lot of lifting."

"Nothing I can't handle." I helped myself to coffee and went to unlock the door that led upstairs. "I moved it all back here myself, didn't I?"

Mom trailed after me. "Let me call someone to help you."

"No way," I said, spotting a familiar gleam in her eye. "No helpers. Do not call anyone."

"But—"

The door jingled, and I waved a hand at the front counter. "You take care of the store, and I'll take care of my stuff."

Charlie had a point, I thought as I surveyed the office again. There was barely room to move from the kitchenette to the table we used as a desk, and the sour scent of so many cardboard boxes made my nose wrinkle in disgust. I made my way over to one of the windows just as something shot from the kitchen to the bathroom. Something orange and white and bedraggled.

"You're not supposed to be up here," I said. The cat, slightly less skinny than it had been when we first met, stared at me without remorse. "There's not even anything to eat, unless you like cookies. And I draw the line at sharing cookies. How'd you get in here?"

If it was possible for a cat to radiate disdain, this one was practically glowing with it.

Once I propped open a window, the cat sashayed past and leapt gracefully to the sill, stretching out to sun itself,

152 | Lucy Kerr

ignoring me as I began shifting boxes and trying to restore order to chaos. A few bags went into the car to take back to the house; another slowly growing pile could go to the thrift store. Progress, however, was slow and tedious—so much so that when my phone rang, I answered without looking, willing to talk to a telemarketer or anyone else.

The good news was, my caller wasn't a telemarketer.

"Hello, stranger," came a familiar voice.

I closed my eyes, tried to talk myself out of the sinking feeling in my chest. "Hello, Peter. How are you?"

I'd meant to call my ex-fiancé. To return one of the many, many messages he'd left me. But every time I'd found a spare moment, I'd also found another excuse to keep from dialing. Peter and I hadn't spoken since the breakup; I'd left for Stillwater before we had figured out how to be around each other without being together. I waited for a pinch of regret or a pang of melancholy, but all I felt was awkward.

"I'm good," he said. "I had a surgery canceled at the last minute, and I thought I might have better luck reaching you in the morning—I wasn't sure you got my messages."

He sounded both wounded and amused, like he knew exactly what was happening to his voice mails.

"Family emergency," I said weakly. "It's been a little busy around here."

"I heard," he replied. "Someone said you were on administrative leave? Does that mean you're coming back once your niece discharges?"

Hospitals were like small towns. It was no surprise that Peter had heard all the details about Rowan and my return to Stillwater. What I hadn't expected was the way my answer seemed to stick in my throat. "I'm playing it by ear," I finally managed.

Peter was silent for a long time, and I fought the urge to fill the gap with some sort of explanation. Finally, he said, "I wanted to talk to you about the wedding."

"Oh?" It wasn't only the cloying scent of the boxes making my stomach churn.

"The hotel said they'd refund our deposit." We'd split the wedding costs fifty-fifty—I would have been happy with something at City Hall, but Peter had wanted the works, so we'd met in the middle: a civil ceremony with a big party afterward. Now that there was nothing to celebrate, the deposit was the last remnant of our failed relationship.

"I can mail you a check in Stillwater, unless you're coming back soon." He tried to sound offhand, but I knew him well enough to hear the hope threading through the words, one last attempt to repair us as delicately as he'd repair a damaged valve or a torn artery. "If you're not sure . . ."

"A check's fine," I said hoarsely. "I'm trying not to make a lot of plans right now. But thank you, Peter. For everything."

He chuckled ruefully, understanding the finality of my words. "You're welcome. Don't be a stranger, Frankie."

I didn't tell him I already felt like one.

We hung up, and I slid to the floor with a thump. I'd avoided Peter's calls because I was afraid it would make me miss my old life too much—not him, exactly, but the world he represented, my hectic, high-octane life, the friends I'd made over the last few years. But hearing his voice and the familiar sounds of the hospital in the background had felt nostalgic at best. There was no yearning to get back to my old life. Peter's call had highlighted the very thing I'd been trying to ignore. I was done with Chicago; it was time to move on.

Annoyed at the realization, I shifted boxes around, attempting to clear a trail, using work to distract myself from the uncertainty facing me. The cat, still watching from the windowsill, yawned hugely.

"You can stay," I told him, "but that doesn't mean I'm going to."

Where would I go? My nursing qualifications meant my options were pretty well limitless. In the past, that kind of freedom gave me a jolt of energy; now it made me feel adrift. How did other people make these kinds of plans? My reasons for choosing a new place had always been haphazard—a postcard from a friend, an article in a magazine, a show on TV. Luck, happenstance, or whim: my impulses had served me well for twelve years. But now, when I envisioned what came next, all I could see were the piles of boxes surrounding me.

*   *   *

A few hours later, I'd arranged the boxes to create narrow pathways around the apartment. It looked like a maze for lab rats, but it was functional, at least for the short term. The apartment was silent, save for my own labored death and the ticking of the kitchen clock, reminding me that Kate's funeral was this afternoon. Not that I needed reminding—I'd been thinking of her all morning, trying to make sense of her death.

What had prompted her to set out the night of the accident? By all accounts, Kate had stayed home from Steven's fundraiser because she wasn't up to socializing. If that were true, why on earth had she been out driving in a storm when she should have been home eating a quart of mint chocolate chip from the carton? Where was she going?

How had Josh Miller known she'd be there?

On impulse, I dialed Noah, intending to find out. As usual, my call went to voice mail, so I left a vague message and got back to work.

I'd just finished dragging a box of snowboarding equipment into the back bedroom, the cat watching me through smug, slitted eyes, when Noah appeared on the landing.

"Frankie, I know the motto is protect and serve, but . . ." He leaned against the doorframe, thumbs hooked in his belt loops, not even bothering to hide his grin.

"I didn't call you over here to help me move," I said, acutely aware that I was sticky with sweat and grime. "I had a question about Kate."

The smile fell away, and he straightened. "Nope."

"Hear me out," I pleaded and outlined all the reasons Kate shouldn't have been on the road that night.

"We've already looked into it," he said. "Even Steven doesn't know."

"She didn't call him?"

"Steven doesn't carry a phone at campaign events."

"What if there was an emergency? What if she'd gone into labor?"

Noah lifted a shoulder. "I'm not her doctor. According to Steven, all his calls go through Ted Sullivan when he's at an event."

I filled a glass at the kitchen sink, relishing the coolness of the water against my dry and dusty throat. "So Ted would have known where Kate was that night?"

"If she'd called him—but she didn't. She didn't even bring her phone with." He dragged a hand down his face, dropped into a chair as if he was about to topple from the weight of the case. "We don't know why Kate was on the road, and my gut says we won't find out until we catch Josh Miller."

"Any luck with that?" I asked, just as my mother poked her head in. Out of the corner of my eye, I saw the very tip of an orange-and-white tail disappear into the bedroom.

"Coffee, Noah?" Mom asked.

"Thanks, Lila, but I'll pass." He fixed me with a glare. "I'm not answering that."

I didn't break his gaze. "Mom, are the police having any luck finding Josh Miller?"

"I don't believe so," she said. "It's a surprise, really, considering how many agencies have been brought in to help."

Noah dropped his forehead into his hands. "Lila, where on earth did you hear that?"

"Oh, around." She fluttered her hands, doing her best imitation of a fluffy old lady, but neither of us were fooled. "You know how people talk. It's hard to remember who said what half the time."

"The police scanner probably helps," I added, and she had the temerity to look offended.

"I don't know what you're talking about, Francesca. I haven't used that thing in years." Before Noah could question her further, she'd escaped downstairs.

"Don't feel bad," I said, taking the chair across from him. It felt so good to sit, I considered never getting up again. "My mom's intelligence-gathering capabilities are so good, she deserves her own acronym."

"Best if I don't think about that too much," he said and then added too casually, "You ever call the surgeon back?"

My cheeks went warm. "We talked."

"And?"

"And nothing. We wrapped up some loose ends from canceling the wedding, not that it's any of your business."

"Oh, *now* you've got a problem with people asking questions?" he scoffed.

The cat sashayed back through the room and nimbly climbed a stack of boxes as if he was ascending a throne. Noah caught sight of him and goggled. "Is that a cat?"

"Yes. Don't tell my mother."

"I have never told your mother a single thing about this place," he said, voice low and his eyes glittering. "I'm not going to start now."

That was for the best, considering what we'd gotten up to here when we were teenagers.

The tension returned—less prickly, more fraught—as if memory had turned the air thick.

"I should go," Noah said eventually, unfolding himself from the chair.

"Yeah. And I have . . . boxes. Lots of boxes." I paused. "Are you going to the funeral?"

"Can't," he said. "Working the case. You?"

"Steven invited Charlie and me."

"And you said yes?" His tone did not imply I would bring comfort to the bereaved.

"It seemed like the right thing to do," I said. "Why—oh. You're worried I'm going to ask a bunch of questions, aren't you?"

"Are you?" he shot back.

"It's a funeral, Noah! I do have some sense of decency."

"But not self-preservation," he retorted. "You're not exactly inconspicuous, Frankie. A town this size, the prodigal daughter returns and solves a murder, then starts digging into another one? You're stirring the pot."

"Are you two going to fight every time you see each other?" Charlie's voice floated up the stairs, and the cat bolted for the bedroom again. I rolled my eyes.

Charlie entered, dumped a stack of bills and orders on the table, and took stock of the room. "Frankie, you were supposed to be working on this!"

"I have been," I protested. "It's just . . . slow going."

"You've barely made a dent." Her eye twitched as she surveyed the towers of cardboard. "You're really going to move all this back to Chicago? I think I'm working that day."

"I am definitely working that day," Noah said, peering into a box filled with rock-climbing gear. "Why don't you just move in here? You've got enough stuff to set up house."

"Did you miss the part about temporary?" I asked, more sharply than I meant. Just because Chicago was my past didn't mean that Stillwater was my future.

"While you're in town." His eyebrows lifted at my tone. "Doesn't it make more sense to stay here in your own place? The five of you have to be getting pretty cramped by now, right?"

"The whole point of Frankie coming home was to be around more," Charlie replied, her tone chilly as a meat locker. "But obviously, it's up to her."

They turned to me, as if awaiting my decision.

But I'd already made my choice, hadn't I? No matter how cramped the house, no matter how maddening my mother or how much I missed my privacy, I'd promised to help out.

Not to mention, sleeping on the bottom bunk and living out of boxes felt temporary. Nobody expected I'd share a room with Riley indefinitely. Setting up in my own apartment felt dangerously close to settling in.

"Seems like a lot of effort for a couple of months. Easier to stay at the house," I said, acutely aware of Noah's scrutiny—and Charlie's relief.

I stood and dusted my hands on my jeans. "Let's finish up those boxes. We've got a funeral to get to."

FOURTEEN

By afternoon, the clouds had cleared, even if my mood hadn't. The sky was a bright crystalline blue, and the bite in the air warned that summer was truly over. No more reprieves, no more gifts of unseasonably warm weather.

My efforts in the office had yielded clothing I'd nearly forgotten I had, including my go-to little black dress. It was made of some sort of miracle fabric—soft as my favorite yoga pants, impossible to wrinkle, dressy enough for cocktails, and conservative enough for church.

Or funerals.

"Black is a terrible color on you," my mother said once I was home and had finished dressing. "It washes you out."

"It's a funeral, not a party." I fastened tiny jet studs at my ears. "Nobody will care."

"You could meet someone," she pointed out. "I'm sure Steven knows a lot of eligible bachelors. Lawyers. Businessmen. Politicians."

"Any guy who's looking to pick up chicks at a funeral is not a guy I want to meet."

Her eyebrows lifted as she considered this. "Fair enough. At least do something about your hair, Francesca. It's disrespectful to leave it all . . ." She waved her hands around her head.

"It's not that bad." When I looked in the mirror, though, I could see her point. The curls were even more wild than usual, brushing the tops of my shoulders and refusing to stay tucked behind my ears. I eyed the pair of safety scissors on Riley's desk and considered a last-minute emergency trim, but my mother snatched them away before I could act.

"Come here," she said with a familiar, long-suffering sigh. She opened the jar of styling goop on the dresser and briskly rubbed some into my hair. Then, extricating one of Riley's less exuberant barrettes from the top drawer, she smoothed down one side, pinning it above my ear.

"I look like a refugee from the thirties," I grumbled. Sure, my hair had been tamed, temporarily—but it left me feeling like Betty Boop's redheaded stepsister.

"You look presentable," she said with a sniff. "Maybe a little lipstick?"

"Enough." I swiped a ChapStick across my lips. "You're sure you won't come with?"

"Someone needs to mind the store," she said. "You and Charlotte go."

"Frankie, move it!" Charlie yelled. "We're going to be late."

I flew down the stairs. Charlie was waiting in what I could best describe as church clothes: black skirt, pale-blue blouse, gray sweater. Her hair was neatly pulled back in a bun and a tiny gold cross nestled in her throat.

She looked sensible and respectable, and my hand went to my hair again, feeling every bit the scatty sister.

"Maybe I should change," I murmured.

"Too late," she replied with a wry smile, and I got the feeling she wasn't talking about my wardrobe. "You're fine, Frankie."

"Thanks for going with me," I said as we drove.

"I've talked with Steven in the NICU a few times. I feel so sorry for him."

"Even with his perfect teeth?" I teased.

"I'm not going to hold good dental hygiene against anyone."

"Did he say anything about the investigation?" I parked down the street from the church, avoiding the snarl of traffic around the parking lot. News crews had lined the street as we approached, but there were plenty of sheriff's deputies handling crowd control—nobody with a microphone or a video camera was allowed on the block.

"Why would I ask him that? Do you really think I'd *gossip* with him in front of his child?"

"To be fair," I said, "it's not like Trey would understand."

"You're impossible," she hissed, then plastered on a smile and nodded at a group of funeral-goers.

"So he didn't say anything?"

"Good grief," Charlie said. "You solved one murder, Frankie. That doesn't make you a detective."

"Two murders," I whispered as we entered the church, the nave crammed with so many flowers my nose itched. "One killer."

A technicality, maybe, but since I'd nearly been victim number three, the details mattered.

We fell silent as we joined the crowd filing into the sanctuary. Inside, the air smelled of beeswax, lemon oil, and lilies. It wasn't just politicians and political groups who'd sent offerings—there were arrangements from people I'd never heard of too, small clusters of carnations with heartfelt notes attached, often in childish print. "Thank you for finding me a family," read one of them, and something prickled behind my eyes.

Each card was a testament to the lives Kate had touched, as was the overflowing church. I caught a glimpse of Steven in the front pew, flanked by family members, somber and contained. The shock and unguarded emotion he'd displayed in the ER had gradually settled into a deeper, more sorrowful grief as he'd waited by Trey's bedside. Now he was the picture of resolute sadness, the sort of noble suffering the cameras outside would love to see.

Ted Sullivan stood nearby, working his way through the pews, shaking hands with a variety of well-dressed, self-important people. He was *networking* while Kate's white-and-gold casket stood not twenty feet away. He paused to say something to the sheriff, then went back to looking for his next victim, the next person to schmooze.

Disgusted, I turned away and scanned the room, hoping that someone in the wall-to-wall crowd would jump out at me. I wanted to take in the crowd, absorb its mood, let any stray impressions snag my attention and direct me toward whatever didn't fit. I could watch myself and be watchful simultaneously, no matter what Noah thought.

The honey-colored wooden pews were full, so Charlie and I found a place along the side of the church beneath a stained-glass window depicting gently frolicking lambs. I turned to watch the people still streaming in, and Charlie elbowed me. "Don't stare."

"I'm observing," I said primly.

"Quit it. You're being weird."

The collection of mourners was odd, to say the least. Politicians in custom-tailored suits rubbed elbows, uneasily, with people wearing black T-shirts and jeans. I even spotted Norris Mackie in one of the pews, his wife by his side, hands clasped and heads bowed in prayer.

Several people, including Kate's sister and a coworker, gave eulogies during the service. Steven must have been expected to speak—the minister beckoned him forward, but after an excruciating pause, he merely nodded and continued with the service. A little surprising, considering Steven was accustomed to giving speeches, but as he covered his face with his hands, shoulders shaking, I felt ashamed at my snap judgment.

When my father had died, people had been quick to tell me how to mourn. Later, I realized that their well-meaning advice wasn't just for my own good, but for their comfort. Grief is messy and awkward. It's hard to know what to tell people when they're living through a terrible hurt, and harder still to watch them suffer. Often, our instinct is to fix things. In truth, what people need is for someone to bear witness to their sadness, not try to stop it.

We followed the casket outside. There was no way to hide from the press now, unfortunately. Cameramen with long lenses clicked away as the procession trailed out of the church toward the waiting hearse. When we left for the cemetery, the television vans followed close behind. Police positioned themselves at the entrance, preventing the news crews from getting any closer.

We reached the cemetery and wound our way through the gently sloping terrain to the burial site, our feet crunching on the gravel path. Though the sky stayed clear, a biting wind crept under our coats. My dress slapped at my legs, and Charlie's heels sank into the damp ground with every step.

"Awful," she said, wiping her eyes ferociously. "Absolutely awful."

For once we were in total agreement. We stood on the outskirts of the crowd as the minister began speaking. As unobtrusively as possible, I let my gaze drift over the assembly, mindful of Charlie shaking her head next to me, letting my instinct take over. I recognized plenty of people but only remembered a few. I'd been away too long.

The service concluded, and the mourners lined up to toss ivory roses onto the casket and offer last condolences to Steven. The line stretched down the hill, and judging by the glacial pace, we'd be here for some time. "Lovely service," Charlie murmured, one of those inane niceties meant to fill the silence, and I nodded, surveying the manicured grounds and neat rows of graves.

My father was buried here, in another section of the cemetery, down the hill and past the columbarium, near a small pond with a stone chapel. I hadn't been there in at least five years, I realized with a guilty start. No doubt my mother visited regularly, but I'd neglected him. As the line inched forward, the urge to visit my father's grave grew stronger.

"Back in a few," I whispered to Charlie.

"What—" she hissed.

"Dad," I mouthed, and her scowl transformed into something like pity.

I skirted the crowd and made my way back toward the main drive, my footsteps overly loud on the gravel path.

The columbarium, shining white marble next to a small pond, marked the entrance to another, older part of the cemetery. Ancient, gnarled oak trees dotted the landscape, offering shade and casting shadows across the tombstones. Generations of Stapletons had been buried here. The closer I got to my father, the more tombstones bore our name, especially when I veered off the path and began making my way across the plots. I trailed my fingers over weathered marble and granite, my footsteps careful and measured, relying on faint memories to guide me.

And then there it was: a simple granite rectangle, a dual headstone. Matthew Stapleton, beloved husband and father. His dates, a stark reminder of how fate had robbed us all. And next to it, an empty space, meant for my mother someday.

I pressed a fist to my stomach, drew a steadying breath, and lowered myself to the ground.

"Hi, Daddy."

My mom, of course, kept the grave immaculate. Only a few leaves had dared to land here since her last visit, and I picked one up, cradling it in my palm. It had been years since I visited. I should have had so much to say, so much to fill him in on. Instead, I fumbled for words.

"I came home," I said softly. "I don't know how long I'll stay, but they needed me, and I came home. I'm sorry that I—" *That I left*, I'd been about to say. But it wasn't true. I'd needed to go out into the world, and I wouldn't apologize, not to my father, or his headstone, or anyone. "I won't leave like that again. Not while they need me."

I rested my hand on the icy granite and waited for some sense of his presence. That was how these things were supposed to work, right? A heartfelt confession, followed by a sense of peace, a swell of comfort. A sign that the departed was still with us, in some intangible way.

There were none of those things. Geese winged across the sky, trees rustled. I tugged my sleeves down over my fingertips, shivering.

I'd hoped that coming here would help me to feel a sense of connection to my dad. Instead, I felt lonely. My father's spirit, any trace of his expansive, exuberant self, wasn't here. I would find him at the store—in the creak of the floorboards and the hum of the table saw, in the gleam of the back counter and the mingled scent of varnish and powdered sugar. Those reminders had been too painful for too long; they were part of what had sent me running. Now those same memories welcomed me back. I wondered what Trey Tibbs would think of when he visited Kate's grave. What memories he'd use to console himself, what stories people would share with him so that he'd know some aspect of Kate.

I stood and brushed away the bits of grass clinging to my dress. I needed to get back to the service. Surely, the line of mourners would have trailed off by now, and Charlie would be checking her watch and huffing with annoyance that I'd disappeared.

Retracing my footsteps, I saw that not only had the line trailed off, it had disappeared completely. I'd spent more time at my dad's grave than I'd realized, and the crowd had moved to the parking lot, heading back to their everyday lives. Rather than join them, I headed back to Kate's grave; it seemed wrong to leave without paying my respects.

The cemetery workers had yet to return and finish the burial; no doubt they'd wait until everyone had left. For now, a single figure still hovered at the far edge of the clearing, half-hidden behind a tree.

"Charlie?" I called, shading my eyes and squinting.

The figure ducked away, but not before I caught a glimpse of flannel shirt and baby fat.

Josh Miller.

"Wait!" Without thinking, I scrambled after him, "Josh, wait! Stop, or I'll scream! There're a million cops in the parking lot—they'll be all over you in a minute!"

I had no idea if it was true, but Josh must have believed me, because he skidded to a halt midway down the hill. I approached him slowly, hands up to show I was defenseless, wishing I hadn't left my purse and phone in Charlie's car.

"You're that nurse," he said. "The one who fixed my shoulder."

"You're Josh Miller," I shot back. "You killed Kate Tibbs."

He didn't deny it.

"What are you doing here?" I fisted my hands in the fabric of my skirt to hide their shaking. "Are you coming after Steven too? Kate wasn't enough?"

"I didn't mean to kill her." He swayed on his feet. "It was an accident."

"Right. You just happened to see her driving that night and decided to follow her? You didn't mean to run her off the road?"

"It was an accident," he said again, his voice vague and petulant. "I only meant to scare her, but she overreacted. The roads were bad, and she swerved, and . . . you don't believe me."

He took a step toward me, and I eased away, saying, "If it was an accident, why'd you run?"

The fugitive lifestyle was not treating Josh kindly. His hair was stringy and matted, his cheeks sallow, and his gaze unfocused. The scent of sweat and body odor hung in the air, and he rubbed at his forehead, growing agitated. "It wasn't supposed to happen like this. I didn't mean . . ."

I drew a shuddery breath. "Why did you go back to your house?"

"My house?" His head jerked back to stare at me.

"I spoke to your neighbor. She said you came back in the middle of the night. You knocked over some garbage cans. Were you looking for something?"

He laughed, and I scrutinized him—his pupils were contracted to a dot, and his movements were almost languid, even as he rocked back and forth. He was high.

"Were you looking for your stash?" I said, taking a step forward, then another. "Money, maybe?"

From his back pocket, he whipped out a knife, and my knees turned to water. "Stay away."

I held up my hands, making myself look as nonthreatening as I could. "I'm staying right here. Promise."

"I don't want to hurt you, but you have to stay away." He shook his head like he was trying to clear it. The jackknife, its blade long and curved, gleamed as it pointed directly at my heart. He stumbled backward a few paces. "I never wanted to hurt anybody."

I was losing him. In a moment, he'd be gone, and I'd be no closer to understanding Kate's death. "Why did you go after Kate? Did someone hire you?"

"It was an accident," he repeated, his voice thin and panicked. "It wasn't about money. It was never about money."

"Then what was it about? Please, please tell me. I promise I'm listening. What is this about?"

The knife trembled, then lowered. "Proof," he said, as if it were obvious.

Nothing about this was obvious to me. "Proof of what?"

"Frankie?" Charlie's voice, high-pitched and alarmed, floated down the hill toward us.

Before I could tell her to stay back, Josh lunged, grabbing my arm and throwing me to the ground. Momentum carried me down the rest of the hill. I glimpsed Josh running away and Charlie racing toward me as I tumbled down the slope, bones jolting and teeth rattling.

"Frankie!" Charlie said as I came to a stop. "Oh, my God! Was that—"

"He's getting away," I mumbled and pushed up on my hands and knees.

"You're not going after him," Charlie ordered and helped me to my feet. "He had a knife!"

"I'm adventurous, not stupid," I said, gingerly testing my arms and leg. Nothing broken, though my dress was covered in grass and dirt, and I'd lost a shoe somewhere. "We need to call Noah."

"My phone's in the car," Charlie said. "But there are a ton of cops in the parking lot. We can let them know. Are you okay to walk?"

I took a few wobbly steps and managed to stay upright. Charlie retrieved my shoe and slipped an arm around my waist, and it was only when the parking lot came into sight that it hit me: for the second time in a week, I'd let Josh Miller escape.

*　　*　　*

By the time we arrived at the parking lot, Steven had already started his statement to the press. Cameras clicked and whirred as reporters jostled for position. It was hard to hear everything Steven said, but his demeanor was calm and determined. Snatches of his statement floated toward us, words like "tragedy" and "determination," "privacy" and "child," "commitment" and "campaign."

Rehearsed, I thought absently, noting the smooth cadence of his delivery, but painful nevertheless. I turned my back and continued searching for an officer, aware that every single second I wasted, Josh Miller was getting farther away. Charlie pointed to Sheriff Flint, standing to one side of Steven, Ted Sullivan on the other, but I wasn't about to tell Steven I'd let his wife's killer escape on national television.

Travis Anderson, hat pulled low to hide his stitches, was directing traffic. I shook off Charlie's grip and ran toward him. His face lit with recognition, then darkened as he realized I probably wasn't sprinting across a cemetery parking lot for a social visit.

Before I could speak, another squad car pulled up, lights whirling but sirens silent, parking a few feet away. A moment later, Noah climbed out, jaw set, eyes hard. Everything about him was grim and unyielding and tightly wound fury. Someone must have spotted Miller already and called it in.

I whirled and reached for his arm.

"Not now," Noah said and brushed past me.

"Noah, listen. I saw Miller. He was on foot, but he might have a car stashed somewhere, on a back road or something. Southwest side of the cemetery."

"What?" He stopped and looked at me as if he'd only just realized I was there. "Who?"

"Miller," I repeated, and somewhere behind me, Charlie made a noise of distress. "He was here. But he got away, and he's armed."

"Josh Miller?" he said, anger darkening his features. "He's here?"

"Yes! I mean, he was. I tried to follow him, but he—wait. Isn't that why you're here?"

"No. We have a situation," he said dully, and he dragged a hand across his face. He twisted away to speak into his radio, and I heard him ordering all available units to the southwest side of the cemetery, repeating the information I'd blurted. The entire time he spoke, his gaze was locked on Steven.

And that's when I understood. Noah wasn't here because someone had spotted Miller. Noah had come to the cemetery to deliver bad news, and it must have been very, very bad indeed for him to intrude on this moment.

Steven was taking questions from the reporters clustered around him, barely visible behind the cameras and mics. Noah started toward them, but I caught his arm and hung on. "What happened?"

He opened his mouth, closed it again, then glanced over at Steven and the press corps, shaking his head.

"Noah, it's his wife's funeral. You can't barge in, especially with all those reporters standing a foot away."

"I need to talk to Steven." But he stayed rooted to the spot, his eyes gone distant and unseeing.

Behind me, Charlie said in a low voice, "People are starting to stare, you two."

"Noah," I said sharply, and his gaze refocused on me. The wind snaked beneath my skirt, and I shuddered and tried to brace myself for whatever he was going to say next. "Tell me."

"It's the baby," he said. "He's gone."

"Gone?" I said as Charlie gasped. My fingers tightened on Noah's arm, anchoring myself to his solidity.

"Gone. Taken. Somebody kidnapped Trey Tibbs."

FIFTEEN

I could only imagine how the scene would play out in the national news. Everyone in America would witness Steven's anguish, every moment captured in high definition from every angle, parsed by pundits and gossip rags alike. Noah's approach. Sheriff Flint slipping away to confer with him. Ted Sullivan following a moment later. One reporter noticing, then another, and another. Steven, puzzled and frustrated when he realized his audience was drifting away.

Ted and Sheriff Flint tried to usher Steven back into the car, where there was a modicum of privacy, but he wasn't having it. Finally, they each took an arm, but he threw them off, face flushing, voice rising. "What the hell is going on?"

Noah leaned in to give him the news, and Steven's face went slack. Seconds passed, my heart thudding in the silence, and then his shock transformed to trembling fury like someone had flipped a switch. For a moment, I thought he'd take a swing at Noah, but Ted grabbed him by the arm, shielding him from the cameras and speaking in a low urgent voice.

"This is your fault," Steven snarled, but it was impossible to know who he meant. Noah? Ted? Sheriff Flint? Whatever

Ted said convinced Steven to let himself be hustled away, even as he continued shouting orders and insults at everyone.

"Come on," Charlie said, tugging at me. "We have to go."

"Where?" I said, wrenching away as she led me back toward the car. "I should help."

"How?" she snapped. "Nobody's hurt. Nobody's sick—except the monster who stole Trey, and I guarantee they're not here. I need to check on Rowan."

"She's fine, Charlie. Noah said the other kids were safe and the NICU is on a hard lockdown."

A noise emanated from deep in her throat—half growl, half sob. "They aren't his kids, are they? Keys. Hospital. Now."

So we went.

"It doesn't make sense," I said as we drove to Stillwater General. Charlie was flying, easily twenty over the limit, but I wasn't brave enough to tell her to slow down. "Josh Miller couldn't have taken him—he was at the funeral."

"Who else would have a reason to take Trey?"

"Forget who," I said. "How? The NICU's the most secure ward in the hospital. You know how carefully those kids are watched. There are cameras and ID badges and security anklets on each baby. Taking a kid through NICU without deactivating his anklet sets off alarms on the entire floor—*everything* goes into a hard lockdown."

"Not hard enough," Charlie said. "Maybe Miller had a partner."

"He's already on the run," I said. "Even if he had a partner, why would he want to make things harder for himself?"

"Maybe he doesn't see it that way," Charlie replied. "Everyone says Josh went after Kate out of revenge, right?

Because she took his little girl. What if taking her child is his way of evening the score?"

It made a horrible sort of sense: justice, twisted beyond recognition. I did not point out that kidnapping Trey might be better than the alternative.

"Do you think the baby will be okay?" Charlie asked. "If it were Rowan . . . she's not ready to leave the NICU. What if Trey isn't ready either?"

Once again, I had no good answer. According to Donna and Jess, Trey's stay in the NICU had been more about security than any specific medical concern. He would have been discharged in the next couple of days, but that didn't mean he was out of the woods. He might have needed a home CPAP machine to help with breathing, or medicine, or special formula. I couldn't envision Josh, strung out and desperate, providing that level of care.

We raced inside the hospital. Police were stationed everywhere, and they scrutinized my hospital badge while Charlie showed her driver's license and the security bracelet that matched Rowan's. We had to repeat the procedure three more times—once when we left the elevator, once when we'd been buzzed onto the maternity wing, and again when we entered the NICU.

Charlie rushed ahead of me, scooping Rowan out of her isolette and holding her close, murmuring something indecipherable. I couldn't help but stare at the empty place where Trey's isolette had stood. He'd been ten feet away from Rowan. Ten feet, and someone had snatched him. They could have taken Rowan too. What if one of the nurses had intervened, and it escalated to a hostage situation? Every infant in this room had been in danger. My hands shook, and I didn't know if it was relief or rage.

Whatever investigating the police were doing, it wasn't happening here. The only other people in the room were staff and parents, all stricken and solemn, the tension in the air ratcheted up to an unbearable degree.

"What happened to Trey's isolette?" I asked one of the other nurses as she rocked a baby whose parents hadn't yet arrived.

"The police took it," she said. "Dr. Solano won't let them work in here, but they're questioning all of us, one by one."

"How did it happen?"

Her voice was flat, nearly defeated. "Jess."

I drew back, looking around for her familiar blonde head. "Jess Chapman? Did the kidnapper . . ."

"No." Her arms tightened around the baby. "Jess *is* the kidnapper. She stole Trey."

I sank onto the nearest chair, cold sweat trickling down my sides. "Are you sure?"

"She switched shifts today," the nurse said. "Something about needing to help out a relative. Trey doesn't need one-on-one care like some of the others, so she volunteered to take him along with her other assignment. Jess really bonded with him the night of the accident, and we all thought she wanted a chance to say good-bye before he was discharged this afternoon."

I pressed a fist against my stomach, trying to quell the oily rush of nausea. I'd seen the bond between Jess and Trey, the way she checked on him even when she was assigned to other patients, and assumed it was harmless. Healthy, even, as if it

178 | Lucy Kerr

was her way of making up for freezing in the ER. How could I have misjudged her so badly?

"So she walked off the floor with him? How is that even possible?" There was no reason for a baby to leave the NICU during their stay—the whole point of the unit was to centralize care, to make sure their specialists were nearby.

She wiped at a tear. "Dr. Solano had ordered one last kidney ultrasound before discharge." I nodded. Standard procedure if there had been any suspicion of internal bleeding from the accident—an all-clear before sending the patient home. "Jess said the machine was broken, so she took him down to imaging instead."

"And they never showed."

Her fingers twisted together, over and over. "Jess called to say they were backed up and squeezing him in would take more time than expected. It was a slow day, so we figured we could manage without her."

It was a good cover story. Imaging never went as quickly as you expected. Emergencies threw off the schedule, machines went down, software glitched. We'd all been there before, so a delay wouldn't send up any red flags. "How long were they gone before you realized something was wrong?"

"An hour," she said miserably. "Dr. Solano called the imaging lab to ask for the results, and they said she'd told them the order was cancelled." Her voice cracked. "We called the Code Pink in minutes."

Code Pink: infant abduction.

Things would have moved quickly once the code was called. An immediate lockdown and room-by-room search of the entire hospital from patient rooms to janitor's closets; the police brought in for a second sweep; every infant on the ward double-checked and guarded until their parents arrived. Trey's chart and blood samples would have been put in a secure location for identification purposes. I forced myself to take slow, even breaths, trying to keep from throwing up.

"Is there security footage?" I asked, once I could speak again.

"They're not telling us much, but the cameras must have caught something. I heard she left a note in the isolette, but . . ." She lifted her hands. "What could she possibly say?"

What could any of us say?

"They'll find her," I said. "Every police department in the country's going to be looking for them."

People disappear more often than you'd expect. I saw it all the time in Chicago—patients who managed to slip off the grid, go underground, and leave their old lives behind. Not easy, but manageable in a big city.

Here, though? Where the land was flat, the vistas wide, and everyone's lives were on display? It would be nearly impossible to hide.

Then again, if you'd asked me this morning, I would have said it was impossible to steal a baby from a locked ward.

"Is Garima on duty?" I asked.

"Dr. K? She's in her office. The police asked her a bunch of questions since she was with Jess on the night of the delivery, but I'm not sure how much she was able to tell them."

True enough. Once Garima handed off the baby to the neonatologist, her work was done; postpartum, she focused more on the mother than the baby. But she and Dr. Solano were the driving force behind the department, the ones who'd developed a NICU facility instead of requiring families with high-risk pregnancies to drive to a larger regional center. This department was her baby, she'd told me more than once, and I knew she'd feel responsible.

"Was Trey receiving any kind of treatment that's going to be a problem if we don't find him quickly?" I asked.

"No. He'd stepped down to regular feedings." It was the only bit of good news in this entire nightmare. "What could Jess want with him?"

None of the answers were positive, so I mumbled something reassuring and went to find Garima. She was on the phone, promising the person on the other end that everything was well in hand, though I could tell she didn't believe it.

"You heard?" she asked when she'd hung up.

"I was at the funeral when they told Steven." I sank into the chair across from her. "How are you holding up?"

"I'm okay," she said, but the skin beneath her eyes looked bruised, and her dark skin had a grayish cast to it. "We have to find him."

"The entire sheriff's department is on it. So are the state police and the FBI. They've questioned all of the staff?"

She nodded. "Some of us more than once. Grace Fisher asked the night shift to come in early for questioning too. They're talking to the parents, and anyone who was buzzed onto the floor. I'm sure they'll want to interview you."

"Of course," I said. "Was there any sign Jess was unbalanced?"

"None," she replied. "I know she had a hard time in the ER the night of the delivery, but she bounced back quickly enough. Her work until now has been exemplary. Solano says she's rock-solid."

"She left a note in the isolette?"

Garima glanced up sharply. "We're trying to keep that quiet."

"Good luck," I said. "What did it say?"

She dragged in a breath. "'Please let him go. Kate would want it this way.'"

I felt the blood drain from my face, suddenly light-headed.

"Exactly." She took off her glasses and rubbed her forehead. "You were at the funeral? How did Steven handle it?"

I searched for the words, trying to make sense of not only what I'd seen and heard but the undercurrents.

"Josh Miller was there," I said, and Garima's jaw dropped. "I spotted him during the graveside service and tried to follow him, but . . ." I waved my hand. "That's a whole different story. By the time I got back to the service, Steven was giving his statement, and I was trying to find a cop to go after Miller. That's when Noah pulled up, and once the press smelled blood in the water, it turned into a circus."

"Today of all days," Garima said softly. "Steven's already been through the wringer. It's cruel."

I nodded. "It couldn't have been a coincidence. Jess must have planned it down to the minute." Had she and Josh planned it together? I filed the thought away for now, focused again on Garima's question. "You've seen patients in shock. They shut down. And Steven did, for a minute. He kind of staggered, and the sheriff and his campaign manager were holding him up, and then he snapped. He nearly tried to take a swing at Noah."

Garima's eyes widened.

"Kate's death really devastated him, but he seemed to handle it pretty well," I said. "After a loss like that, some people lash out. They've got so much rage that it burns right through their control. Steven was hurting, but he was turning it inward, you know? He almost seemed to blame himself, like if he hadn't gone to the fundraiser or had made Kate go with him, he could have stopped it."

"Survivor's guilt," she murmured. "He should be blaming Josh Miller."

"He does. But he's also been pretty realistic about the odds of a successful conviction. Working as a prosecutor has jaded him, I think. This is different."

"How so?"

"He was furious. Once it sank in at the cemetery, he started ordering the sheriff around, cursing at Noah, demanding they bring in other agencies."

"Bet that went over well," she murmured.

"The press ate it up. It's got to be all over the news by now."

"He'll sue," Garima said wearily. "Whether we find Trey or not, we could lose our NICU designation. It could shut the whole hospital down. I feel terrible even thinking about it while that poor baby is missing, but—" She spread her hands wide. "We've done so much good here, Frankie. Now it's over."

"Maybe not," I said. "We'll find the baby. Once we do, the hospital will recover, even if he does sue. Nobody here was negligent."

The words sounded hollow, even to my own ears. Garima sighed and stood. "Guess I should get back out there. Check on my people."

"Hey." I punched her arm lightly as we left her office. "You do good all the time. I should know—Rowan and Charlie are alive because of you."

She smiled weakly and headed out while I returned to the NICU.

"I'm not leaving," Charlie said before I could get a word out. "She can't stay here by herself."

"She'll be fine," I said, though I couldn't help running a hand over Rowan's downy head, reassuring myself she was safe. "There's a cop outside, and the entire ward's on lockdown. You'll be lucky if they let you bring her home at discharge, security's so tight."

"Security didn't help Trey Tibbs, did it?" She practically snarled the words.

"Trey was targeted, Charlie. It was personal."

Personal and baffling. Had Jess's bond with Trey warped somehow, pushing her over the edge? It was the easiest explanation, though by no means a comforting one. I could almost have bought it if Kate's crash had been an accident. But it seemed like too big of a coincidence that the baby that Jess bonded with, out of all the infants she'd taken care of in the last few years, was the one whose mother had been murdered. More logical to assume that Jess and Josh were working together from the start.

It fit, I guess, if you wedged the facts together and ignored the people. By all accounts, Jess was devoted to her patients. It was hard to imagine someone who loved children taking up with a guy who'd lost custody of his own. I was missing something.

"Rowan is safe. Nobody's going to steal her. Someone is targeting Steven's family—we just have to figure out who."

"We? We are not detectives. *You* are not a detective. You are a nurse, and you should not be going toe-to-toe with a killer at someone's funeral!" I bit my lip as Charlie continued, voice rising. "This family has been through enough in the last month, Frankie. I know you feel bad about this Josh Miller guy walking out of the ER, but you need to step back—way, way back—and let Noah and the police handle this. You want to save something? Focus on the store, or there won't be much left to save."

SIXTEEN

It took several hours, but I finally managed to convince Charlie to come home. Rowan was several weeks away from discharge, and there was no way the hospital would allow Charlie to sleep in the lounge for that long. Not only that, but Riley needed her too.

We waited for shift change—Charlie wanted to be sure that she knew exactly who would be watching Rowan for the night, and the sight of Donna's familiar face seemed to ease her fear.

"Fingerprint ink," Donna called, taking longer than usual to scrub in. "I had to talk to the police."

"They're fingerprinting people? They already know Jess is responsible," I said.

"They're just being cautious." Donna lowered her voice. "Frankie, I know Jess. She's a good person. She's a good nurse. She loved that baby, sure, but we all have patients who are special. There's nothing wrong with that."

"I think Steven Tibbs would disagree."

"There has to be an explanation," she insisted. "She'd never hurt Trey. I'm sure of it."

"Let's hope you're right," I said.

After I'd dragged Charlie out of the hospital, we stopped in at the store, where Riley was assembling a miniature mansion out of building scraps. My mother, naturally, had the grapevine's take on Trey's abduction. It wasn't enough that Jess had taken Trey. There was always another layer to the conspiracy, and theories ranged from the Chicago mob to St. Louis gangs, ex-clients of Kate's to ex-cons Steven had prosecuted. I was surprised nobody had proposed alien abduction and said as much.

"It's only been half a day, Francesca," my mother said primly. "Give them some time."

"How was traffic today?" Charlie asked, scanning the receipts with a scowl.

"Slow. It picked up after the news about Trey broke."

"Why?" I asked. "Is there some correlation between major crime and home improvement?"

Mom brushed a stray wood shaving from the counter. "I have a granddaughter in the NICU and a daughter on staff. People assumed I might have insights."

"You mean gossip," I said sourly.

"People are scared, Francesca. Things like this don't happen in Stillwater. Knowledge makes them less afraid."

"And boosts the bottom line," Charlie added.

Mom smiled. "How was the funeral?"

"Before the police came? Sad." Charlie slanted a glance in my direction. "Until Frankie chased after Josh Miller."

"Francesca!" My mother threw up her hands. "For heaven's sake!"

"What was I supposed to do?" I asked. "Wave at him from the grave site?"

"So you took matters into your own hands?" Mom glared. "That's not what I meant when I said to take initiative, and you know it."

"I talked to him a little." Perhaps it was the coward's way out, but I decided against telling her about the knife. "He said the crash was an accident."

"Of course he'd say that. Murder carries a longer prison term than manslaughter," Charlie said. When we gaped at her, she shrugged. "What? When you watch as much *Law & Order* as I do, you pick up a few things."

Mom turned back to me. "Francesca, you could have been hurt."

The gleam of the knife flashed through my mind, but I kept my voice steady. "I wasn't. And we told Noah right away."

"He's going to strangle you," Charlie said, "as soon as he gets a spare moment."

"Well, that won't be for a while," my mother said dryly. "What on earth did Miller go to the funeral for? Was he trying to rub it in? Did he want to revel in all the misery he's caused?"

I frowned. "Why would he do that if it really was an accident? He certainly didn't *look* like he was enjoying himself."

"Maybe it was a guilty conscience," Charlie said. "He wanted to atone for what he'd done. Or maybe he wanted to establish an alibi for Trey's kidnapping."

"What's an alibi?" asked Riley, popping out from behind the counter.

All three of us jumped. She'd been playing so quietly, we'd forgotten she was there, and from the beatific expression on her face, that's exactly what she'd banked on. I'd used the same trick plenty of times when I was her age to eavesdrop on conversations my mother deemed "not appropriate" for small ears.

"It's a grown-up word," my mother said firmly.

Riley stuck out her chin. "I know lots of grown-up words."

Before she could demonstrate, I cut in. "An alibi is a way to prove you weren't around when something bad happened. For example, if we know that someone ate the last of the cookies this afternoon, but you were at school the whole time, that would be your alibi."

"Daddy ate the cookies," she said promptly.

"Now that we've all learned a new word," my mother said with a firm and deliberate change of subject, "let's finish closing up so we can head home. Riley, start sweeping. Charlie, are you nearly done cashing out?"

Charlie, less interested in vocabulary than register totals, looked up from a pile of receipts and said, "We need a way to boost traffic that does not involve felonies. Our numbers are falling off again."

"A Get Ready for Winter sale?" I asked. "Snowblowers and ice melt?"

My mom pursed her lips. "Not yet. Firewood and rakes, yes. Maybe some of that cast iron."

"People like to be prepared," I argued. "Don't they?"

"Not when it comes to hardware," Charlie said. "People only buy snow shovels when it's snowing. No one buys salt before December first. It's still autumn. They're thinking about playing in leaves instead of slogging through snowdrifts."

"One last cookout while they watch football," my mother agreed. "They're not ready to hunker down yet."

True enough. Still, there had to be something that would draw people in. My stomach growled inspiration. "Cornbread," I said abruptly.

"Ooooh, cornbread," Riley said, popping up again. The kid had a sixth sense when it came to food. "I love cornbread. Can we make some tonight?"

"Daddy's making spaghetti and meatballs," Charlie replied. "Cornbread wouldn't go."

"Not for dinner," I said. "For the store. Make a bunch of cornbread and a vat of chili. Use the cast iron, hand out samples. Give them your recipe."

"I will do no such thing," Mom said, outraged.

I ignored her. "Make it an autumn celebration. You don't need to give them a huge discount—ten percent, at most. Get 'em in here, show them all the things we've got to enjoy fall—one of those steel fire pits, a new rake, tulip bulbs they can plant now and enjoy in spring. People want to get together; they want the chance to gossip. Give them that right here in the store."

"We're not a social club," my mother said.

"Really?" I gestured to the row of personalized mugs our regulars kept next to the coffeepot. "People didn't go to HouseMasters when the news about Trey broke—they came here. You're losing sales to big box stores because they beat you on price every time. You're never going to win that battle, so stop trying. Give people something else. Something they won't get at some generic chain."

"Connection," Charlie said slowly. "Community."

I nodded. "A woman is dead. Her baby is missing. People are scared, so why not give them a way to fight it?"

"And you want to play off their fear? That's not who we are, Francesca," said my mom.

"Not play off their fear. Bring them together so they're not afraid. You don't have to make it about money. You can donate the proceeds to Trey's college fund if it makes you feel better. The important thing is that we create a space for them to be together. Show we care about Stillwater. About the people."

"It might be nice," Charlie said.

My mother considered. "I'm not giving out my chili recipe."

SEVENTEEN

"You're still here?" Costello asked when I came on duty the next night. "Thought maybe you'd changed your mind."

"And miss all the fun?" I replied, looking over the whiteboard where our current cases were listed. "Appendicitis in Exam Three?"

"Stomach flu in One, strained rotator cuff in Two."

"I've got the appendicitis," Esme called from the other side of the nurses' station.

"Guess that leaves you on puke duty," Costello said. I opened my mouth to protest. "You're the newbie, Stapleton. You take the dregs."

"I've got five years on Esme," I protested.

"Not here you don't," he replied. "Zofran and IV Ringer for the flu, then get the shoulder down to imaging."

I ground my teeth and got to work, grateful I'd brought an extra pair of scrubs.

As it turned out, the flu patient was easier to deal with than the shoulder. Antinausea medication and IV fluids to rehydrate had her quickly improving. The shoulder was a different story. He'd been in three times since summer, claiming a different injury every time, demanding painkillers at every visit.

"I really need to be able to work tomorrow," he insisted. "If I don't make it through my shift, I'll lose my job. Can't you give me enough for a couple of days? Even fifty milligrams would help."

Educated patients are fine. Overeducated patients—the ones who think Google is as good as a medical degree—are a nuisance. Patients who want to order their own pain meds, especially when their injury is invisible, however, are a problem.

"The doctor prescribes things, not me, but I'll let him know you're concerned about missing work. He can give you an official letter if that will help with your boss."

The muscles in his shoulders—yes, even the injured one—bunched, and his hands curled to fists. The room seemed smaller suddenly, and yet the door seemed farther away. "I need those meds."

"You can discuss it with the doctor when he comes in."

I strode out, the weight of his gaze landing like a blow between my shoulder blades. I was careful to keep my stride even and unhurried, my head high, and went over his patient history more closely. Then I tracked down Costello.

"The shoulder's an addict," I said. "Repeat patient, pain out of proportion, wants specific meds, and he's getting surly about it. How do you want me to handle him?"

"Get him out," Costello said sharply. "I'll write a script for physical therapy after the exam. Otherwise, he gets ibuprofen and ice. You can give him the brochure from the health department if you're feeling generous. Make sure to note it in the system and on his chart."

All standard procedure, but it wouldn't solve the underlying problem.

"How long has this been a happening?" I asked.

"What? The opioid crisis?" He snorted. "We've always had a few cases, but it's gotten worse in the last two or three years."

"Isn't the county doing anything? I know they've got a few programs, but at Chicago Memorial . . ."

"We're having a budget crisis at the moment, or haven't you heard? County health department can barely afford tongue depressors." He shook his head. "They're doing the best they can, and so are we."

"Dr. Costello, we've got an MI, sixty-year-old female, ETA twenty minutes," Alejandro called.

"Get Dr. Beach to discharge the shoulder, check in on the flu patient again," Costello ordered, downing the rest of his coffee and heading out. I bit back a complaint about being sidelined yet again. He glanced back at me. "Do it fast, Stapleton. I want you in on the MI."

"Got it," I said, trying not to sound too eager—or too grateful. Myocardial infarctions were heart attacks and infinitely more interesting than stomach flu.

"Stapleton," he barked again as I started toward Exam Three.

I glanced back.

"Take security with you."

In the past, I might have resisted asking for help, but Josh Miller had turned me more cautious. Besides, there was no reason defy an order from an attending, especially if I wanted to avoid being the go-to girl for food poisoning and strained shoulders when acute cases were coming in.

Dr. Beach, the other ER physician on duty, finished the exam in near-record time. His instructions were identical to Costello's, and I went through the standard discharge spiel, conscious the entire time of the khaki-shirted security guard standing a few steps away. The patient's gaze darkened when he realized I wouldn't be giving him anything stronger than ibuprofen, his eyes jerking from me to the guard and back again.

"You're supposed to *help* people." Spittle formed at the corners of his mouth.

"Giving you those meds won't help," I said. "This might, though."

I set the brochure from the county health department, a listing of all the resources and support groups in the area, on the edge of the gurney, and then eased back. I kept my hands up, palms outward to show I wasn't carrying anything else, not a single tremor despite the tension poisoning the air. Behind me, the guard shifted his weight ponderously.

I kept my expression neutral, my voice easy and soft. "It's yours if you want it."

His ragged breaths were the only sound in the room, and I forced myself to stay still—not threatening, not cowering. Simply present, hoping that it would give him the chance to pause before his anger and his desperation propelled him into violence.

With another curse, he pushed off the bed and stormed out of the room, pausing only to slap the paper out of my hand.

I exhaled shakily. "Can't say I didn't try. Thanks for sitting in."

"No problem. Wasn't the first time I've had to."

No, it wouldn't have been. Not if Stillwater was dealing with the same sort of opioid epidemic sweeping the rest of the country. We saw plenty of it in Chicago, but everything I'd read—and everything I'd seen since arriving at Stillwater Gen—suggested that prescription abuse was worse in rural communities.

Now, though, I had a heart attack to deal with. I ducked into Exam One and made sure the patient was keeping down her apple juice, then headed over to the ambulance doors.

"I want MONA first, then get the leads on him, draw a rainbow for type and cross, blood gas, and cardiac enzymes," Costello was saying as I arrived.

"Got it," Esme said. "Trauma One's prepped and ready."

MONA wasn't a person, but a protocol—a standard treatment given to a specific condition. Ask anyone who's worked in cardiac, and they'll tell you: when a patient comes in with a suspected heart attack, MONA, a lifesaving combination of morphine, oxygen, nitroglycerine, and aspirin, greets them at the door.

"Vargas, did you call the cath lab?" he demanded.

"They're standing by," Esme replied.

"Time?"

"Forty minutes since they called in," Alejandro said from the desk.

Sixty minutes was our window. Treating a cardiac patient within the first hour of a heart attack made a crucial difference in outcomes. If we were at minute forty, the window was starting to close.

Costello flashed a grin like a kid who'd just accepted a dare.

"Plenty of time," he said, slapping his hands together. A moment later, the ambulance arrived, and we were careening through the halls, Costello shouting orders as fast as I could follow them.

We were fast, and we were good, and we saved the patient.

When we were done, I realized it was the first time I'd ever seen Paul Costello truly smile.

★   ★   ★

Meg Costello caught sight of me on my way back from the cath lab. "Miss Stapleton!"

"Meg, you've gotta call me Frankie. Miss Stapleton sounds like a substitute teacher. How's the art going?" I asked.

She glanced around like someone might overhear. "Okay, I guess."

"Have you checked out the School of the Art Institute online yet? I've heard they have an amazing program."

She shook her head so hard, her glasses nearly slid off her face. "I don't think my dad would like that."

"There's no harm in looking," I said firmly. "I grew up hearing that I had to take over the family business. Not just from my mom, but from everybody in this town. My dad died when I was a kid, but I was a Stapleton, so everyone expected I would take over, even though the *last* thing in the world I wanted was to stay in Stillwater and run the a hardware store."

Her voice dropped to a whisper. "What did you do?"

"I went away to college, got my nursing degree, and started crisscrossing the country."

"Wasn't your mom mad?"

"She was disappointed." The memory pinched at me, even now. The way her lips had trembled, the way her eyes had sought out the picture of my dad on the mantel. She hadn't spoken to me for days. "Which was worse, in a way. But if I'd stayed, I would have been miserable, and I would have made everyone else miserable. I don't think either of my parents would have wanted that for me, no matter how my mom felt at the time. I'm guessing your dad feels the same way, deep down."

Very deep down. Like, Grand Canyon–level deep down. Mariana Trench–style deep down.

"Have you told him you don't want to be a doctor?" I prompted.

She dug her toe into the ground. "I want to make him proud."

I knew exactly how she felt. My dad was gone, but I had to believe that if he were alive, he would look at the work I did—grueling, heartbreaking, frenetic, exhilarating, important work—and he'd ruffle my hair and rumble, "*Stapleton girl. Tough as nails,*" exactly as he had when I was a child. The knowledge went a long way toward assuaging my guilt over being gone for so long.

"Your dad will be proud no matter what you end up doing, Meg, because you'll be the one doing it. But it would probably help if you were honest with him about how you feel."

Charlie, I thought, would be impressed. It was the sort of advice a responsible adult would give. I only hoped it was the *right* advice.

Meg ran a hand across her eyes and nodded, but there was no conviction to it. "I'm really sorry, Frankie."

I slung an arm around her shoulder and gave her a quick hug. "What for?"

"Ms. Fisher wants to see you. Right now."

Grace Fisher. Hospital president.

I was sorry too.

Most hospital administrators kept regular office hours. While part of me was impressed that Grace didn't seem to object to working late, another part of me wondered why—and what she wanted.

"I'm on duty," I said. "Your dad . . ."

"She already called down and told him he could page you if the ER ran into trouble," Meg said, her voice barely above a whisper. No doubt Costello would be a delight when I returned.

If I returned to the ER. Whatever the reason for my summons, it couldn't be good—Meg's nonstop hand-wringing as we walked to the office was proof enough that this wasn't a social call.

Finally, she stopped in front of a solid wood door, gesturing to the nameplate beside it. "This is Ms. Fisher's office."

"Thanks," I said. "Don't suppose she mentioned what this was about?"

"Sorry," Meg said again.

I couldn't tell if she was apologizing because she didn't know or because she did. Either way, she scurried away as I knocked. The sound reverberated down the empty hallway. Everyone else in the administrative wing must have gone home hours ago.

Grace answered the door herself, confirming my suspicion. The reception area was empty, the secretary's desk tidied for the night and a single lamp left burning on a side table. She shook my hand, her grip firm and brisk.

"Frankie, come on back." She gave me a small, tight smile, as if she was trying to make this seem a pleasant visit. I forced a smile of my own and followed her inside. The office, like Grace herself, was quietly tasteful. Bookcases lined one wall, the shelves filled with everything from thick volumes on health care administration and management to neatly labeled binders. A few family pictures in gleaming silver frames were interspersed with the books, along with a row of starched white nurses' caps from different eras.

"Shut the door, please," she said, taking a seat behind her heavy oak desk. "I'm glad you were able to stop in. How's your niece doing?"

"Great," I said cautiously. "We're hoping to bring her home soon."

"Good," she said, and the warmth seemed genuine this time. "Did you know I got my start as a NICU nurse? It was years ago, well before I came to Stillwater."

I hadn't, but the effortless way she handled Costello made more sense now. I waved at the collection of caps. "Are those yours?"

"Only the last one. The rest belonged to other women in my family—they're a nice reminder of where I came from." She gave them a fond glance, then returned her attention to me. "Are you enjoying life in the ER? Adjusting to the slower pace?"

People often want to put you at ease before they deliver bad news. It's as if they think that building a rapport, even a temporary one, will somehow soften the blow. It never does—if anything, it makes the damage worse.

"I'm enjoying it very much." Before she could make more small talk, I said, "Is there a problem with my performance?"

"Not at all." Her expression clouded for a moment, and she glanced down at her desk, remarkably free of knickknacks or paperwork. A pair of stacked brass trays sat on the right corner next to the phone, and on the left, a large computer angled toward her. A single teacup—ivory bone china, roses twining along the rim—sat in the very center of the desk. A credenza along the back wall displayed the rest of the service. She touched the edge of the saucer with a fingertip, then spoke. "I understand you have some questions about Norris Mackie. More specifically, about the fundraiser he attended last week."

I curled my fingers around the arm of the chair, willing my face not to betray my surprise. I'd been expecting to defend myself against a complaint from Costello—about Art Gundersen, perhaps, or taking my breaks up in the NICU. How had Grace heard about my visit to Mackie's office?

Riley. She'd told Mackie and his staffer that I worked at the hospital. She'd used my name. Easy enough to put it together and reach out to Grace.

The real question was, why?

"I visited the Congressman's office," I said, pleasant and noncommittal. Until I understood what was happening, I wasn't going to volunteer anything.

"I've known Norris for quite some time," she said. "In fact, I attended his fundraiser that evening."

"Did you enjoy the event?" I asked, since *Do you think Mackie hired someone to kill a pregnant woman?* seemed gauche.

"I did," she said and folded her hands in front of her. Her wedding band, a slim circle of diamonds anchored by a single large stone in the center, glinted. "I want to assure you, Frankie, that the Congressman never left the hotel that night."

People often assume that not lying is the same as telling the truth. They're not the same thing at all. I, for example, don't lie, especially when I'm dealing with a patient or their family. It's a point of honor. But while I won't lie, I will evade. I will distract, or not answer, or parse my words more carefully than any lawyer or linguist.

Which meant that I could recognize when someone was not-lying to me.

"What about the fundraiser? Did he leave before it was over?"

The pause before she answered was all the truth I needed. "I'm not in charge of his schedule. However, *if* the Congress-man left early, he would have had an excellent reason."

An excellent reason that involved Kate Tibbs, perhaps? As Charlie had said, Mackie could have hired Josh Miller. Maybe he'd ducked out to get confirmation the hit had gone as planned.

I searched Grace's expression, looking for some sign that she was complicit, or aware, or involved in what would surely be a massive conspiracy.

She looked worried—frown lines bracketed her mouth, and her body canted forward, but she didn't look *guilty*.

"Did Mackie ask you to talk to me?"

She picked up the teacup and sipped, giving herself time. "He mentioned your conversation, and I thought it best if I clarified the matter."

Hospital presidents didn't memorize their staff's schedules—especially their temporary staffers. Grace had looked up my schedule, waited around after business hours, and sent Meg to pull me off the floor midshift. This wasn't a clarification. It was warning.

"Frankie, I know you were instrumental in solving the Jensen murder. Your willingness to act in that situation is what prompted me to bring you on board. In this case, however, you're overstepping."

I straightened as my hackles rose. "Is this an official reprimand?"

"Not at all," she replied quickly, and the flush of her cheeks told me she recognized that I wasn't the only one overstepping. "Norris is a good man. A respected man. To publicly suggest otherwise this close to an election would be reckless, and I don't believe you're reckless."

With a visible effort, she relaxed her hold on the teacup and sipped, waiting for me to promise I would leave Norris Mackie alone.

Mackie was hiding something. Grace had all but admitted he'd left the fundraiser early that night. Was he having an affair? Was he involved in something shady? Regardless, it seemed as though his secret could cost him the election if it ever came to light, and I couldn't help but wonder if Kate Tibbs had died to keep that from happening.

EIGHTEEN

My return to the ER was met by a steady flow of minor cases, a few genuine emergencies, and a very vocal kidney stone patient that had the entire department wincing in sympathy. Busy enough to keep Costello from grilling me about the visit to Grace's office, but not so busy that I could avoid his suspicious glares. When I finally left, after finishing a mountain of charts under Costello's eagle eye, the sun was a pale smudge in a cloudy morning sky, and I was exhausted simply from keeping my head up.

"You're late," my mother said when I arrived home.

"Long shift," I said. The stairs seemed like too far to walk, so I flopped facedown on the couch and pulled an afghan over my shoulders, not even bothering to change out of my scrubs. The couch was soft, the afghan smelled like lavender, and I could feel myself sinking as sleep overtook me.

"Francesca!" Mom sounded like she'd already called my name several times.

With an effort, I opened my eyes. "Sorry. What?"

She gestured toward the kitchen. "You have a visitor."

"He's not my cat," I protested, burrowing farther under the blanket. "You should be glad he's catching all those mice, anyway. He's doing us a favor."

"I didn't say a word about that creature." Her mouth twisted in momentary disgust, then smoothed, overly bright. "I said you had a visitor."

"This is not the time for a setup," I grumbled.

She drew herself up, offended. "I wouldn't dream of it."

"Not a setup," Noah called from the kitchen, and I groaned.

"I tried to tell you," Mom said. She took her coat from the hall closet and picked up her purse. "Have a nice chat, you two."

"Thanks, Lila. You have a good day."

She fluttered her fingers at Noah, frowned at me, and disappeared.

I considered pulling the afghan over my head and feigning sleep, but Noah was likely to drag me off the couch. Instead, I heaved myself off the couch and stomped into the kitchen, elbowing past Noah, who was filling the doorframe and looking very official. "What?"

"You went after a murder suspect. On your own. Do you have any idea how dangerous that was?"

"He pulled a knife on me. I have a pretty clear picture of the danger, thanks."

"Why didn't you call nine-one-one?"

"My phone was in the car."

"Why engage?" he pressed. "Why not scream your head off and run the opposite direction?"

"He would have gotten away." Before Noah could point out that was exactly what happened, I added, "Before we'd had a chance to talk."

"There is nothing Miller could have said that's worth your life, Frankie. Not a damn thing."

"You don't even know what he said," I replied, then recapped our conversation. The frown lines in Noah's forehead deepened as I spoke. "Miller was working for someone, I'm sure of it. That's why he went back to his house—to get proof."

"What makes you think he was telling you the truth?" Noah replied. "We've been over that house more times than I can count and the only thing we've found proof of is his drug dealing. That's it, and we've practically taken the walls down to the studs. We've also dug through his finances. There's no unusual bank activity, no suspicious payments. Nobody remembers him throwing around big wads of money, and based on the amount of cash we turned up, I'd say if someone paid him to kill Kate, they got an excellent deal."

"He said it wasn't about money," I reminded him as I rummaged in the fridge. "What about Jess? Have you found a connection between her and Josh?"

"Not yet," said Noah. "One will turn up."

I sat down at the table, yogurt in hand. "Jess wouldn't be involved with a dirtbag like Josh. It doesn't make sense."

Noah folded his arms. "It makes perfect sense, once you know who you're dealing with."

"What does that mean?"

He prowled around the room, picking up various chicken-themed knickknacks, giving them a cursory inspection, and setting them down again. "I shouldn't tell you this."

"My mom will have the full story by dinner," I pointed out. "Might as well save us both some time."

He sighed and sank into the chair opposite mine. "Jess's last name isn't Chapman."

I gaped at him. "She's an identity thief? All hospital employees have to go through a background check. Anyone with access to meds goes through even more rigorous screening. If Jess was using a fake name, they would have flagged her before she ever got a job."

"Not fake. Changed. Jess was adopted. It took us a while to find it because it happened when she was a juvenile and the records were sealed. Once we were able to get into those records, guess what we found?"

My appetite vanished, and I pushed the yogurt away.

Noah said, "Jess Chapman—or Bennett, as she was back then—spent most of her childhood on the radar of Children and Family Services. Mom and Dad were addicts, so she and her younger brothers spent a lot of time shuffling between various relatives and temporary foster care."

"That's awful," I said softly. Noah hadn't had an easy childhood, but it sounded like a picnic compared to what Jess had endured. *We survived*, she'd said, talking about how she shared a room as a kid. Clearly, survival had been no small feat.

"Not done yet." His voice was a near-monotone, the control belying how deeply Jess's story must have affected him. "The parents don't lose custody for years, even though the kids have been taken out of the home. The little brothers, at least, end up in a long-term situation, but Jess has a history of running away, of getting mouthy with adults. She's a hard one to place, according to the report. Boys, drinking, violating curfew, barely passing her classes. Finally, a new caseworker comes in and says enough is enough, right about the time Jess turns fifteen. The birth parents lose custody, clearing the way for the boys to be adopted. Jess still has some struggles, but just after her sixteenth birthday, a couple of empty nesters take her in, and eighteen months later . . . they adopt her. Jess Bennett becomes Jess Chapman, and because she's technically a minor, we don't see the name change until we start digging."

"So it's a happy ending," I said, though his recitation felt bleak.

"Is it?" He leaned back in the chair, lacing his hands behind his head. "Three guesses who her caseworker was."

My eyes met his. "Kate Tibbs."

He nodded. "One of Kate's first cases when she came to the county."

"And you think Jess wanted revenge?" I couldn't hide my skepticism. "For what? Finding her a good home?"

"Breaking up her family, for starters. Taking her away from her brothers. Letting her flounder in the system for so long. I've got a million reasons, Frankie, but the fact is, I don't need a single one. I've got video of Jess taking Trey. A motive's nice, but it isn't necessary for me to throw her in jail once I find her."

"You honestly think that Jess waited eight years before she swooped in to exact vengeance?" That kind of calculated patience was typically reserved for TV show serial killers.

"I don't think she sat around plotting it," Noah said. "Kate and Steven did a VIP tour of the maternity ward a few months ago. We think Jess must have recognized Kate, and it was too much for her. She snapped."

"Jess froze when Kate was brought in," I said, remembering the shouts. The blood. The tiny bear-shaped charms. "I thought it was nerves, but it wasn't. She recognized Kate."

"Guilty conscience."

"Broken heart," I countered. "You don't know for sure that Jess hated Kate. Isn't it possible she was grateful, instead?"

"She stole Kate's child!" Noah said, slamming his fist against the table so hard the silverware jumped. "You said yourself it was dangerous for him to be out of the hospital. If she was grateful, why would she put Trey at risk?"

"I don't know," I said miserably. "Has there been any sign of them?"

He dragged a hand over his face. "We've searched her apartment, her locker at work, every place we could think of. We found her car abandoned at a rest stop, but no sign of her or the baby. The state police have been canvassing baby stores in the area, the big ones, closer to Springfield."

"And?"

"And they remember her. She came in a few days before the funeral and bought a bunch of supplies: diapers, bottles, some cans of formula, and a travel crib. Some of those outfits with the feet attached too. It's not much to go on, but at least it's a sign that she wants to take care of him. She wouldn't buy all that if she was planning to do him harm."

"What's next?"

"We keep going. Try to find a connection between Jess and Josh, hope that one of them screws up and uses a credit card or shops somewhere with an observant clerk."

"You think they're together?" I still couldn't picture it: seedy, strung out Josh and delicate, tenderhearted Jess.

"It's a possibility. I don't know if I like it better or worse. Harder to hide three people than two, but Josh is getting twitchy, showing up at funerals and pulling knives on people. I'm not crazy about him having access to Trey." He paused.

"I'd appreciate it if your mom and her friends didn't find out about Jess's background, at least not yet."

"Not a word. I promise."

Noah looked haggard—hollowed cheeks, shadowed eyes, three days' stubble on his jaw. The jaw was actually quite nice, stubble and all, but my heart twisted to see the toll this investigation was taking on him. "You're not sleeping."

"Can't," he said shortly. "A catnap here and there, but I can't sleep while Trey's out there."

"Have you told Steven?" I asked and began clearing away the breakfast dishes.

"That I can't find his son?" Noah asked bitterly. "He's aware."

No one had ever held Noah to a higher standard than himself. The temptation was to step back, to leave him alone. That's what he wanted, no doubt. Instead, some impulse had me leaning forward, brushing a hand along his arm in sympathy.

"You'll find him," I said.

He froze for an instant, then covered my fingers with his own, holding me in place. "Yeah? How do you know?"

"Because it's you. I've never seen you give up on anything in your life."

"You're missing a whole chunk of my life," he reminded me. "Same as I'm missing yours."

"You're you," I said firmly. His radio squawked at the same time my mom's police scanner—the one she swore she didn't use—beeped. I pulled away to switch it off, adding, "You'll find that baby or die trying."

NINETEEN

When I woke later that afternoon, the house smelled like heaven. I splashed cold water on my face and made my way downstairs, where Riley was slumped at the table, scowling at her homework, and my mother was pulling pans out of the oven.

"Dinner smells great," I said, peering over Mom's shoulder and reaching for a Tater Tot.

She smacked my hand. "Not for you."

"What?" I looked closer. Two pans of Tater Tot casserole—my childhood favorite—stood on the counter, steaming gently. "Mom. Who are these for?"

She turned and beamed. "Steven, of course. I made cookies too."

"Snickerdoodles," Riley grumbled and stomped into the other room, saying, "We can't have any."

I watched her go, startled by the return of Riley's dour doppelgänger. "I know your inclination is to stress-bake anytime someone hits a rough patch, but this is a little excessive, don't you think?"

"He's one of us," she replied, "and he could use a homemade meal."

"Are you doing this to get the scoop?"

"Of course not," she replied, hand over her heart, the very picture of wounded outrage. "Why would you think that?"

"Because I've seen you in action. This casserole comes with questions."

"I don't know what you're talking about, Francesca."

"Really?" I pinned her with the same look she'd used every time I'd told her I was going to hang out with friends when, in fact, I was sneaking off with Noah. "You're telling me you're not planning to take this dish to Steven's, wait on the stoop until he invites you in, and then pump him for details so you can tell all your friends what you've witnessed firsthand?"

"Absolutely not. It's hardly my place to do something like that." She sounded utterly sincere.

"Good."

"It's yours." When I started to protest, she cut me off. "You're Steven's classmate. You had a connection to his wife, you've seen his baby in the NICU, and you attended the funeral. You can be a pillar of strength for him, Francesca. A shoulder to lean on."

A familiar warning began to sound in the recesses of my mind. "I don't think . . ."

Deftly, she wrapped the snickerdoodles in aluminum foil. "If that support evolves into a friendship, so much the better. You could use more friends here. And oftentimes, a friendship can evolve into more."

"*Mother.*"

"What's the harm in reaching out?"

"His wife was murdered a week ago. He's not back on the market, and even if he was, I'm not interested."

"Oh? Is there someone else?" she asked, beaming at me.
"No!"

"Well, then, you should keep an open mind," she chided.
"I'm sure there'll be plenty to see over there, regardless."

"Mom, I'm not going on a reconnaissance mission for you
and your cronies."

"You're the one who wanted to build community,"
she said with a sniff. "It seems like the least you could do
is offer him some support, especially with the election so
close. Bring Charlotte with you too. She can talk to him
about the fundraiser for Trey. We're going to have it Friday
evening."

"You know Charlie's married, right? She's off the market."

She smiled serenely. "I know that Steven was up twelve
points in the latest poll. And I know it's good business to make
sure your local politicians can count on you. Take Charlotte.
Take the casserole. Be a good neighbor."

"Fine," I muttered. "We'll go before work tonight."

"Excellent," she said. "Make sure to tell me all about it
when you get back."

★   ★   ★

"I can't believe she bamboozled you into this," Charlie said
as we walked up the flagstone path to Steven Tibbs's house.
He lived on the outskirts of town, one of the few subdivisions
that had sprung up over the years. A pleasant-yet-staid colo-
nial. Not a McMansion, but certainly more modern and spacious than most of the houses in the downtown area. "You're
losing your touch."

"I'd just woken up," I said. "My defenses were down.
Besides, she wasn't going to let it go. She's got some crazy idea

that Steven and I could pair up. After an appropriate mourning period, naturally."

Charlie grimaced. "Ew. That's a little much, even for Mom."

"Right?" I'd thought the same thing. I rang the bell, balancing the plate of cookies in one hand. "We'll drop these off, mention the fundraiser, and go."

Ted Sullivan opened the door, frowning. I bobbled the cookies and stammered a hello while Charlie held out the casserole dish invitingly.

"What?" he asked in the same tone people used with telemarketers and solicitors and other uninvited guests. Which, technically, we were—but his displeasure startled me so much that I spoke without thinking.

"Food. For Steven. What are you doing here?"

Next to me, Charlie sighed.

"Running a congressional campaign," Ted said coolly, scrutinizing us. "You're that nurse. From the ER. The funeral too."

He didn't say it like a compliment.

"Frankie Stapleton," I said. "This is my sister, Charlie."

I nudged Charlie forward, letting her take over. She continued the introduction, hitting just the right note of sympathy and goodwill. I'd give her this: Charlie knew how to handle people.

Once Ted was convinced we were harmless well-wishers and not members of the press or spies sent from Mackie's campaign, he led us into the kitchen.

It was an airy, spacious room with a round pine table tucked into a bay window, vintage French posters on the wall, and an island with a built-in wine rack. It looked comfortable and cozy, with pictures of happier times displayed everywhere—Steven and Kate on vacation, at their wedding, on the campaign trail. Ultrasound pictures of Trey were posted on the refrigerator, along with an invitation for a baby shower, and I was struck again at how very unfair life could be, that so much joy and anticipation could be stolen in a single moment.

Steven looked up from the dining room table, where he was surrounded by file folders and stacks of paperwork. Three laptops sat open, one of them streaming the news, and he shut it with a snap as he greeted us.

He'd lost weight since I'd first seen him in the NICU. I could see him struggling to focus on us, his gaze drifting to the file-covered table in the next room.

"We brought you something to eat," Charlie said with a winning smile. "I'm sure you're overrun with food right now, but it'll freeze. We figured it might be good to have a lot of meals stocked up, once the baby . . ."

She trailed off.

He grimaced. "Once the baby comes home? *If* the baby comes home?"

"I'm so sorry," she said, setting the food on the counter. "For everything you've been through. It must be a nightmare."

He turned up his hands as if he couldn't find the words. "I never . . . this wasn't how it was supposed to be. We were supposed to stand up on the podium together. I can still picture it, you know? On the day of my swearing in, the three of us together on the steps of the Capitol."

Charlie reached out. "They'll find him. I'm sure they will."

Ted's phone rang, shrill in the suddenly silent room. He excused himself and took the call out on the back deck.

"Steven," I said, "I know you've already talked to the police about this, but do you have any idea—any idea at all—where Kate was going the night of the accident?"

The noise Charlie made was something between a squeak and a wheeze.

"She didn't tell me," he said after a long moment. "I wish she had. I wish I'd made her go to that stupid fundraiser, or stayed home with her, or gone out on whatever errand she needed." His voice wavered, then strengthened again. "But I didn't, did I?"

"I'm sorry," I said, both apology and condolence in the words. Next to me, Charlie was scarlet with embarrassment.

"Me too, more than you'll ever know." He spread his hands wide, a gesture of helplessness. "But I can't change the past. All I can do is protect my son—assuming we can find him."

"They will," Charlie assured him.

He turned to her. "You should bring your daughter home, Charlie. She's beautiful. She deserves the best, and that hospital isn't remotely capable of keeping our children safe." His gaze flickered to me. "I know you work there, Frankie, but you have to admit it's a travesty. That woman walked right in and stole my son."

"It's appalling," I said, not wanting to disagree but certain the hospital wasn't to blame. "The police are working nonstop, Steven. They're doing everything they can to find Trey."

"You always had a soft spot for Noah MacLean." It was desperation that lent a jeering note to his words, I told myself, and tried not to react. "I'm not willing to leave it to the police. It's been nearly forty-eight hours, and they've got nothing to show for it. I want my son back, and I don't care how I get him."

"Do you have the nursery ready?" Charlie asked, breaking the tension. "It might help if you could focus on that, on making sure it's perfect for when he comes home. I could help, if you wanted. Tell you if you're missing anything vital."

Steven nodded slowly. "Kate was working on that," he said. "I haven't been in there since . . ." He straightened his shoulders. "Would you like to see it now? You could tell me if we're—if I'm—missing anything."

Charlie glanced at me, and I nodded. "You two go ahead," I said. "I'll put the food away."

She followed Steven through to the front of the house, their footsteps nearly inaudible on the carpeted stairs. Out of the corner of my eye, I saw Ted pacing the length of the back deck, listening intently and responding, his features animated. The sliding door was ajar, and now that Steven was upstairs, I could hear Ted's conversation.

"Nobody knows," he said into the phone. "It's a bunch of Podunk deputies spinning their wheels, but what did you expect?"

I bristled at hearing Noah's hard work dismissed so easily. I circled the kitchen island, keeping my back to the door so my eavesdropping wasn't so obvious. If Ted looked in, he'd assume I was bustling around the kitchen. "Exactly," he said with a laugh. "Did you see the latest numbers from CNN? We keep spinning this, keep it in the news cycle, and one more ought to do it."

One more what? One more poll? One more press conference? Ted's voice dropped, like he was trying not to be overheard. I busied myself with the food, smoothing down the foil, stacking and restacking the dishes, trying to look like my attention was on casseroles and not his creepy conversation. Listening to Ted capitalize on Steven's grief was nauseating.

"The money's not a problem," he said, voice dropping as he moved farther away. "Handle it however you want, as long as it's handled, and let me worry about the optics."

Not about the money, Josh Miller had said. But for Ted, perhaps it was. Had he done more than capitalize on Kate's death? Had he *caused* the accident, even arranged Trey's abduction, all in the hopes Steven would get a bump in the polls? What were the optics he wanted here: the image of Trey coming home or the one where a devastated Steven, having lost everything else, dedicated himself to public service? Which one furthered Ted's agenda?

Ted's footsteps grew louder as he continued pacing, his side of the conversation punctuated by the occasional "uh-huh" and "yeah, yeah" as he approached the sliding glass door. I yanked open the freezer door, only to find it was already full; at least six other pans were neatly stacked inside. The gossips of Stillwater had been busy, but considering what I'd just heard, they'd missed out on the biggest scoop.

From this distance, Ted's voice was an indistinct rise and fall, and I took advantage of it to look around the dining room, wondering if there was anything I could bring to Noah. A half-heard conversation wouldn't be enough. After a cursory sweep of the room, my gaze fell on the folders stacked haphazardly on the dining room table.

The cream-colored file folders had yellowed with age, their corners bent, their edges rubbed soft, and their seams split from overstuffing. Some were held shut with industrial-sized rubber bands. I moved close enough to read their labels, each written in a messy script—last name, first name, and a pair of dates.

Election files, presumably, were about issues, donors, or pending legislation. They would have held opposition research or talking points. They would have been crisp and new, or at least newish. These looked more like old medical records.

With a quick check over my shoulder to make sure Ted was still outside, I flipped open the nearest folder, and my suspicion was confirmed. These were DCFS files. *Kate's* files. How had Steven gotten them?

I backed away and gazed around the room. In the corner, perched atop a dining room chair, was a box full of desktop odds and ends—framed pictures, including one of an ultrasound; a coffee cup full of pencils; a variety of handheld puzzles and games; even a few worn-out stuffed animals.

Kate's desk, Kate's files. Steven must have taken them when he cleaned out her office. He was conducting his own investigation, and I wondered if Noah was aware of it. Considering Steven's earlier comment, it seemed unlikely. What if Steven's investigation pointed back to Ted?

Ted, whose conversation was no longer audible.

I dashed into the kitchen and whipped the foil off a platter just as the back door slid open.

"What are you doing?" he asked.

"Thought I'd put out some cookies," I said cheerfully. "My mom makes amazing snickerdoodles, and I figured you guys could use a snack while you worked."

He didn't reply, and I held up the ball of aluminum foil and smiled as if I were Charlie. "Do you know where the recycling is?"

"Just throw it out," he said and strode into the dining room as if checking to make sure I hadn't touched anything.

I trailed after him, crinkling the foil. "So how'd you end up in Stillwater, of all places? I would have thought someone like you would have your pick of candidates."

He crossed to the sideboard, poured himself a tumbler of good bourbon, not bothering to offer me any, and then faced me with a smooth, campaign-ready smile. "I believe in Steven. He's a good man with a clear vision for the country, and—"

I held up my hand. "Come on. Steven's nice, but really? You came to a tiny little river town in the middle of the country because you believe in his *vision*?"

His eyes were dark and cold as river water as he scrutinized me, and fear skittered along my nerves. Maybe I'd miscalculated, challenging him here. Charlie and Steven were upstairs, but whoever had killed Kate was a master of timing. If Ted came after me, he'd pick a moment I wasn't expecting.

He chuckled, dry but genuine, and my lungs eased. "Steven's donors are making it worth my while. And frankly, this district? It's a stepping-stone. I've been doing this a long time, and your boy's got what it takes to go the distance. Might as well get in on the ground floor."

I couldn't help the giggle that escaped. "The distance? Do you mean president? You're not serious."

"Stranger things have happened," he said. "Political careers are all about the story, and his is a great one. Working-class kid from the heart of America, literally risks his life to save people from a burning building, overcomes tremendous personal loss to win an election and put our country on the right path? The story practically spins itself."

"Kate's death is more than a story. It's a crime."

"No reason it can't be both." He held up his drink, let it catch the light, and took a sip. "Look, Katherine Tibbs was a nice woman. It's a shame, what happened to her. But I'm being paid to get results, not to feel sad."

Well, that was a disgusting take on the situation. Charlie and Steven's return saved me from having to respond.

"They're planning a party," Steven told Ted, his voice full of doubt.

"A fundraiser," Charlie interjected when Ted looked at her in disbelief. "We wanted to give the community a chance to show their support; all the proceeds will go into a college fund for Trey."

Ted appeared to mull over the idea. "Have you lined up press?"

"Um . . ." Charlie looked at me, bewildered.

Optics, I thought. But Uncle Marshall counted as press, so I smiled and said, "Naturally."

"It'll make a nice story," he mused, trading his whiskey for his smartphone, scrolling through contacts. "Community coming together, taking care of one of their own. Downtown, right? Can we have it close to where the fire was, all those years ago? It's a great angle to lead with, really brings things full circle."

Next to me, Charlie huffed out a breath. I couldn't make my good-byes fast enough.

When we were safely out on the porch, Charlie's smile dropped away. "What were you doing while we were upstairs?"

"This and that," I said vaguely. "Putting away the food, making small talk . . ."

"Pfft. You were snooping."

"Says the girl who went up to 'see the nursery,'" I said, making air quotes. "How was it?"

"Sad," she said, with a look that told me we weren't done discussing my snooping. "Decorating the nursery, especially your first one, is such fun. You're making the perfect, cozy home for this little person you can't wait to meet. It's obvious how much fun Kate had in there—new furniture, fresh paint. She stenciled his name on the wall; the changing table's fully stocked. There's a monogrammed blanket and a little rocking chair with his name painted on it. It's the perfect room . . . and now it's as far from perfect as it can be." Her voice was thick with tears, and she stared out the window as I drove home.

"Did Steven say anything about the investigation?" I asked.

"He's furious. Scary mad, almost. He wouldn't leave off raving about how he was going to sue the hospital to have the NICU shut down. He wants Sheriff Flint tossed out of office, says the whole department is incompetent or corrupt or both. I tried to get him talking about Trey, thinking it would give him something else to focus on, but he's pretty obsessed." She considered. "I don't blame him. What if it had been Rowan?"

True. He'd been so supportive of the police when Kate died—patient with the investigation and realistic about its outcome. But people could only take so much before they snapped, and Trey's abduction had pushed him over the edge.

"Why did you ask him about where Kate was going that night? Why would you dredge that up?" Charlie asked.

"Because it's weird," I said. "I've never been pregnant, but I've seen plenty of women that far along in the ER. You know what every single one of them tells me? Her feet are too swollen to fit into her shoes, her back is killing her, and her hips feel like they're coming out of their sockets."

"The last month is so uncomfortable," Charlie said. "There's nothing weird about that."

"Sure. But when you were eight months pregnant, would you go for a leisurely drive in the middle of the night?"

She drummed her fingers on the dashboard. "Depends on how bad my cravings were."

"During a terrible storm? Without your cell phone?"

Her fingers stilled. "What are you saying?"

"I don't know," I replied. "When I have a patient, we give them the obvious tests and treatments first. People are so different that even for something like strep throat, the symptoms can be all over the board. But if the obvious stuff doesn't work, we look at the symptoms that *don't* fit. Sometimes we find more than one illness; sometimes we end up with a totally different diagnosis. But we never ignore the weird stuff. We might decide, eventually, that it's insignificant, but we always check it out."

Charlie hummed. "So Kate's going out is weird, but it might not be significant."

"Exactly. Did Steven tell you he's running his own investigation?"

"Kind of hard to miss," she said. "The more people looking for that baby, the better, as far as I'm concerned. What's the harm?"

"If someone took Rowan, what would you do if you found them before the police did?"

"I'd kill them," she said promptly. "Preferably with my bare hands."

"Right. And if Steven finds Trey and the kidnapper before the cops do . . . ?"

Charlie's eyes widened. "Oh."

"Yeah. That baby's already lost one parent. I'd prefer he not lose another."

TWENTY

I dropped Charlie at the store, leaving her to fend off Mom's interrogation while I went to work. I felt jittery, flooded with adrenaline, unable to settle my thoughts. Should I tell Noah about overhearing Ted's conversation? Warn him that Steven was spiraling out of control?

Too many loose ends—that was the problem. It was like looking at a tangle of wires, impossible to tell which ones carried live current and which ones would simply fall away when the knots were undone. And the more I tried to tug on the wires, the tighter the tangle.

The temperature had dropped again, and I stuffed my fists deep into my pockets as I dashed from the parking lot to the ER doors. I hoped Trey was somewhere warm. Somewhere safe.

An hour later, I was wrapping an ACE bandage around the arm of a twelve-year-old skateboarder when the door to the exam room slammed open. "Are you completely incapable of minding your own business, Stapleton?" Costello demanded.

"I'll be with you in a minute, Doctor," I said and smiled at my patient. His mother glanced nervously at Costello, but I continued wrapping the arm. "Almost done."

Costello fumed as I finished reviewing care instructions and reminding the mother to follow up with an orthopedist in the morning. Then, mindful of our audience, I slipped out of the room and headed for the staff lounge, knowing Costello would follow.

"How may I help you?" I asked when we were inside.

He slapped the Art Institute literature I'd given Meg on the counter. "On what planet do you think it's appropriate to push this kind of thing on my daughter?"

I made a show of paging through one of the booklets. "It's a college brochure, not porn. I thought you wanted Meg to go to college."

"This isn't college; it's art school."

"It's both. And one of the best in the nation," I pointed out.

"My daughter is not going to art school."

"Because you've decided she should be a surgeon? Have you ever asked her what she wants to do? Or are you so busy dictating to her that you can't be bothered to listen?" No wonder Meg didn't want to stand up to him if this was his reaction to a simple brochure.

A vein pulsed at his temple.

"I've seen her work," I said. "She's a good artist, and it makes her happy. Why not let her pursue it? Medical school is grueling even if you love it, and she doesn't. Would you really make her go through that just to impress you?"

"Meg has never said she doesn't want to go into medicine," he said, but there was a flicker of uncertainty in his expression.

"Really? I've known her for less than a month, and it seems pretty obvious." I took a breath. "She's a good kid, you know. She wants you to be proud of her."

"I am. Of course I am. Meg knows that." He seemed to deflate a little, then pointed a finger at me. "You're a decent nurse, Stapleton. But you don't know a damn thing about kids. Quit interfering."

"Good talk," I called as he threw the door open. "Let's do this again soon."

He stepped outside, then stuck his head back in, smirking. "Looks like I'm not the only one annoyed with you today. Can't say I'm surprised."

I followed him out to the nurses' station, baffled until I caught sight of Noah striding down a side hallway. I chased after him, wanting to pass along the details of my visit to Steven's, but he didn't seem to hear me.

When I finally caught up, only slightly out of breath, I said, "Hey! I need to talk to you."

"Not now," he said without breaking stride. His jaw was tight, his eyes stony and bleak.

My heart squeezed. "Did you find Trey? Is he—?"

Noah spared me a glance, though he didn't slow down. "It's not Trey," he said, and I nearly stumbled with relief. "It's Josh Miller."

"You found him?"

"No. Manager of a local junkyard did, behind the office."

The news should have been happy, but Noah didn't look happy. He looked furious. He should also have been on his way to police headquarters to interrogate Miller. Instead, he rounded a corner and was heading down a back hallway I'd barely seen, except for on my first-day tour.

Noah was heading toward the morgue.

*　　*　　*

In Chicago, murder victims go to the medical examiner, located in a dedicated building inside a medical school with its own morgue and full autopsy capabilities. Stillwater didn't have those resources. The coroner had an office at the county courthouse, and suspicious deaths were taken to the hospital morgue, where the autopsy could be performed and evidence collected under the watchful eye of the sheriff's department.

Based on Noah's brief description, an autopsy wouldn't be necessary to find out what killed Josh Miller. Three bullets to the chest at point-blank range were a pretty good indicator of cause of death.

Unfortunately, the bullets didn't tell us who had put them there—or why.

Noah left while I was in with a patient and returned again around midnight. I leapt from my chair at the nurses' station. "Anything? Have you found them?"

He shook his head. "I took a team out to the junkyard where Miller was found and checked it over. There's no sign of Trey or Jess anywhere near there. Found his car, though. It was in the back of the lot, with the passenger's side all smashed up. Tire treads match the ones at the scene, and we took paint samples, but it seems pretty obvious. Medical examiner says the bruises are consistent with the accident."

"That's something, anyway," I said. One link in the chain, one bit of closure for Steven. "Here's something else," he said. "Six months ago, Miller was brought up on drug charges, and Steven was the prosecutor."

"More motive for Josh." I ushered him into the lounge and handed him a cup of terrible coffee. He grimaced in anticipation but drank it anyway.

"The case never made it past the grand jury, so he walked without ever being indicted. It's not much of a motive, especially compared to everything else we've got, but every little bit helps."

"And Steven never made the connection?"

"With as many cases that come across his desk?" Noah shrugged. "Not a surprise he wouldn't remember, especially since the case went nowhere. We missed it initially because his secretary only flagged cases that had gone to trial."

"So who killed him?"

He took another sip of coffee and winced. "Smart money's on Jess. Sheriff likes her for it, anyway."

I goggled at him. "You've got to be kidding me. You have zero evidence they know each other, much less that they're in this together."

"Miller kills Kate, and Jess kidnaps her child within the span of a week?" He lifted an eyebrow. "Pretty big leap to say they're not connected, especially since they both have reason to hold a grudge."

"That doesn't mean Jess was the shooter," I protested.

"Hard to see it any other way." Noah stretched, the lean, rangy lines of his body reaching for the ceiling, twisting to relieve the strain of the evening. "I had two fugitives tied to the same case. Now one of them is dead. If Jess didn't do it—and logic says she probably did—I'd be very interested to hear her take on the matter."

"What about the person who hired him?" Before he could explain why I was wrong, I rushed on, the words spilling over each other. "I know you're not convinced he was working for someone else, but what if he was and the proof was hidden at the house? It would explain why he risked going back, even when you were watching the place. If the person who hired him realized Josh had real, tangible proof, it makes sense that they'd want to eliminate him."

"Eliminate him?" Noah's eyebrows lifted.

"It's a good theory," I said stubbornly. "Especially if it's about the election. Josh made the perfect patsy because his history with Kate gave him a plausible motive. It probably helped convince him to take the job."

"Maybe," Noah said, his expression betraying nothing. "We're still running down a few leads. They should show us if there's anyone else involved."

"What kinds of leads?"

"The usual. Phone records, background checks, financials."

I picked at the fraying upholstery of the couch. "Like Norris Mackie's financials?"

"It's not so simple when you're dealing with a sitting congressman," Noah said. "I'm working on it."

"What about Ted Sullivan? Are you looking at him?"

His eyebrows lifted. "Something you want to share, Frankie?"

Quickly, I filled him in on our visit to Steven's house.

His frown told me he wasn't convinced. "That's how those people talk. Ted Sullivan is a shark."

"Exactly," I said. "Steven's lead was pretty slim before Kate died. Ted could have decided they needed the sympathy vote for insurance, maybe even started rumors about Mackie's involvement."

"It's possible," he said in a way that made it sound as if he thought it was very, very unlikely. "But the man has put senators into office. Governors. Hard to imagine he'd take this kind of risk for a tiny district in Illinois, no matter how good he thinks Steven's chances are."

"You didn't hear him talking about the optics of a missing baby. Made my blood boil."

"Soft heart," Noah said with a rueful smile. "I'll look into it, but don't get your hopes up. Save that for Trey."

TWENTY-ONE

The rest of my shift was a steady flow of minor cases, the kind of things that were time consuming and required lots of charting and phone calls and lab work, but no actual emergencies.

Easy for me to say, of course. I wasn't the one with the broken wrist or double ear infection. That's one of the challenges of ER nursing—you might know that someone's situation isn't life-threatening, but to them in that moment, it's painful and all-encompassing. I've had patients interrupt me while I was in the middle of CPR to ask for a cup of juice. They're not bad people; they just can't see outside their own situation. Their own pain.

I wondered what kind of pain had driven Jess to steal Trey. I'd seen the surveillance tape of the abduction—everyone in the country had since it was leaked to the local news. She must have known what the fallout would be: the uproar, the manhunt. Yet she'd been calm and steady the entire time, speaking softly to Trey, smiling politely at everyone she'd passed. She'd rolled Trey's isolette into a janitor's closet and emerged with him tucked against her chest, well-wrapped against the cold. The footage had spliced together her escape, and every shot, every angle, showed a desperate, terrified young woman who'd guarded the baby in her arms with tenderness and resolve.

I tried to take solace in one of the last clear shots—Trey bundled under Jess's coat, only his knit cap and the curve of his cheek visible in the grainy shot as Jess approached a side exit door. She kissed the top of his head, adjusted her coat to better shield him, and left without a backward glance. Surely nobody who took that kind of care with a child could bring herself to harm him.

Finally, my shift over, I went upstairs to visit Rowan. A security guard was permanently assigned to the NICU now, and he scrutinized my hospital ID and driver's license before allowing me inside.

Rowan was awake, and I talked to her about Riley and all the fun we'd have once she came home. I described her tiny pink nursery and snuggled her as I explained what Christmas was and all the presents coming her way. "Milk it, my friend," I confided. "You only get a first Christmas once, and you're in an excellent position to clean up."

"She's not likely to ask for a pony," Donna said, overhearing our conversation. She too was off-shift, already wearing her coat and carrying an enormous flowered purse.

"I know. But this is probably her only shot at convincing Matt and Charlie." I kissed Rowan's downy head and tucked her back into the isolette. "How have things been in here?"

She tipped her hand side to side, lowered her voice. "So-so. The parents are angry and worried, so they're spending a lot more time in here, asking a lot more questions."

I glanced around. Many of the rocking chairs were indeed taken with exhausted-looking mothers and fathers. "Second-guessing?"

"A little, at least to start. Once they see us in action, they usually come around. I can't blame them, you know. Scary enough to have your baby here, but when you think it's not safe . . ."

I stood and stretched, feeling the twinge in my back. Tension, a not-very-old injury, and a series of long days had left me moving a little gingerly when I'd been sitting in one position for too long. Along the far wall of the NICU, I noticed a poster. "Stillwater General NICU" was lettered across the top in pink and blue marker, followed by "Our Family Is Your Family." I'd never noticed it before—I always scrubbed in at the sink closest to Riley's isolette, and the poster hung on the far side of the counter. Now I inspected it carefully.

Every NICU staff member had contributed a photo of themselves with their family. Husbands, wives, children, parents, even pets. There was a photo of Garima with her parents, wearing traditional Indian dress, and one of Donna surrounded by grandchildren. I skimmed over the familiar faces, looking for one in particular.

"There," Donna said, coming to stand beside me. She tapped at a picture in the corner. "That's Jess."

Jess sat on a bench with three teenaged boys, her arms around their shoulders, all of them mugging for the camera with wide identical grins.

"I still don't believe it." Donna's voice was thick with tears. "I can't. Jess would never hurt that baby. You saw how she was with him."

"Do you think she snapped?"

"Not a chance. That girl was as sane as you or me."

"She needs to turn herself in," I said. "If they think there's even a chance she might hurt him . . ."

I didn't finish the sentence, but I didn't need to. Donna understood perfectly.

"Do you have any idea where she could have gone?" I asked. No doubt Noah and his team had already grilled every nurse on the floor, but maybe a friendly conversation would uncover more details.

"None," Donna said. "They've searched her locker, they've pulled all her files, they've looked everywhere they possibly can."

"Not everywhere," I said. "Did they see this picture?"

Empty nesters, Noah had said. A couple whose kids were already grown when Jess came into their lives. But the boys in this picture, with their gangly limbs and scattering of acne, were definitely younger. I'd bet every penny in my checking account that these were Jess's biological brothers.

"I don't think so," Donna admitted. "It's a recent one, though. See that purple streak in her hair? She had that put in over the summer."

Noah was wrong. Jess and her brothers hadn't lost each other after all. I gently freed the photo from the poster and examined it more closely, tilting it under the light.

"Can I keep this?" I asked.

Donna blinked. "I suppose. It's not as if we want parents to have a reminder. Is it important?"

"It might be," I said and tucked the picture in my pocket as we left.

★　　★　　★

By the time I arrived home, everyone had left for the day. I dropped my stuff on the kitchen counter and studied the picture, something about the image making me feel prickly, like a song you couldn't get out of your head. Eventually, I gave up, leaving the picture on the table while I went upstairs to sleep.

When I woke, my mother was home, sitting at the table, reading glasses on, picture in hand.

"I thought you'd be at the store," I said to my mother as I came into the kitchen.

She didn't look like she was dressed for working behind the counter. She was wearing a brighter lipstick than usual, and her silk blouse and spotless wool trousers would show dust in a heartbeat.

"I'm meeting a friend for lunch." Her cheeks turned a faint pink.

"Awfully fancy for the diner."

She stood and passed me the photo. "What is this, Francesca?"

"A clue, I hope. Jess Chapman and her brothers. I hope so, at least. I'm trying to make out the background."

"Ask Marshall," she said, pulling off her reading glasses. "He has all those photo-editing programs for the newspaper."

Rather than watch Uncle Marshall enter the information age, I pulled out my cell and snapped a picture of the picture, then began zooming and editing, cropping out everything except the background.

My mother was not normally a patient woman. But I had to hand it to her—she managed to hold her questions until I set the phone down.

"Well?" she finally asked.

"Jess didn't hate Kate Tibbs," I said finally. "They were friends."

"How do you know?"

"The reflection."

She snatched up the phone and peered at the image I'd enhanced.

Jess and her brothers had been seated in front of a large plate-glass window. I'd cropped out Jess and the boys and instead had zoomed in on the reflection of the photographer, lightening the shot and boosting the contrast. The resulting image was blurred, and her eyes were hidden behind the camera, but it was enough. The smiling face on my phone was the same one I'd on the news countless times over the last week.

"That's her. Kate," my mother whispered.

"If Kate and Jess were taking pictures like this, I don't think Jess was plotting her murder."

"It doesn't seem likely," Mom said, picking up the original photo and reaching for her glasses again. "But why would she have taken Trey?"

"And *where*? She wouldn't go to her brothers," I said, thinking out loud. "She planned this out. She would have known they'd dig up the information on her biological family. They'd be sending officers to check the houses of anyone related to her by blood or adoption."

I stared at my screen, willed the smiling faces to speak. Jess couldn't have traveled far—everyone in the world would be looking for Trey. She must have holed up somewhere,

waiting for the worst of the attention to pass before she . . .
what? What was her end game? She couldn't possibly hope
to kidnap the child of a potential US congressman and evade
capture indefinitely.

"This shop," my mother said hesitantly. "I know it.
They're renowned for their fudge."

"You've been there?"

"Oh, yes. It's not a far drive—it's in Hale, near Cumber-
land Lake. Plenty of people rent little cabins and such in the
summer. But it's popular with tourists year-round because of
the antiquing and festivals and so forth. This place is known
for its candy but especially their fudge. See? The kitchen has
windows so the tourists can watch them make it. Maybe she's
gone there?"

"Wouldn't she do better in a city, where she could
blend in?"

"She's a pretty enough girl," my mom said, pursing her
lips. "But she's not particularly striking. Her features aren't
memorable. The news is showing a blonde woman with a
baby. If she dyed her hair and kept Trey out of sight, nobody
would give her a second thought." She set the picture down.
"You should call Noah. Tell him to have a SWAT team go
down there."

"Because of a picture? He'd never believe me."

"He might," she retorted. "It's not as if they're exactly
overrun with leads. And time is of the essence, isn't it?"

I envisioned a group of black-clad officers kicking down
the door of a vacation cabin, guns at the ready. The number of
ways that scenario could go wrong was breathtaking. "Even if
Jess is in Hale, a SWAT team is the wrong approach."

"Francesca."

"Let's say they go there and find Jess. They don't need to storm the place right away. They can try talking to her first. If they go in there with guns a-blazing, there's no telling what might happen. Someone could die."

"Someone *has* died. Call Noah," she repeated and checked her watch. "I'm late. Promise me you'll call him."

The sense of foreboding that swept over me was so strong, I had to grip the back of a chair to stay upright. Forcing a smile, I said, "I promise. Go have lunch."

She nodded and left, secure in the knowledge that I always kept my word.

Which is why I'd been careful not to say *when* I would call Noah.

★   ★   ★

"I'm sorry," said the receptionist at the sheriff's department. "Deputy MacLean is in a meeting and can't be interrupted."

"Okay," I said slowly. "What about Sheriff Flint?"

"He's unavailable as well. Would you like to be put through to voice mail? If not, I can try to find another officer for you to speak to."

I wanted the officer I knew would listen to me, who'd take me seriously. Who would act without overreacting.

"Go ahead and put me through to voice mail," I said as the sign outside my car window welcomed me to Hale, Illinois.

TWENTY-TWO

Hale was as quaint as my mother had predicted. A covered bridge, cobblestone streets, and block after block of tiny, colorful shops offering antiques, art, gourmet foodstuffs—particularly fudge. I cruised around for a few minutes, my pace slowed by the hordes of tourists in town for the harvest festival, my mood growing worse with every fanny pack I spotted. Could Jess really have come here? And if she had, how was I going to find her among the throng of tourists? She wouldn't be browsing the shops or enjoying a lunch at one of the fussy little tea shops. She would have gone to ground.

Kate had taken the picture of Jess and her brothers only a few months ago. Obviously, even after all this time, they were in close contact. *Friendly* contact. So why would Jess have taken Trey? Grief could warp even the strongest person—maybe losing Kate in such a graphic, immediate way had twisted something inside her.

Maybe I was wrong not to have waited for Noah.

I stopped in at a vacation rental office where the elderly woman behind the counter made it very clear that spur-of-the-moment lodging was simply not done. There were no available cabins.

Then again, Jess hadn't stolen Trey on the spur of the moment.

"What's a reasonable amount of lead time, then? Like, could I call two days before? Three?"

"We recommend at least three months," she said with a sniff. "Minimum."

"Three months?" My shoulders slumped. There was no way Jess had planned this three months in advance. It was a good thing I hadn't spoken to Noah, because bringing him out here would have been a colossal waste of time and resources—not to mention, I would have gotten Steven's hopes up for nothing. I started for the door. "Sorry to have bothered you. Thanks for your time."

"You could try our wait list," the woman called, misunderstanding my disappointment. "We have cancellations occasionally."

I paused, gripping the strap of my backpack. "How likely is that? I mean, have you had one recently?"

"Yes, actually. Within the last . . . month or so? I didn't actually handle that booking, but I seem to remember that we had a cabin open up unexpectedly, and the next person on the wait list accepted immediately."

My throat was suddenly very dry. "What cabin was that? Are they staying a long time?"

"That's Dove Cottage," she said. "It's lovely. One bedroom plus a loft, right on the lake, with a private dock. The current occupant is only staying another week or so, but I'm afraid it's booked solid until after the holidays. I was just telling someone else the same thing yesterday, in fact."

I pasted on a smile. "It sounds great. I'll have to plan ahead next time."

"Take a brochure," she offered, and by some miracle, my hands were steady enough to accept it.

Only when I was back in my car did I trust myself to open it, the paper rattling in my hands. It was a short drive to Dove Cottage. Fifteen minutes, at most. I could pop out there, look around, and if anything looked suspicious, call Noah.

I'd probably end up surprising some middle-aged couple on their anniversary.

I took a few deep breaths, steadying myself the way I did before facing a particularly rough trauma—locking away the fear, focusing on the plan.

I was halfway to the cottage when my phone rang.

"Where are you?" Noah thundered.

I winced. "I left you a message."

"I heard it," he replied, "but I'm having trouble believing I heard it *correctly*."

Briefly, I explained about the picture I'd found and my certainty that Jess and Kate were friends.

"We have her on video! You've *seen* it, Frankie. Not to mention the fact she may have killed Josh Miller."

"I'm not saying Jess didn't take the baby," I said, turning onto a gravel road. "I'm saying there's a good reason. But I don't believe she killed Josh, and neither do you."

He didn't deny it.

"Noah, if you storm in there, you might lose the chance to get any answers at all. Don't you want to know why she took Trey?"

"There is never a good reason for kidnapping." Noah fell silent, as if the call had dropped. But I could hear the sounds of the station house behind him. My shoulders crept higher with every passing second, waiting out the battle between his disbelief—*she wouldn't*—and his instinct—*of course she would.*

It took less time for instinct to win than I would have guessed.

"Frankie," he said, his voice full of warning, "where are you?"

"About three minutes away from Dove Cottage."

I heard him inhale, as if the simple act of taking a breath might keep the fuse of his temper from lighting.

"Are you sure she's there?"

"I don't know." I spotted the sign and pulled over, killing the ignition. "I don't want to drive all the way up to the cabin; it'll spook her. I'll walk in and try to get a closer look."

"Don't," Noah ordered, but I was already climbing out of the car, easing the door shut.

"You're going in, aren't you?"

"Shhh." I crept down the gravel drive. The cottage was as sweet as its name, painted a soft gray with white trim, shutters on the windows, and a wide front porch. It was quiet here. The only sounds were the lake, the trees, and the intermittent honking of geese. The other cabins on the map were spread out far enough that I couldn't see them, adding to the sense of solitude.

"There's a car. Silver Volkswagen," I whispered, keeping the vehicle between me and the house.

"Get back into your car and get out of there," Noah said. Then grudgingly, "Is it hers?"

"How would I know? You said she abandoned her car at some truck stop." I peeked in the window. "There's a car seat base."

"She's got him?" Noah's next words were muffled, like he'd covered the receiver to shout orders. I couldn't hear exactly what he said, but the urgency in his voice was hard to miss.

"It's only a base," I warned him. "We don't even know if it's her car."

"Why are you defending her?" he asked. "What if it was Rowan who was missing? Don't tell me you wouldn't be barging in there raising hell."

He was right, but I couldn't shake the feeling that I was looking at this through the wrong lens, missing the whole picture. Then I remembered Steven, how desperate he was to find his son, the sheer agony of not knowing. Whatever Jess's reason for taking Trey, it couldn't justify the horror she was putting Steven through. Nobody deserved that kind of pain.

"Fair enough," I whispered and turned toward the house.

"Frankie, do not go in there," Noah said, as if he could see me. "I'm on my way, and I'm bringing backup. The local sheriff's department will be there in ten minutes and the state police are sending a chopper right now."

I ignored him, spurred on by adrenaline and fear and a need to see Trey safe. Jess wouldn't have hurt him; I was certain of that. But once the police arrived, the situation would escalate; there'd be no going back. If I could talk her into handing him over before they reached the house, it would be safer for everyone. The last thing we wanted was for Trey to become a bargaining chip.

There's a fine line between risk and recklessness, and there was too much at stake for me to cross it, even by accident.

The strain in Noah's voice—fear and fury and frustration—nearly stopped me in my tracks. "Get back into your car, drive to the nearest gas station, and wait for me. Do not move from that spot until I send someone to escort you back to police headquarters."

I hesitated. It was the reasonable thing to do.

"*Now.*"

Being ordered around, however, tended to make me unreasonable.

I hung up the phone and peered in a window. The room, decorated in knotty pine and inviting, slipcovered furniture, was deserted—no shadows, no noise from inside. Nobody having lunch at the farmhouse table, nobody watching TV or getting ready for a day at the harvest festival.

I tried the door, expecting it would be locked, but the knob turned smoothly under my hand. The door swung open with the barest squeak, and I stepped inside, my footsteps near-silent.

My phone was buzzing like mad—Noah trying to reach me again. In the absence of any other noise, even the vibrations seemed loud, filling the empty room. I turned it off, shouldered my backpack, and began a slow, cautious walk around the first floor.

"Jess," I called softly. "It's me. Frankie Stapleton from the NICU? Rowan's aunt?"

There was no reply.

"I'm here by myself," I said, making my way around the first floor, peering out at the empty deck that led to the glass-smooth lake. "The cops are on their way, but we have a little time before they get here. Can we talk?"

Silence. Had they run again? Had someone tipped Jess off? Or was she hiding upstairs, lying in wait for me? Was I walking into danger, or was I too late? I couldn't let myself believe that, couldn't consider what "too late" might look like.

"Jess, I'm sure you had a really good reason for taking Trey. Can you tell me about it?" I pushed open the door to the bedroom, talking all the while. "I can help, you know. I'm friends with one of the deputies. If you want someone to plead your case, I'm your best shot, but I need to see Trey. Everyone's worried about him; we'd all feel a lot better if we knew he was all right."

I thought about Rowan and how noisy she was, constantly squeaking and sighing. If Trey was here, wouldn't he make the same sorts of noises? But the car seat was still outside—he couldn't have left.

My search of the bedroom—opening closet doors and peering under beds—had turned up nothing. They couldn't have run out the back; the cottage wasn't big enough to sneak out without me spotting them. If Jess and Trey were here, they must be upstairs. I approached the staircase, heart hammering and palms damp.

"Kate helped you, when you and your brothers were kids, didn't she? She found you a home, made sure you could stay in contact with them. She was your friend." I eased up the stairs, the treads creaking underfoot. Every instinct I had was screaming at me to get out, to run, to turn back. "You must have been so devastated when she came into the ER that night, and none of us realized it. I'm so sorry. I'm sure it gave her some peace to know that you were helping Trey into the world. That you were taking care of him."

Something hovered at the edge of my mind, gossamer and haunting as the brush of a moth's wing, but it disappeared under the fear shrieking at me. I forced myself up the stairs, up to the eerie, echoing loft.

"Jess, we don't have much time." My voice faded to nothingness, my mind going blank. My words hadn't made a difference up to this point; there was no reason to think that was going to change.

The loft came into view slowly. The air up here carried a thick, unwashed scent, like a house closed up too long in the heat. Jess and Trey must have been cooped up here the entire time they'd been missing. Another step, and I spotted the baby gear Jess had purchased: a box of newborn diapers, and a stack of neatly folded onesies on the nightstand next to the bed. A half-empty bottle and burp cloth were tucked into the seat of a rocking chair. The bed itself was a massive four-poster, the kind you'd need a step stool to get into, and my feet made no noise on the plush carpet as I moved closer. A baby name book lay facedown atop the patchwork quilt. And tucked into the corner, an empty crib.

I swore under my breath. They'd been here. I'd missed them, and the knowledge tasted bitter and ashen. Noah was going to be furious, I was certain, but it's not as if I'd scared her off. The house had been empty the moment I stepped inside. Maybe she'd always planned to run, or maybe something had spooked her. Either way, I was about to be in trouble.

I could hear the sirens, far away but growing louder by the second. Resigned, I sat down on the edge of the bed, paged through the baby name book, noting all the ones Jess had marked. Would she try to forge a birth certificate? Take him out of the country? How was it possible that a girl who'd spent her entire life in the system could disappear so completely?

A rhythmic thumping joined the sirens. A massive picture window overlooked the lake, and I could see its deep-blue surface churning into whitecaps, signaling the helicopter's arrival. Might as well face the music, I thought and then stopped short at the sight of a not-quite-closed door in the corner. A closet? A bathroom? Either way, it was the one place I hadn't checked.

"Jess?"

I set the baby name book down and crossed the room on graceless feet, as if some invisible hand was prodding me. I reached for the doorknob, then drew my hand back and gave a gentle push, the noise of the helicopter outside drowned out by the sound of blood rushing in my head.

Then I stopped, helicopter forgotten at the sight of Jess.

Or rather, Jess's body, splayed in the bathtub.

★   ★   ★

I've lost count of the number of gunshot wounds I've seen. GSWs, we call them in the ER, because we see them so often, we need an acronym.

The thing about a gunshot wound is that you *expect* it to be a bloody, gaping mess. But unless the bullet is designed to explode upon impact—hollow-point, for example, the kind people call cop-killers—they're actually small wounds. It's the damage that they do inside that is so deadly. The damage you can't see.

I've seen patients where the entry wound is so small, you could fit a pencil snugly inside, but once we're in surgery, we discover that the patient's entire chest cavity has been shredded.

So if you didn't look at Jess's stomach, you might mistake her expression for shock, as if she was aghast to find herself lying fully clothed in a bathtub, blood pooling around her.

But the sky-blue T-shirt she wore was soaked through with blood from neck to hem, the material stiffened and nearly black. Her expression was contorted in pain, not dismay. And the smell, thick and unmistakable, was one I'd encountered in the ER too many times to count. Without thinking, I reached for a pulse, knowing I wouldn't find one.

I tucked my hands in my back pockets, mindful of how angry Noah had been the last time I touched a body, and knelt next to her. My mom had been right. Jess had dyed her hair a flat, unremarkable brown, the ends darker where the blood had soaked in.

She'd taken a single shot in her lower left abdomen. Tear tracks marked her cheeks, salt trails that spoke of her struggle to live. Not that there was a pleasant way to die, but this was one of the cruelest—a slow, painful bleeding out. Hard to fix in surgery. Impossible to save away from a hospital. Bile rose in my throat.

There was blood on the floor, where she must have fallen before the killer shoved her into the tub, and smeared red handprints on the wall where she'd tried to boost herself out, maybe to call for help.

More likely to try to get to Trey.

"Trey?" I gasped, as if he might answer me. There was no sign of him. I checked in cabinets and behind doors, ran to the bedroom to check underneath the bed. Nothing to see but a wide expanse of carpet. I'd already searched downstairs, and there was no other place in the loft to hide a baby.

Whoever had shot Jess had fled, taking Trey with them. No doubt it was the same person who'd killed Josh Miller. Was the killer their partner, or were Jess and Josh merely pawns?

The police would be here any moment, and I didn't doubt they'd lock the cabin down. Quickly, I stood and returned to the small stack of baby gear on the nightstand. Without touching the bottle, I sniffed it—the formula inside was definitely going off. Combined with the sticky, drying blood on Jess's shirt, I guessed it had been at least half a day since she'd been shot. The killer had left all the baby gear behind, even the diapers and cans of formula I'd spotted downstairs. Why not take them with?

I returned to the baby book. My fingerprints were already on it, so there was no reason not to. Jess had used a credit card receipt to mark her place, and I peered at it, hoping it would be just that easy to find out who her accomplice—and killer—was.

Naturally, I was wrong.

Kate Tibbs had bought the book a month ago. How had Jess gotten hold of it?

I felt that whisper at the back of my neck again, the touch of ice in my gut. Before I could figure out why, I heard the front door bang open downstairs, the sound of boots on the hardwood and the shouting of cops.

"I'm up here!" I called. Then I knelt on the floor, put my hands on my head, and waited for the cavalry.

TWENTY-THREE

Noah had one of the deputies to follow me home and ordered me to stay put once I got there. "I'll deal with you later," he said as coolly as he'd speak to any criminal.

I tried not to feel hurt. After all, when I was knee-deep in a crisis, I did the same thing: narrowed my focus to the most acute problems. Anything on the periphery didn't just fade—it fell away completely. Even so, the dismissal rankled.

Police swarmed over the building, gathering evidence and processing the scene. As I pulled away, a police cruiser in my rearview mirror, I tried to figure out what would be next.

Had Jess wanted a child of her own? If that was the case, why wouldn't she adopt? She knew from experience what the foster care system was like and how adoption could transform a child's life. With Kate vouching for her, she could have easily been approved.

I knew what the police and Steven would say: Kate's death caused Jess to snap. She'd pivoted from grief to greed, wanting to take over Kate's life, wanting to raise Trey as her own.

It was a convenient explanation, but it didn't fit. It relied on coincidence, dismissing the interactions we knew about—Kate and Josh, Steven and Josh, Kate and Jess—in favor of the one we'd never proved: Jess and Josh. The killer was in the middle of it all, the spider at the center of the web, picking off prey one by one. Now he—or she—had Trey.

By the time I got home, all I wanted was a shower and perhaps a cookie the size of my head. Noah had assigned Travis, the boy deputy, to follow me. Now he rolled down his window as I stumbled toward the house. "Ma'am? Deputy MacLean wanted me to remind you that he expects you to stay here unless he tells you otherwise."

I resisted the urge to remind him that Deputy MacLean was not the boss of me. Instead, I raised a hand in acknowledgment and trudged up the front walk.

Riley came tearing down the steps to greet me. "Company for dinner!" she cried. "Grandma made me to set the table with the good silver."

"Fancy," I said, and she bobbed her head eagerly. "Who's the company?"

"Reverend Tim."

"Grandma invited a priest to dinner?" I followed in Riley's wake, my steps leaden.

"Francesca," my mother trilled when I walked inside. Her bright expression dimmed as she took me in—bedraggled, bereft, with bloodstains marring my clothes. "What on earth? We have a guest."

She nodded meaningfully to the man on the sofa. A platter of her famous artichoke dip and slices of French bread sat on the coffee table, nearly gone. Riley dashed by and scooped up another helping, then ran upstairs.

"Sorry?" I said, though I was fairly certain I didn't have anything to apologize for.

Her lips pursed, she gave a sharp nod. "Reverend Tim, my daughter, Francesca. Francesca, Reverend Tim is the new assistant pastor at the Methodist church."

I gave a small wave. Reverend Tim, eyebrows raised at my appearance, returned it.

"We'll let you get changed," Mom said pointedly, "and then we can eat."

"Mom . . ." I was in no mood for a meal. Any appetite I might have had vanished every time I thought of Jess's blank eyes, and I couldn't stop thinking about it.

"Upstairs," she said in a voice that brooked no argument. Too tired to argue, I made my way to the bathroom and scrubbed up as thoroughly as if I was heading into surgery. Despite multiple rounds of soap and water, I still *felt* Jess's blood on my skin.

Back in my room, I stripped off my clothes and dropped them in the trash, pulled on the first clean pajamas I could find, then crawled in bed. Guest or no guest, I was done.

"We're eating soon," said Riley from somewhere above me.

"I'm not hungry," I said into my pillow. "Who is that guy?"

"Reverend Tim. He works at a church."

"I know that," I said, rolling over to face Riley, who was hanging upside down from her bunk, pigtails dangling. "Why is he here? Is someone's soul in danger?"

She shrugged, an impressive feat considering her position. "Grandma invited him. She said you had a lot in common."

"Reverend Tim? And me?" Somehow I doubted this. "Like what?"

"You're both from Stillwater."

"So is everyone else in Stillwater."

"He spends a lot of time at the hospital. On the Jerry floor."

"Geriatric," I corrected absently. "It's not a person, it's . . . oh. She's trying to set us up."

Riley bit her lip to keep from grinning.

"I do not want to be set up."

"I didn't invite him!" she protested.

"I don't need a relationship right now. I don't *want* a relationship right now. I'm only going to be here for a few months. Does she really think a minister is going to be interested in a no-strings—?" It occurred to me that Riley, who was staring at me, mouth agape, was probably not the best audience for that line of argument. "Never mind. The point is, Riley, a woman should be safe in her home. She should be able to walk in the door after a long, unspeakably awful day and put on pajamas, eat some breakfast for dinner, and go to bed."

Riley jumped down with a thud. "This isn't your home."

I blinked at her. "Well, not technically. But—"

"You said you're only going to be here for a few months. That's what you tell everyone." Her little face darkened. "But if this isn't your house, then you're a guest. And guests are polite," she said, warming to her theme. "Guests have *manners*."

"I didn't mean . . ."

"So if you're a guest, you should go downstairs and make conversation, like Grandma says."

"Riley," I wheedled. On top of everything else, I hadn't expected to have to make my case to an eight-year-old. But she wasn't interested. What had I said to anger her?

This isn't your home.

Realization smacked into me like a two-by-four to the back of the head. "Riley, you know I love being here with you, right?"

"No, you don't. Grandma makes you nuts. You miss your cool apartment, and Chicago, and all your friends at your big hospital."

"Hey, Grandma makes *you* nuts sometimes too."

She folded her arms and looked away.

"But you know what?" I continued. "My apartment doesn't have you. Which makes this place infinitely cooler than Chicago. And I'd *much* rather hang out with you than with Reverend Tim or anybody at my old hospital." I tipped my head toward the closet, where the board games were stacked up. "In fact, why don't we forget dinner? We can stay up here and play Monopoly."

"Can't. Company," she said and skipped out of the room, pigtails swinging. "And no wearing pajamas."

Riley, it seemed, could hold a grudge.

I switched clothes again, into jeans and a polka-dotted blouse, giving the pajamas on my bed a longing look. "Soon," I promised and went downstairs.

*   *   *

"How are you settling into Stillwater?" Reverend Tim said as I passed him the platter of roast chicken.

"It certainly hasn't been boring."

"Your mother was telling me about your involvement in the Jensen case." He shook his head. "Tragic, really, how greed can motivate people to do such terrible things."

"I don't think we need to rehash that situation," my mother cut in smoothly. "Certainly not over dinner."

"No shortage of tragedies around here," I said, ignoring her. I was still rattled from finding Jess, and my fear for Trey had robbed me of my appetite.

"Kate Tibbs, you mean." He nodded sadly. "Hard to fathom how someone could harbor such evil in their heart. Certainly, she worked with troubled souls . . ."

"Did you know her?"

"A bit. First Methodist does quite a lot to help social services when we can—a coat drive for the children, a food pantry, other initiatives. Several of our families have fostered children, so we've interacted with her. The entire congregation is praying for Baby Trey's safe return." He gave a rueful smile. "People are always looking for connection, aren't they? Tragedies carry greater meaning if there's even the most tenuous of threads to bind you to them. We can only trust that the poor troubled girl who took him will see the error of her ways."

"Jess," I said hoarsely. "Her name was Jess Chapman."

Noah, of course, wouldn't have said anything. He would have held his cards to his chest, followed the appropriate protocols. But I was tired, and sad, and my own tenuous connection had bound me so tightly to Trey Tibbs that my worry overrode any thought of discretion. "And she's dead."

TWENTY-FOUR

"Of all the ways to ruin a dinner party, Francesca," my mother scolded as we washed up from dinner. "We didn't even get to the pie."

"If you would stop trying to set me up, I wouldn't have had to ruin your dinner party," I retorted.

"New rule," she said, handing me a baking dish to dry. "No talking about murder at the table."

"He was going to hear about it anyway. I'm surprised you didn't hear it over the scanner."

She glanced over at it. "Why on earth would I? They're so cautious about what they say over the radio these days, it's hardly worth turning the thing on. Regardless, the Reverend didn't need to hear you're involved. How are we supposed to find you someone if you're constantly getting caught up in these horrible crimes?"

"I don't need you to find me someone," I said, frowning at the scanner. I could have sworn I'd turned it off earlier. "A relationship is not in the cards for me right now. I have work. I have the store. And I have you guys. Isn't that enough?"

She softened. "But I'm worried you'll be alone."

"I am *never* alone," I said grimly, just as the doorbell rang.

"I'll get it," shouted Riley, shooting down the stairs and across the living room.

"Officer Noah!" she squealed from the other room. "Hi, hi, hi! Daddy has a night class."

Matt and Noah had become friends while I'd been away, but I didn't think this was a social call.

"Actually, I'm looking for your Aunt Frankie," Noah said.

"Ohhhhhh." Riley drew out the word. "Is she in trouble?"

"I need to ask her a few questions, that's all."

"She's in the kitchen." I heard the screen door open, then shut, and Riley confided, "She has dish duty because she ruined Grandma's dinner party."

"She did?" For a moment, amusement overtook the strain in his voice. "What did she do?"

"Talked about dead people. Grandma wanted Aunt Frankie to make a good impression on Reverend Tim, and she says talking about dead people during dinner isn't polite."

I shot a glance at my mother, whose shoulders were shaking with laughter.

"Well . . ." Noah began.

"But Aunt Frankie said that Reverend Tim deals with plenty of dead people. And then Grandma said that proved they had a lot in common, and then Aunt Frankie said . . ."

"Aunt Frankie said it's your turn to dry," I said, coming into the room, tossing the bright-yellow dish towel over her shoulder.

Noah's amusement faded as he caught sight of me, though not entirely. "Entertaining clergy? You in need of spiritual guidance?"

"I'm in need of a nap," I grumbled.

"Naps can wait." He looked as haggard as I felt. "I need your statement about today."

I shrugged. "I told you everything back at the cottage."

"I need an official statement. Give me any lip, and the sheriff has authorized me to bring you down to the station."

"On what grounds?"

"Obstruction. Interfering with a police investigation. Tampering with evidence. Shall I go on?"

I glanced behind me. Riley and my mother were both standing in the doorway, wide-eyed.

"Outside." I bit off the word.

"Noah, do you need anything to eat?" my mother asked as I led Noah through the kitchen and onto the back deck. "I can fix you a plate."

"Thanks, Lila, but this is an official call."

The cold night air was just short of bitter, the shock of it after the overheated kitchen stealing my breath.

Twelve years ago, Noah would have wrapped his arms around me to ward off the cold. Now he watched me shiver and deliberately stuffed his hands in his pockets. I hugged myself to keep warm and studied him closely.

Did he always push himself this hard? I remembered what Reverend Tim had said about personal connections and wondered if he'd known Kate well or if there was another thread I hadn't yet seen. Something I'd missed.

Twelve years away meant I'd missed plenty, and Noah might not be inclined to fill me in, even if I asked.

My pride wouldn't allow me to ask.

"Let's start from the beginning," he said.

"Aren't you going to use your little notepad?"

He sighed deeply. "You're in a mood."

"So are you," I shot back.

"I'm in a mood because I'm trying to find a stolen baby and close what is now a triple homicide. I am in a mood because for several days running, you have seen fit to insert yourself into a police investigation when I very specifically asked you not to, putting both yourself and my case at risk. I am entitled to my mood. *You're* in a mood because your mom has resorted to setting you up with the local clergy. How'd that go, by the way?"

I boosted myself onto the porch railing and tried not to let my teeth chatter. "I thought you wanted to talk about the case."

He reached into his back pocket and withdrew the notepad, waggled it at me. "Why did you decide to go to Dove Cottage?"

"Because I found the picture of Jess and Kate in Hale, and it seemed like a good place to hide. Touristy, so she wouldn't stick out, but definitely not the first place you'd think of. She had good memories of her time there with Kate, so it seemed like a natural fit."

"You got lucky."

"I paid attention," I shot back. "Jess and Kate were friends, Noah. It doesn't make sense that she'd want to hurt Kate or the baby. She was taking good care of him."

"Maybe she wanted to keep him. Maybe she and Josh decided they were going to start a family of their own?"

"With her friend's child? And then some random person kills them both and steals Trey a second time?" I scoffed, even though I'd entertained the same idea, at least for a while. "You don't believe that."

"I believe we need to find Trey."

"Find the killer, and you'll find the kidnapper," I said. "Did you turn up anything strange at the cottage?"

"Strange?"

"When I found Jess . . . there was something . . ." I trailed off, trying to remember what I'd seen. What I'd felt.

Spiders on the back of my neck. Ice in my gut. Something wrong, something that didn't add up. Something that should've been there but wasn't; something that shouldn't have been there but was. The harder I concentrated, the further it skittered away.

"We didn't find anything weird," Noah said, watching me closely. "Baby stuff—clothes, blankets, bottles, diapers. Medical supplies, but they were all unopened. Pretty much the usual. A baby name book. It's not a good sign that the killer left all the supplies behind."

The chill that ran over my skin had nothing to do with the temperature. The killer hadn't taken the supplies because they weren't planning to need them. Newborns needed to be fed every three hours or so; assuming Trey was still alive, he wouldn't last long without formula. "We're running out of time, aren't we?"

"Looks that way." He sank into a patio chair. "Steven's holding a press conference tomorrow afternoon. He wants to update the public on the case. Like we're not already doing that."

"He's upset," I said softly. "Anyone would be, in his situation."

"I get that, but he needs to step back and let us do our job. He's constantly asking for updates; at this point, he knows as much as the sheriff, but I've got no guarantee he won't spill it all to the press tomorrow. We've asked him to hold off, but he refuses."

"That's Ted Sullivan," I said. *One more should do it.* One more press conference, perhaps? How would he have known something newsworthy was going to happen, unless he'd been the one behind it? "Have you looked into him yet? Checked his alibi?"

"I've been a little busy with all the dead bodies," he replied. "But yes, he alibis out for everything—the accident, the kidnapping, Josh's shooting. If he's not with Steven, he's schmoozing the press."

"We should be logical," I said. "Go over the suspects. Alibis, motives, all of that."

"What do you think I've been doing, Frankie? We have an entire conference room devoted to this case at HQ."

"Yes, but I haven't seen it."

"Because you're not a cop." He sighed. "Our official theory is that Jess and Josh were an item. Kate took Josh's daughter away, and the two of them hatched a plot: kill Kate, take the baby. An instant family for the happy couple, plus revenge on the side."

"That's crazy," I said. "And who shot Jess and Josh, then? Kate's ghost? Trey? You don't have a scrap of evidence to support that theory, do you?"

His shoulders slumped. "Not really. One toothbrush at the cottage and her apartment, no men's clothes at either location."

I frowned. "You don't buy the official theory, do you? You never have. That's why you kept going back to Josh's house after the first search. It's why you've been sharing information with me, because you want someone to look at it with fresh eyes."

He stayed silent but put the notepad away. The time for official statements was over, and we could talk about the truth. He crossed the back porch to stand in front of me, his voice low enough that not even my mother, who was no doubt trying to listen, could overhear.

"We're seeing a lot more drug cases lately," he said. "Steven's office is in charge of prosecuting them. He's campaigning on his reputation as a family man who's tough on crime; he's promising all sorts of new funding for treatment and prevention if he gets in."

"'Steven Tibbs, Stronger Tomorrows,'" I parroted.

"Exactly." He studied me for a moment, as if weighing exactly how much to tell me. "I think Kate's death was meant to send a message. Trey's abduction is more of the same. There's been no ransom demand—at least not that Steven's told us about. Maybe whoever's in charge wants something other than money."

"Like they want him to make a case go away?" I suggested, and then it hit me. "What if they want him to drop out? What if that's what the press conference is about? He's announcing his withdrawal from the race?"

"Could be," Noah said finally. "Like I said, the sheriff believes Kate's death was about revenge and getting the baby. Steven agrees, even though he's unhappy with how we're handling the investigation."

That didn't mean he wasn't being blackmailed—just that he hadn't told the police about it.

"What if . . . ?" I flexed my hand, the answer hovering just beyond my fingertips, and grabbed his arm. "What if we moved too fast?"

His mouth curved slowly despite the gravity of the situation, and he stepped in closer. "I don't remember you ever complaining."

"Focus." I dropped his arm, ignoring the warmth that flooded my cheeks. "We jumped from the crash to the abduction. Everyone assumes they were basically the same thing—same motive, same criminals. They've blurred together. But if we look at them separately, there's no evidence Jess was involved in the crash at all."

"If that were true, she'd have no reason to kidnap Trey."

But Jess always had a reason, according to everyone who knew her. Even taking Trey had been carefully orchestrated. She wasn't impulsive or flighty—she'd grown up in a world that careened out of control at a moment's notice, and it had made her cautious. Thoughtful. She understood contingency plans, but she craved order.

"Let's agree to disagree," I said.

"Story of my life," Noah muttered. He stepped away, and the cold rushed back in. I hadn't realized how much heat the man radiated. "You're saying Jess had nothing to do with the crash, and . . . what? Josh had nothing to do with the kidnapping? It's all a coincidence?"

"Not a coincidence," I said. "Someone else is manipulating them. It's all part of someone's agenda, whether that's trying to get Steven elected or force him out of the race—or is related to one of his cases."

"Ted alibis out," he reminded me. "And before you ask, so does Norris Mackie."

"What about Norris's staff? Politicians never do their own dirty work."

His eyebrows lifted. "You have a lot of experience with dirty politicians?"

"Chicago, remember?"

"We have guys running down some leads on Mackie, but they're not panning out. It's not a great motive, anyway. The polls were tight, but he's been doing this long enough to know that a stunt like this could increase Steven's lead. Without Kate's crash, he might have pulled out the win." He paused. "What about Steven?"

I punched his arm lightly. "Not Steven. He has a better alibi than Mackie."

"He also has a staff."

"What's his motive?" I asked. "The polls were tight, but he was still ahead, wasn't he? He didn't needed a sympathy vote."

"Marital problems?"

"Everyone says they were happy. He's devastated, Noah. You've seen him. Does he really seem like the kind of guy who would kill his pregnant wife? And then steal the baby? He doesn't even need to steal Trey; he's the dad. You can't honestly tell me you think it's him."

"Not really. It's reflex, you know? To look at the husband first." He shook his head. "It's gotta be the drugs angle, doesn't it?"

Exhaustion and frustration were taking a bigger toll on him than I'd realized. Noah might be my friend, he might respect my judgment, but if he was actually asking me to verify that his police work was sound, he was in bad shape.

"It's got to be," I agreed. "That's the only motive that makes sense."

But even as I said it, I knew that sense had little to do with it. Motive was a deeply personal thing. Entirely justifiable. A worthy risk for the reward, whether that reward was financial or emotional. Outsiders couldn't understand the calculus of what drove a person to murder; they could only recognize it.

And we were running out of time.

TWENTY-FIVE

We went over my statement a few more times, Noah coaxing details out of my tired brain, both of us concocting and discarding theories. He jotted down some things to follow up on, and each time I felt a sense of accomplishment.

"We make a good team," I said, sitting next to him on the steps.

His pen stilled for an instant, then resumed. "Yep."

"Is this what you do when you're not out actively catching criminals? Talk over the case with the guys?"

"Women too," he said. "And yeah, sometimes."

"Are you going to tell everyone I helped?"

He slanted me a look. "Probably not."

"I had some good ideas."

"It's not about the ideas. It's that I am sharing case information with a member of the public. Someone who's involved in the case, no less."

"Why are you?" I asked. The question had been gnawing at me all evening.

"You've always been nosy," he said with a grin. "Seemed like I might as well put that to work."

"Noah, you're talking over a case—possibly the biggest case of your career—with me, instead of your team of trained professionals. And don't give me the line about needing fresh eyes. With the number of agencies involved in this, you've got more eyes than an optometry convention."

He groaned, and I jabbed his shoulder with my finger. "Do you honestly expect me to believe it's because I have a well-developed sense of curiosity?"

"That's what you call it?" he said. "Nosy."

"Nice try," I said. "What gives?"

For a moment, he didn't reply. He'd put the notebook away, and now he sat on the steps, his leg pressed against mine, solid and warm. "Do you remember, back when we were in high school, and you'd keep me company while I was working on a car?"

When we were seniors, Noah had worked at an auto shop after school and on the weekends, trying to bring in enough money to help at home. I used to visit him at the garage, sitting amid the tool chests and oil pans, listening to him explain how power steering worked, the difference between an alternator and a timing belt, or about how to properly gap a spark plug. Twelve years later, I couldn't remember any of those things. I remembered Noah and the way his hands had looked, nicked and scratched and covered with motor oil. I remembered the sound of his voice, warm and rough, and the way his laughter seemed to vibrate through me. I remembered that the itch beneath my skin, the one that made me desperate to leave Stillwater and see the world, eased whenever we were there, because the rest of the world disappeared, and for those few brief afternoons, I was content.

"I remember." The words caught in my throat.

The back of his hand brushed mine. "You didn't care about cars."

"Not really."

"But you let me talk about them nonstop."

"It mattered to you," I said. "Besides, it wasn't always cars."

Sometimes when it had been late, or he'd been tired, or his dad had been on a particularly rough bender, we'd talk about other things: his younger siblings, what he was going to do for his next English paper, where we'd travel when we finally escaped. We'd argue politics or rank the best movies of all time. We'd plan road trips and train trips and chart a course through Europe. We'd talk about anything, and nothing, and everything.

"I had so much going on back then. So many worries crammed into my brain, I could barely keep them straight. It was like listening to the radio and someone was flipping through the stations, so fast you couldn't tell the difference between music and static." He rubbed the back of his neck, almost bashful. "You cut through the static. We'd talk, and all the worry, all the craziness would drop away. The world would make sense again. I didn't know what I wanted back then—nobody does when they're seventeen—but when you were there, it felt like I had a shot at figuring it out."

I bit my lip, tried to ignore the prickling behind my eyelids. I'd known, at seventeen. I'd known exactly what I wanted: Noah and freedom. I hadn't yet realized that the two were mutually exclusive.

He laced the very tips of his fingers with mine, staring at something far beyond the backyard. "I'm a good cop, Frankie. I'm good at what I do, and I care about the people in this community. But this case . . . I feel like I'm back in the garage again. I can't figure out what's real and what's noise or how to make sense of it. But if I don't, and soon, that baby will die."

I didn't say anything.

"*That* is why I'm talking to you." He turned and met my gaze, and something both defiant and hopeful was in his eyes.

"Well," I said, trying and failing to keep my voice from cracking. My heart wasn't far behind. "As long as there's no pressure."

His smile quirked, but he continued to watch me, the seconds slowing and the air between us shimmering with something indefinable.

And then the back door swung open.

"I thought you might be hungry, Noah," said my mom as I scrambled to my feet. She hefted a tray of food. "We had plenty of leftovers."

"We're wrapping up," he protested. "I'll eat back at the station."

"Vending machines do not count as dinner," she said, crossing to the glass-topped table on the other side of the porch and setting down the tray. "You need to keep your strength up."

I glared at her, but Mom ignored me to smile brilliantly at Noah. "I seem to remember that you liked my roast chicken."

"Nobody makes better," he admitted, joining her at the table and eyeing the spread.

She smacked his arm with a napkin. "Flatterer. Have seconds, if you like."

She switched on the battery-operated lantern in the middle of the table, bathing us in warm, flickering light. "I'll leave you two alone. No hurry."

She disappeared into the house again.

I pressed my hands to my cheeks, feeling them heat. "Sorry about that."

"Are you?" he asked. When I didn't answer, he nodded thoughtfully and sampled a bite of chicken. "She is a determined woman. Maybe I should hire her."

I took my cue from Noah, gliding past the strange, fraught moment, tucking away the raw emotions for a time when I was steady enough to handle them. I threw myself into the chair opposite his. "Do you see what I have to put up with? Every time I turn around she's trying to ambush me. I can't live like this."

He watched me over the rim of his water glass. "So don't."

"What choice do I have? I promised Charlie I'd stay and help. I've sublet my apartment, so it's not like I can move back in."

"Move in above the store," he suggested. "Your stuff is already there, and you'd be on-site when Charlie needs help. It's not as private as Chicago, but it's more than you have here."

"Nobody would be ambushing me with dinner guests." I paused, stealing a bite of chicken from his plate. "It's not a bad idea, but . . . you heard Charlie before. She's not a fan of the idea."

"It's worth considering," he said.

"Grandma said I have to go to bed," Riley said sullenly. I turned in my seat to see her silhouetted in the doorway.

"Sounds about right. Gimme a hug."

Riley padded out onto the deck in purple zebra-striped pajamas but didn't come over for a hug. Instead, she eyed

Noah. "Are you guys talking about the dead lady from dinner?"

"Kind of," Noah said.

She nodded sagely. "Are you going to find the person who did it?"

"We're going to try," I said.

"Actually, Riley, that's my job," Noah cut in. "Your aunt's answering a few questions for me, that's all."

Riley nodded, her wide eyes telegraphing that she didn't believe this for a second. "You should have come for dinner," she told him. "You're more fun than Reverend Tim."

"Thanks," Noah replied, "but I wasn't invited."

"You could come tomorrow," she said.

"Why the sudden interest in dinner guests?" I demanded.

"Company means dessert," she said and turned her attention back to Noah. "We could go for a ride in the squad car too, with lights and everything."

"Maybe soon," Noah hedged with a look at me.

"C'mon, Riley. Time for bed." I gave her a hug, but she squirmed away from me. "Sweet dreams, buddy. Love you."

"Love you too," she muttered. "G'night, Deputy Noah."

"Night, Riley. See you soon."

After she'd left, Noah grinned. "That is a highly focused kid. Must run in the family."

"Dessert brings out her mercenary side."

He studied me. "You're going to Steven's press conference tomorrow afternoon, aren't you?"

"What do you think?"

"I think I couldn't stop you even if I wanted to. You scared me today, Frankie."

"I'm sorry," I said, meaning it. "You said it yourself, every minute Trey's gone, the danger is worse."

"Doesn't mean I want you running into danger," he said softly.

"Doesn't mean I'll stop."

TWENTY-SIX

Finally, I slept. Twelve solid hours of unconsciousness, with my dreams filled with images of Jess bleeding out on the floor of the ER while I tried to patch her back together with preemie-sized supplies. I dreamed of Rowan, of reaching into her isolette and finding only a pile of blankets and wires. I dreamed of the photograph of Kate and Steven, smiling for the voters, their arms around a chubby, laughing Trey—a picture that had never existed, and the closer I looked, the faster it faded away.

Twelve hours should have left me rested, but I woke gritty-eyed and irritable.

"Where is everyone?" I asked when I stumbled downstairs.

Matt glanced up from the papers he was grading. "Riley's at school, your mom's at the store, and Charlie's at the hospital. I'll head over there in a bit. Coffee's fresh," he added.

"Thanks," I said and poured myself a cup.

"Heard we had all sorts of company yesterday," he said.

I sighed. "Were you in on the Reverend Tim scheme?"

"Me?" He snorted. "I know better than to get involved in your mom's plans. She gets that gleam in her eye, I keep my head down and my mouth shut. This, actually, is my strategy with all Stapleton women."

"You could have warned me."

"What's the fun in that?" He frowned at the essay before him and scribbled a comment. "Your mom wants you to stay here. She thinks we're not enough to convince you."

"It's not a question of enough," I said, staring into my coffee cup. "It's . . ."

Matt waited.

"It's me. And where I fit. I'm not sure it's here." The coffee was good—strong and rich without being bitter. Matt was in charge of the coffee, I'd learned, and for that I was grateful. I was also coming to learn that while my sister's husband might be happy to let the Stapleton women run the show, he was the one who kept things going while all those personalities battled it out. "Noah suggested I move into the apartment above the store."

He leaned back in his seat, the gesture more considering than surprised. "What do you think?"

"I don't know," I said. "It seems like a lot of effort if I'm going to turn around and move out again in a few months."

"Easier to stay put in the short term," he agreed.

I sat back, feeling vaguely annoyed. It was an amiable enough response, but I'd expected more of an argument—to stay here because I was needed or to move in and make this a more permanent arrangement.

"Are you always so neutral?" I asked.

"Are you really asking for advice?" he returned with a smile. "We love having you here, even if Charlie doesn't say it. Riley adores you. Your mom is over the moon. We'd love it if you decided to stick around longer too, but not if the idea makes you miserable."

"I never said I was miserable," I said quickly. "Except when Mom is in matchmaker mode."

"Fair enough." He tapped his pen on the stack of papers, considering. "It's a big change, you coming home. Everyone needs some time to get their feet under them, Lila included. Moving to the apartment would be another change, and we'd have to adjust."

"You think it's a bad idea." Was that relief I felt or disappointment?

"If it's temporary, there's no need to disrupt everyone again. But if you're thinking about making it a longer-term situation . . . people are more adaptable than we give them credit for. A little breathing room might be the thing that makes it *possible* for you to stay here long-term."

It did not escape my notice that Matt, English professor, who taught composition for a living, was carefully avoiding the word "permanent."

"It's easy to feel like you're taking a step backward right now. The apartment would be a step forward, only on a path you hadn't expected." He stood, scooping the papers into his battered leather briefcase. "I'm off to the hospital. Is this a conversation I should mention to Charlie?"

"Will she take it better coming from you?"

"She'll take it best if she thinks it's her own idea," he said. "Barring that . . . yes."

"Go for it." The coward's way out, perhaps, hiding behind my Viking of a brother-in-law. But I was fresh out of courage.

★   ★   ★

The clouds had been gathering all day. By the time we arrived at the press conference that afternoon, they'd turned the sky ugly, threatening rain. The chill in the air had settled in for good, iron-hard and implacable. The wind was already kicking up when Steven made his way down the front steps of the house, pausing to check his phone before crossing to the podium at the edge of the lawn.

News crews had settled into position, and the constant staccato clicking of shutters filled the air. The reporters surged forward as Steven faced them, hands gripping the sides of the podium, searching the crowd as if he was looking for a friendly face—or the kidnapper.

I spotted Noah off to one side, standing with a group of sheriff's deputies, a wall of navy uniforms and set faces. Next to me, Charlie hugged herself and bounced ever-so-slightly on her toes, trying to keep warm.

"This feels ghoulish," she said. "Like we're here for entertainment."

"Support," my mother said firmly, standing on the other side of her. "We want him to know we're thinking of him."

Half the town had shown up for support. In a couple of hours, they'd come to Stapleton and Sons for another round. I spotted Donna and Garima nearby and gave a small wave. The crowd fell silent as Steven cleared his throat and began.

"Good morning, everyone. I know that Sheriff Flint, the state police, and the FBI task force have been keeping you all updated on the details of my son Trey's abduction. I'm not going to spend my time today going over all the details. As you may know, the woman responsible for his kidnapping was found dead yesterday."

A murmur of sympathy rose from the crowd. They'd heard the news, but somehow having it come from Steven himself, having it laid out so baldly, was even more horrifying.

He waited until the murmurs died down. "We believe Trey was with her, based on items found at the scene, but there was no sign of Trey. I want to emphasize that there is no evidence that Trey has been harmed up to this point."

"Why does he keep saying the baby's name?" my mother grumbled. "It's not as if we're likely to forget it."

"It's to remind the kidnapper that Trey's a real person with a family. Humanizes him. Now shush."

But I wasn't watching Steven anymore. I was watching Ted Sullivan, a few feet away. His eyes were fixed on Steven as he continued speaking, mouthing the words along with his candidate.

"We have every reason to believe Trey is alive, but that does not mean he is safe. All my energies now are focused on bringing Trey safely home, and we're suspending the campaign indefinitely. When we resume, it will be with Trey in my arms, and my beloved wife, Kate"—he swallowed hard and continued—"looking down on us from Heaven."

The speech was scripted, which made perfect sense. Hard enough to stay composed in this situation. Writing out your comments beforehand would reduce some of the pressure. Still, it was disconcerting to watch how pleased Ted was by the performance, to watch Steven wait for the applause he knew was coming.

Steven continued, thanking the crowd for their support, asking for the usual thoughts and prayers, taking a few questions. After a moment, Ted pulled out his phone, listened, and turned his back on the cameras.

"Something's wrong," I murmured to Charlie.

My mother leaned over. "What is it? What's going on?"

I shushed her, keeping my eyes on Ted. He'd put the phone away and crossed over to the sheriff, drawing him away from the crowd.

"Frankie, don't," Charlie said, following my gaze.

"Gotta," I said and edged closer.

The men were arguing in low, furious voices. I tried to overhear what they were saying, but Noah spotted me. Moving swiftly, he cut me off.

"What's going on?"

"Nothing you need to worry about," he said, taking me by the elbow and guiding me back to my family.

"Noah, come on. There's a ton of press here. Whatever's happening is going to get out, so you might as well spill. I can *help*, remember? Like you said last night."

Behind us, Steven was wrapping up the press conference and heading back into the house.

"Not this time," he said. "Go home. All of you."

"Not likely," I said and watched as the sheriff, the FBI agent in charge, and the state police chief trailed into the house. Ted looked longingly at the press but followed dutifully.

"Let's go," Charlie said, tugging at my arm. "It's late and I need to . . ."

"You two go ahead," I replied. "I'll walk back."

"You'll catch your death of cold," my mother said. "Besides, we need to finish getting ready for the fundraiser. I have five vats of chili sitting at home, and I need help getting them over to the church."

The fundraiser had taken on a life of its own—so many people had wanted to come, my mom and Reverend Tim had moved it to the basement of First Methodist to accommodate the crowd. My mother, both soft-hearted and savvy, had hung posters for the event all around town and convinced Marshall to run ads in the *Journal-Standard*. "Sponsored by Stapleton and Sons Hardware, your neighbors since 1875" was emblazoned across every one. Even so, the chili could wait, and I said as much.

The press felt the change too—something in the way the honchos had marched inside, all tension and purpose, had caught their attention. Instead of dispersing back to their vans, they hovered, packing up their equipment with deliberate, maddening slowness.

"Noah will tell you soon," Charlie said reasonably. "He always does."

I wasn't quite as certain. Noah on the back porch under the moonlight was very different than the one who'd grabbed me by the arm and ordered me home, and the latter didn't seem inclined to share.

One of the reporters was idly checking his phone when he straightened and gestured to the cameraman, who quickly set up for another shot, a tight-focus interview with the front door of the house in the background.

I pushed my way through the crowd, everyone jostling to hear the scoop so they could turn around and report it themselves.

"A message has appeared on the Find Trey Tibbs web page—an anonymous commenter has posted a message saying—and this is a direct quote—'I don't want any more trouble. He's at Henderson's, and I am long gone.' End quote. We're not clear yet who this 'Henderson' is, but you can be sure that Channel 6 is on the story, and we'll be the first to bring you answers." The reporter signed off and dashed toward Steven's front door.

"Henderson?" my mother said blankly. "There haven't been Hendersons around here for years. The daughter moved away, didn't she? To New Mexico? Some kind of hippie?"

"The dairy's still there." I thought back to my conversation with Meg Costello. "Kids use it for parties and stuff."

"And stuff," Charlie echoed, waggling her eyebrows. "But it's huge—didn't there used to be a ton of outbuildings?"

"Yeah, when we went . . ." I began as my mother narrowed her eyes. "Lots of outbuildings. All deserted."

"Trey could be anywhere on the property," Charlie said and tilted her face upward. "There's a storm coming in. They can't leave him out there."

The sheriff had emerged from Steven's house by now, and the reporters rushed to the door. He confirmed the report, adding tersely, "We're sending all available units to the scene. So as not to impede the operation, we're asking that all members of the press stay outside the perimeter until we have something to report. The terrain we're talking about is large—it's an abandoned commercial dairy farm, approximately twelve hundred acres, with an unconfirmed number of outbuildings centrally located on the land. We're asking all available first responders in the surrounding counties join us as well. As you can see, the temperature is dropping and the situation will become increasingly dangerous as night falls and the storm picks up, so time is of the essence."

I looked at Charlie.

"We can help," she said. "We know that farm."

"They won't want us."

"Text Noah."

"I don't think he's looking at his phone right now." I'd learned enough about Noah's phone habits in the past week to know he didn't check his messages during breaks in the case.

"Fine," she said. "Which of those cruisers is his?"

"Unit twenty-three," I said, waving a hand toward the line of police cars down the street.

Charlie marched off, chin stuck in the air. I glanced at my mother.

"What if the kidnapper is still there?" Worry lines creased her forehead and carved furrows around her lips. "What if it's a trap?"

I didn't have an answer. The rain began, fat cold drops that soaked into my coat immediately. "We can't *not* look."

"We, is it?" she said, and my only reply was a shrug. "Go, then. I'll handle Riley and explain this to Matt."

"Thanks, Mom." I bent to give her a quick kiss.

"Francesca," she called as I jogged over to Charlie, "take care of your sister."

I raised a hand in acknowledgment. Charlie was standing next to the cruiser, huddled into her jacket.

"I'm not leaving unless Noah takes me with," she said.

I tipped my head, curious. "Why?"

"Because that baby is out there. Alone. He's already lost his mother. And his poor father . . ." she trailed off, looked away for a moment. "Stupid postpartum hormones," she said with a toss of her head. "I'd want someone to look for Rowan, if I couldn't. Don't you dare try to talk me out of it."

"Me? Hardly," I scoffed. "It's Noah you're going to have to convince, and I don't see that happening."

"Why not?"

"Because all he has to do is get in and drive away," I said. "Standing next to the passenger's door isn't really effective. You need more leverage."

I circled around to the front of the car, boosted myself onto the hood.

"Is that legal?" Charlie asked suspiciously. "Sitting on police property?"

"Probably not." The police came streaming out of Steven's house, Noah included. I patted the hood. "Let's find out, shall we?"

TWENTY-SEVEN

"Get off my car," Noah said a few moments later.

I didn't point out that we had spent plenty of time lying on the hood of his car when we were teenagers. Of course, that had been a rusted-out Chevy, not a police cruiser, but he'd never complained before.

"You'll need medical personnel on the scene," I said.

"We'll have an entire fleet of ambulances on-site," he said. "Besides, it's not my call. The FBI is going be running the search pattern, and neither of you are trained."

"You need more people," I said. "Henderson's is huge, and there are approximately eight million outbuildings, and they're all falling down. In fact, they were falling down a decade ago, and I doubt they'll be any better now."

"All the more reason to let me get to work," he said. "I'll do my best to keep you updated. Now go home."

I folded my arms across my chest. "Make me."

His hands flexed as if he was about to try but caught himself.

"Charlie," he said, obviously hoping to appeal to her better nature, "talk some sense into her."

We exchanged glances, and Charlie flipped her braid over her shoulder. "She is making sense. We know the area—both of us do."

"I know it better," I put in. "You didn't spend much time out there."

"Like you were around to know?" Ignoring my sputter of outrage, she returned to Noah. "We both know Henderson's. Wouldn't it be good to have people on the ground who are familiar with the terrain?"

"One of whom has medical training?" I added. "You know we're right."

He frowned. "Stay put."

I patted the car beneath me. "Bet on it."

He jogged back to one of the FBI agents, and they spoke for a few minutes. The other man glanced over at us, squinting through the increasingly heavy rain, and I lifted a hand in greeting. Charlie put up her hood.

Noah shook his head, and they continued speaking. Finally, they both approached.

"You volunteering to help in the search?" He stroked his mustache, considering.

"Yes, sir," Charlie said eagerly.

"Which one of you is the nurse?"

I raised my hand again.

"Which one of you found the body of the kidnapper?"

I kept my hand up.

He eyed me. "This isn't that, got it? You two help out today, you're just searching. The agents at the scene will direct you. If you find the baby, you start yelling—someone will hear you and come running. You will do exactly what my agents tell you at all times. You do otherwise, and I'll bring you up on federal obstruction charges."

"Yes, sir," we echoed.

He jerked a thumb at us. "Take 'em over, make sure they've got vests so nobody thinks they're the kidnapper and accidentally shoots them. It's on your head if they get in trouble, MacLean."

"They won't," he said, scowling at me.

The agent left, and Noah stared at us for a long minute. "Get. Off. My. Car."

We scrambled to obey.

"Sit in the back," he said. "Both of you. Hand to God, Frankie, if you give me the slightest hint of lip, I will leave you locked in there until the case is over, whether that's tonight or two weeks from now."

"Thank you" was all I said.

He shook his head and climbed into the driver's seat.

★   ★   ★

Henderson's farm was sprawling, acres and acres of overgrown fields and tumbledown buildings. In the cold gray rain, flashlights dancing across the grounds and across shed windows, it was nearly postapocalyptic.

"How long?" Noah asked tersely once we'd arrived. We were pulling on neon-yellow vests with reflective stripes, the same one cops wore during traffic duty. The word "POLICE" was stenciled front and back in large letters, presumably so the other agents didn't shoot us.

"We'll stay until we find him," I said, and Charlie nodded agreement.

"No," Noah replied. "How much time do we have? Trey's a baby; the temperature's dropping, and we don't know the last time he was fed. How long before . . ."

Next to me, Charlie made a noise of distress.

"I don't know," I said honestly. "There are too many factors in play. Standing around talking won't help, though."

"Got it." He led us over to a woman crouched in the back of a van, a lamp trained on a large map of the area. "Two more volunteers. Where do you want them?"

"The message said Henderson's," she replied, handing us heavy-duty flashlights. It wasn't full dark yet, but the storm had flattened what the daylight remained; everything looked murky, dirty, and ominous. "We're moving our way across the property, searching the buildings off the main routes first, working our way back to the far edges of the land."

"Why?" Charlie asked.

"The kidnapper would have wanted to make a quick getaway," she said patiently. "The longer he was here, the greater the risk of discovery. It makes sense he'd stay close to the main roads and stash the baby somewhere convenient. It's possible he even covered the terrain on foot."

Charlie frowned, as if she didn't believe the woman.

"It's standard procedure," the woman assured us.

"Nothing about this has been standard," I said slowly, picking up on Charlie's skepticism. "Charlie, when you were here, where were the parties held?"

She pursed her lips, trying to orient herself on the map. Then she tapped a cluster of worker's cottages on the southwest side. "Over here, mostly."

"Those are very isolated," said the woman. "It's unlikely he'd spend so much time on the property."

"That's why he'd go there. They're out of the way, so they're less likely to be seen."

"In fact," I said, "this part of the property backs up to this grove of maple trees—and on the other side of the grove is the county highway. It makes more sense that he'd pop across that way."

"There's no path through those trees," she argued. "No easy way to access it."

"Nothing marked, maybe. Kids cut through those woods all the time. Hunters too."

She studied the map. "We can reassign some people, I suppose."

"We can head out there now," I said. "Send the rest of the team when they're free."

"I'll take them," Noah said, and the woman nodded, already speaking into her walkie-talkie.

A short while later, the car bouncing and jolting over rutted pathways, we'd reached the cottages. Shacks, really—corrugated tin roofs and scrap lumber walls, windows busted out after years of teen parties.

"You two work together," Noah ordered as he let us out of the car. "No splitting up."

"We'll cover more ground separately," I argued.

"No lip," he said and fingered the handcuffs on his belt, intention clear. "Stay together, or you go back to the squad car."

"Together's good," Charlie said, and I nodded in agreement. I swung my backpack over my shoulder, and we set off toward the southwest while Noah took the southeast.

"Hard to believe anyone comes out here now," Charlie said as we began checking the shacks. The rain was falling steadily, and the rumble of thunder nearly obscured her words.

"It doesn't look like they do," I said. We'd inspected three of the shacks, and none of them showed any signs of recent use. The fourth had a pile of broken glass in the corner, old beer bottles tossed against the heavily graffitied wall, but there was no sign of a fire, inside or out. "Not much, anyway."

"You know what's crazy?" Charlie asked. "Mom had no idea about this place. Even back when we were kids."

"Well, she doesn't have any reason to think about it right now. Riley's still got a few years."

Charlie scowled at the notion. "That's not funny."

"It's kind of funny," I said. "You'll be telling her not to do something you totally did. Can't wait to see her face when she figures it out."

"Parents must know about this place now, don't they? That's probably why it isn't used as much."

"Kids still come out here," I replied. "But I don't think it's common knowledge. You'd have to be a local."

"A local from a long time ago," Charlie mused. She pulled out her phone, hunching over to shield the display from the rain. "Mom left me a voice mail."

"Go ahead," I told her. "Catch up when you're ready."

I thought back to the map the female agent had shown us. I knew those woods. So did Noah. Because while plenty of parties had happened in the worker cottages, we'd wanted more privacy. Deep within the maple grove was a small clearing with a sugaring cabin. Warmer, quieter, and sweetly scented from years of boiling sap, the sugarhouse was a closely guarded secret, even among my classmates. I hadn't seen it on the map, but if the killer had parked south of the dairy and come through the woods on foot, he might have stumbled across it.

"Back in a few," I called to Charlie through the open door of the cottage.

Brow furrowed, she nodded, barely glancing up while she listened to her phone.

TWENTY-EIGHT

The ground was covered with sodden maple leaves, their brilliant colors muted in the deepening darkness. I slogged through them, trying to remember the exact path to the sugarhouse. Overhead, the thunder rolled in a near-continuous pulse. The trees blocked some of the rain but didn't seem to cut the wind.

A flash of lightning overhead had me quickening my pace, relying on instinct more than vision to guide my feet.

Instinct. My instincts had warned me about something else earlier. Something about Jess. Dove Cottage. What was it?

Twenty yards ahead, behind a stand of old maples, stood the sugarhouse. A one-room wooden building with a tall peaked roof, vents on the top and along the sides. Remarkably, almost all of the windows were still intact. As I'd thought, almost nobody knew it was here.

I thought I heard a cry, but there was no way to know from here if it was Trey or simply the creaking of the trees in the wind.

I edged across the clearing, senses straining, hands shaking with cold and fear.

The wind picked up, and lightning ripped across the sky, making me flinch. A moment later, the door swung wide, and Steven Tibbs came out, his coat wrapped around a tiny squalling bundle.

He stopped short when he saw me. "Frankie?"

"Steven?" I took two steps forward, then stopped. "Is that Trey? Did you—?"

He blinked away rain. "I found him," he said, stumbling over the words. "I had a feeling."

"When did you get here? Shouldn't you be home, waiting for news?"

His mouth twisted. "Like I'd leave this to the police?"

"But how—?"

"I had a feeling," he repeated, louder this time. "There's a bond, you know. Between a parent and a child. A father and his son."

Training overtook bewilderment, and I snapped into action. "Is Trey okay?"

"He's perfect," Steven said, awkwardly jostling the screaming child.

"Let me take a look," I urged. "Make sure he's not dehydrated or suffering from hypothermia."

"He's perfect," he repeated. "It's a miracle, Frankie."

I wasn't about to argue. "Let me examine Trey. It'll take five minutes, and then we can get him to the hospital."

He stumbled backward. "They lost him once. I'm not risking it again."

"You want to make sure he's healthy, don't you?" I said, my voice soothing. "Five minutes. A quick exam. I've done a million of them, and you'll be right here. Then you can bring him home."

He shielded Trey as lightning crackled overhead, shadows lunging and flickering around us.

"Steven," I said, trying not to betray my nervousness, "the baby's getting soaked. It's not good for him; he won't be able to maintain his body temp. You want him to be warm, right?"

Wordlessly, he turned and went back inside the sugarhouse.

Once we were inside, I played my flashlight around the large square room. It looked much as I remembered it—metal sugaring vats and a boiler against one wall, taps and buckets hanging along another. Overhead was a vented cupola, and even now, the years-old scent of wood, sap, and syrup combined to turn the damp air sweet. A car seat waited in the center of the room, a shearling-lined bunting covering it, a battery-operated lantern sitting next to it. A few dirty diapers, neatly secured, had been tossed into the far corner. Next to the car seat were a jumble of empty bottles, and a pile of blankets lay on the floor. I spread them out and switched on the lantern, gesturing for Steven to set Trey down on the makeshift bed while I dumped my backpack on the floor.

"He's dressed for the weather, at least," I said, noting the polar fleece pajamas he was wearing. "Hello, sweetheart. Let's take a peek at you, hmn?"

The baby had stopped crying. He was quieter than I would have liked, drowsy with cold and hunger and the unique ability of newborns to sleep through distress. But his color seemed good, his pulse was strong, and he didn't appear to be suffering from hypothermia or dehydration. Steven hovered over me while I worked, saying nothing.

"He looks pretty good," I said. "We need to get him back right away. We have no idea how long it's been since the kidnapper left him here or how long it's been since he ate. His diaper's wet—that's a good sign—but I don't want to change him until we're someplace warmer." I zipped up the his pajamas, then swaddled him in several layers of blankets. "It's amazing he's doing so well. If he'd been out here even a few hours more . . . your timing was perfect."

"It's a miracle," Steven said yet again.

Something in his voice—confidence and certainty, instead of gratitude and relief—sent the back of my neck tingling again. "Two miracles in one lifetime," I said lightly, keeping a hand on Trey. "Lucky man."

He cocked his head, gave me his campaign smile. "What do you mean?"

"The fire, right? You got there at exactly the right time. If you hadn't gone to help your dad with inventory, who knows what might have happened?"

"Two miracles," he agreed.

I wasn't so sure anymore. According to my mom's breathless recap, the downtown fire had started in a trash can when a lit cigarette had been tossed atop a pile of old cleaning rags. They'd smoldered for hours, according to the fire marshal, before they caught fully and jumped to the building.

And Steven had been there. How fortunate, everyone had said, that he came along at exactly the right moment. According to Charlie, he'd been at the scene earlier. Early enough, in fact, that I couldn't help wondering if it was his cigarette that had started the fire in the first place—and when he'd returned and discovered the horrific fallout, he'd made the best of a bad situation.

I wondered if he'd done the same tonight.

I stood, hugging Trey close to my chest and swaying gently. "What gave you the idea to come out here? I didn't know anyone else knew this place existed."

Steven shrugged. "You and Noah MacLean weren't the only people to use it."

"No." My skin prickled a warning. "We weren't. Seems weird that an out-of-towner would, though."

His smile grew fixed. "What do you mean?"

"Well, Jess didn't grow up here. How would she have known about it?"

"Maybe her partner did."

"Maybe," I said softly, "but we haven't found any evidence she had a partner—not Josh Miller, not anyone."

"You haven't looked hard enough," he snapped. "She was working with someone. She colluded to steal my son."

I thought about Dove Cottage. The portable crib. The feeding supplies. The neat, freshly laundered piles of clothing. The baby name book.

Kate's baby name book.

"Trey is for Steven the third, isn't it?"

He nodded cautiously.

"Family tradition," I said, "like how Charlie and I have boys' nicknames. Was that always the plan?" *She stenciled his name on the wall,* Charlie had said.

"Of course. From the day we knew he was a boy." He held out his arms. "I'll take my son now."

I backed up a step. "So why'd Kate buy a baby name book?" *A monogrammed blanket.*

He opened his mouth, closed it again. Finally, he said, "I don't know what you mean."

"Jess had a baby name book with her." *A little rocking chair with his name painted on it.*

"She stole my son. Of course she'd give him a new name. She probably planned to change her own too."

"It wasn't her book. It was Kate's. She'd only bought it a few weeks ago."

Steven stuttered. "I don't—"

"It bothered me, that book, but I couldn't figure out why. And then it hit me. Kate didn't need a baby name book unless she'd decided to name him something else. But you would never have agreed to that."

He stared at me.

"Unless you weren't going to be around," I continued. "Unless Kate was planning to leave you. Here's what I think happened, Steven. She wanted to leave, for whatever reason. Maybe she didn't like being a politician's wife. Maybe she was bored. Maybe you'd done something unforgivable—cheated, maybe? We all know how politicians can be when it comes to interns. So soon before the election, it would be political suicide if she left you. Especially when you were running as a family man with family values. It's all about the optics, right? So instead, you hired Josh Miller to kill her."

A boom of thunder rattled the walls, and I clutched Trey tightly, putting more distance between us. Steven tracked my movements with an unblinking stare.

"He was only supposed to scare her," he said hoarsely. "Make her see that it was better to stay with me, where I could protect her. I never meant for them to be hurt. I loved her. I really did. I only wanted her to stay."

"You killed her."

"I wasn't driving!"

"You hired the guy who did it. How did it work, Steven? Did you pay Josh? Get him drugs? Or did you botch his case on purpose? Make sure it never got out of the grand jury?"

He flinched, and I knew I'd struck true.

"Josh came to the funeral to see you. To let you know he was still in town, and he had proof of your involvement."

"He was going to blackmail me." He sounded insulted.

"So you arranged a meeting at the junkyard to pay him off. And instead, you shot him."

"He deserved it. He was only supposed to scare Kate, not hurt her." He pressed a fist to his temple. "It wasn't supposed to be like this."

It was what Steven told me in the NICU, the night Kate died. He'd told me, but I hadn't understood. He hadn't been suffering from survivor's guilt. He'd been guilty. That's why he'd resigned himself to the police never catching the driver, why the initial search of his files hadn't flagged Josh's case. He couldn't afford a thorough investigation.

"No wonder Kate wanted to leave you," I said. "You're crooked."

"She was my *wife*. I loved her."

"She must have been scared out of her mind when Josh started following her. How did you explain it?"

"I told her I was being pressured to drop some of my cases, and the people involved were intimidating her to keep me in line. I said once I was elected, we'd be safe. She believed me."

"For a little while," I agreed. "But she was a smart woman. Somewhere along the line, she realized you were lying. That you were the one scaring her. Or maybe she stopped believing you would keep your promises." I shrugged. "Either way, it was time to go. She wouldn't have trusted the police, would she? If *you* were crooked, anyone could be. She needed some-one who would help her protect Trey no matter what. Who would be more loyal than Jess, considering everything Kate had done for her?"

It made sense now. Kate had planned to hide in Hale while she figured out how to expose Steven. She might not have trusted Steven's connections, but she'd want her own network, Jess included, close by. She'd waited until the cabin opened up, then waited a little longer, until Steven was busy with a campaign event. Storm or no storm, she'd had to leave that night or lose the chance of escape altogether. And Josh Miller had followed.

"If she'd listened . . ." Steven began.

"She'd what? Be alive? She's dead because you sent Josh after her. When Kate came into the ER that night, Jess knew what you'd done, and she knew nobody would believe her. You were the town hero, a DA, and you were crooked. She was a foster kid who'd been screwed over by the system again and again. What other choice did she have? Jess took Trey to protect him from you, because she'd grown up with a monster and couldn't imagine letting it happen to the child of the woman who'd saved her."

A change settled over Steven's features, a hardening. A different Steven, one I hadn't seen before.

"Give me my son, Frankie."

"How did you figure it out?" I asked. Best to keep him talking, give the other searchers time to reach us. "Kate worked so hard to keep her connection to Jess a secret."

"I didn't, at first. She never came near Trey while I was in the NICU. I'd known Kate had stayed in touch with some of her clients, but I'd never paid much attention. Still, when the police said it was a former case, I knew exactly where to get the information. I asked to clean out her office and took the files I needed. The trip to Hale was an annual tradition for those kids, organized by Kate. I hadn't known where it was, but Kate kept excellent records."

I thought about the chatty woman at the rental office. Someone had called, she'd said, asking about wait lists. "You figured out where Jess was, and then you shot her."

"I was protecting my son. There's a case for self-defense, you know. I was afraid she'd hurt him, and I have a constitutional right to defend myself and my child."

He was doing it again, the rehearsing. Practicing his story the way he had in the NICU that first night, when he'd told me how he wanted to honor Kate.

Thinking of it, I nearly gagged.

"You took him back," I said slowly, trying to fit it all together, trying to buy myself some time. I glanced around the sugarhouse, saw the propane heater he'd used to keep the room warm, saw the empty bottles he'd fed Trey and the pile of dirty diapers. "You've been hiding out here since then, leaving him for a few hours, coming back to check on him. Didn't Ted notice? Or has he been in on it all along?"

"If it's not a poll question or a lead story, Ted doesn't care what I do. He's had plenty of practice looking the other way. Besides," he added, "it's only been a day. I made sure Trey was warm. That he was fed."

All this time, we'd assumed Jess had snapped because of Kate's death. But it was Steven who'd gone off the deep end. The guilt must have caused some sort of mental break for him to risk his son's life like this.

"He's an infant, not a houseplant." I was shaking now, not from cold or fear, but from anger. "He's a newborn baby, and you left him here." I paused. "You left him here so you could find him. Because it would make a great headline. You even posted that message on the website, didn't you, so the news would break while you were on camera. How did you—?"

He held up his phone. "Do you know how easy it is to be anonymous on the Internet? There are entire websites meant to hide your identity. It's dangerous, really," he added with a grin. "Someone should make a law about it."

He'd checked his phone right before he'd stepped up to the podium, I remembered now. He'd sent the message, then given the press conference of his career. He'd orchestrated it perfectly. He was testing out sound bites. Just like with the fire, all those years ago, he'd taken a disaster of his own making and turned it into an opportunity. No wonder he'd sounded so odd when I arrived.

I could already picture it: Steven, emerging from the woods in the storm, triumphantly holding his son. It would be the front-page story of every newspaper in the country, the cover of every magazine. He'd sail into office on a tide of sentiment, and nobody would realize their hero was actually the villain.

Nobody but me.

"Give me my son," he said again, and from the depths of his parka, he pulled a gun. "I don't want to shoot you, Frankie. I'm not a killer. I'm really not. I'm just trying to protect my family."

"By killing people. By killing your *wife*," I said and shrank at the anger that crossed his face.

"I never meant for that to happen." His hand shook, the gun barrel gleaming in the artificial glow of the lantern. "I loved Kate."

"I know," I said quickly, "but you're putting Trey at risk now. Do you really want to do that?"

"You're not leaving me any choice."

"There's always a choice," I said gently. The baby began to fuss, and I swayed from side to side. "Put the gun away, Steven. You could hurt Trey."

"You're upsetting him."

"He's wet," I said, "and hungry. We should get him to the hospital."

"Hand him over."

"So you can shoot me? The woods are filled with FBI agents and cops. They're going to hear the shot, and what will you tell them?"

He thrust his chin out, a show of bravado belied by his trembling. "I'll tell them we ran across the kidnapper together. He shot you while I went for Trey. You'll be a hero."

"I'll be dead. And nobody's going to believe you."

"What do you expect me to do?" he shouted.

"Give yourself up," I said. "Tell your story. Make them understand it was an accident, that you were only trying to protect your family."

Did I believe that would fly? Not for a second. But I didn't need to—I only needed Steven to believe long enough to get Trey to safety. Help wasn't coming, but if I could circle around to the door, maybe we could make a run for it. Steven wouldn't shoot me if I was holding his son, would he? I was no longer sure.

"You're a good man," I said. "If you shoot me, people won't see that. They won't understand. You'll lose Trey forever."

"I'm going to lose him anyway." He sagged as if exhausted.

"You're his father. They'll take that into account. But if you pull that trigger, you won't be able to cover it up or explain it away. The only way to help Trey now is to be honest."

"I can't," he said brokenly and lifted the gun. But this time, he didn't point it at me. He pointed it at himself.

"Steven, please put the gun down. You want to protect Trey, don't you? If you do this, you'll *hurt* him." Inspiration struck, sudden and desperate. "A gunshot this close would damage his eardrums. Would you do that to him? After everything, would you hurt him now?"

He paused, lowering the gun and letting it dangle from his fingers. A flicker of movement near the door caught my eye.

"Just set it down," I said soothingly. "Kick it over to the corner. Everything's going to be okay."

"You'll come with me?" he said, like a lost child.

"We'll walk out together."

"Can I hold him?" Steven asked, still clutching the gun, and I froze.

Kate hadn't died because Steven was concerned about his son—he was concerned about himself. His image, his status, his future. I pictured Kate in the ER, the mama bear charm on her wrist. I saw Jess, bleeding to death in a bathtub. Those women had given their lives to protect this baby. Steven had done nothing but lie, hurt, and manipulate, all in the name of protecting himself.

"Frankie. *Please*," he said, but it wasn't sorrow I heard in his voice. It was another manipulation.

Trey began to cry in earnest, and I pressed a kiss against his forehead.

"Frankie," he repeated as the gun came up again. "Give me my son."

"Drop it, Steven," came Noah's voice. "Drop it right now, or I will drop you."

My gaze flew to the doorway where Noah stood, half hidden in the shadows.

"Noah," Steven said. "You don't—"

"Shut your mouth and drop the gun." His tone was steely as he stepped inside. "Now!"

Wearily, as if the effort of holding it had been too much, Steven let the gun slip to the floor with a crash. Noah quickly kicked it aside. I flinched at the noise and shushed Trey, my own breath shuddering.

"On your knees. Hands above your head," Noah growled. "You've seen it enough times, you should know the drill."

Steven cast me a pleading look but obeyed, motionless as Noah slapped cuffs on him and read the Miranda rights.

"You okay, Frankie?"

"We're fine," I said, though my voice was shaky. "Trey needs to get to the hospital."

"Done," Noah said and bent his head to radio in our status, requesting an ambulance and a squad car meet us at the highway to spare us the long walk through the woods.

Steven's eyes were wet. "Please let me hold my boy. One more time."

I stared at him. "What was it that Kate had on you, Steven? I mean, other than the fact that you're a power-hungry lunatic. Were you cheating on her? Throwing cases? Why didn't she just turn you in? Why would she run?"

"Leave it," said Noah. I glanced at him in surprise.

"He killed her," I said. "He might not have been driving the car, but it was his idea."

"I figured," he said. "Let's focus on Trey for now."

We started toward the road, Noah marching Steven ahead of him, the flashlight illuminating a narrow path. Me clutching Trey with one hand, the lantern in the other, keeping pace as best I could.

"Kate was going to disappear," I insisted as we picked our way through the forest, the rain hammering down. "She didn't need to. The press would have listened to her. Why not go public?"

Neither man replied.

I'd seen it before, of course: women who didn't think they'd be believed. Women who came to the ER battered and bloody, insisting they'd walked into a wall or fallen down the basement stairs while carrying a load of laundry. We always offered to connect them to the police, to domestic violence agencies. Some of them took us up on it. Most didn't. The ones who most vehemently denied our help, strangely enough, were the wives of cops.

Kate wasn't being abused. Steven wasn't a cop. But he was a powerful man who had the ear of the police. He'd have even more ears, even more powerful friends, if he won the election.

"She was afraid," I said to Steven. "She was afraid you might . . . what? Hurt her? Make her disappear another way? But the police . . ."

He smiled slyly, looked over his shoulder at Noah. "I'm not really the person you should ask about the police, am I?"

Steven stumbled and fell, face first, cursing and spitting out leaves. I looked at Noah. "What—?"

"Rough terrain," he said shortly, hauling Steven up and shoving him forward. "Watch your step, Steven, instead of running your mouth."

Ahead of us, the ambulance was visible through the trees, lights flashing like strobes. Noah's face was strangely miserable. "Go on ahead," he said, nudging me. "Get that baby out of the weather."

I nodded and picked up the pace, calling to the paramedics, relief overtaking me. But beneath it all was a low insistent pulse of dread.

TWENTY-NINE

I rode in the ambulance with the baby, which meant we were greeted by none other than Paul Costello.

"I'm going to start banning you from the ER unless it's your shift," he grumbled as I handed over a squalling, red-faced Trey. "Every time you walk in those doors, disaster follows."

"Maybe I'm following the disaster," I said, scrubbing my hands, the tepid water strangely hot on my icy skin. "Cleaning it up."

"Maybe you *are* the disaster," I thought I heard him say, but he was already examining the baby, dictating to me as if I was on duty.

The on-call pediatrician arrived, but Costello waved him off. "We're nearly done. Rustle up some formula—Alejandro knows where it is."

I moved toward the door, assuming the order was for me. Instead, he said, "Stapleton, you brought this kid in, you can stick with him until he's back upstairs. Play mom."

He finished examining Trey and turned to me, balancing him easily in one arm.

"You look like a drowned rat," he said, taking in my soggy and bedraggled state.

"Thanks. I was going to find a dry pair of scrubs, but the attending wouldn't let me leave."

"Bring her some towels," he said to Esme, who had been hovering nearby.

"You okay?" he asked when she was gone.

"Other than looking like a drowned rat, sure. Not a scratch on me."

He eyed me. "Yeah. But are you okay?"

Compartmentalization had always served me well. It allowed me to tuck away the repercussions of one tragedy so I could focus on the next. But from the minute Kate Tibbs had come into the ER, I'd been unable to look away, unable to move on. I'd been caught up in their tragedy—and had almost become another victim. But now it was behind me. Justice would be served. Steven would go to jail. Trey would grow up without parents; Jess's brothers would grow up without their sister. And I would move on—a luxury, I realized, I nearly hadn't been granted.

"I will be," I said, meeting his gaze steadily.

He nodded once. "Sounds like things got dicey out there. Nice work protecting this little guy."

"Thanks," I said, marveling at the sight of Costello holding a baby. He looked almost human.

"That's the thing about being a parent," he said, pretending to examine Trey's hands. "You never stop wanting to protect them, no matter how old they get. You think, 'If I can keep everything under control forever, they'll never get hurt.'"

"I'm not sure it works that way," I said. "You can't control the entire world."

"No," he agreed, "but you can't blame a guy for trying."

It was as close to an apology for my interference with Meg as I was likely to get.

Esme brought in a stack of towels, and Costello placed the baby in the isolette. "Change clothes, get him back up to the NICU, and get out. You're dripping on my exam room."

★   ★   ★

"Ms. Fisher wants to see you in her office," said one of the NICU nurses once Trey had been safely transferred back to the ward. Still wearing the scrubs I'd changed into, with my hair towel-dried but still tangled, I made my way downstairs, knocking on the now-familiar door.

"Come on back, Frankie," Grace called. "Please shut the door behind you."

I wasn't surprised to see her, as composed as always, behind the desk with teacup in hand.

But Norris Mackie in one of the ivory brocade armchairs threw me.

"Tea?" Grace asked, already pouring out a cup.

I accepted it gratefully, warming my chilled hands on the thin china. I didn't think I'd feel warm for a long time to come.

The silence stretched out while we all eyed each other, judging the tension, the currents, the unstated questions. Finally, I spoke.

"You didn't kill Kate Tibbs."

"No, miss, I did not," Mackie said sternly.

"I apologize." I bowed my head. "I jumped to conclusions."

"That you did." He sounded a lot like my middle school principal.

Nettled, I took a sip of tea before replying. "You did lie about leaving the fundraiser, though."

He sighed deeply, exchanged a look with Grace.

"My heart . . ." he said slowly.

If I'd thought this conversation couldn't get any more awkward, I was wrong. I had no intention of sitting through these two exchanging endearments. The day had been much too long for that kind of nonsense.

Stiffly, I said, "Your personal life is your business. Both of your personal lives, I mean. I'm not here to judge."

Grace burst out laughing.

"Oh, Frankie, I appreciate your discretion, but you misunderstand. Norris's heart . . . that's why he left. We're not . . ." She fell into another fit of laughter.

I twisted to face Norris, who was chuckling under his breath.

His labored breath.

The chuckle turned into a cough.

I glanced at his feet, swollen in their polished shoes. Remembered his stiff, careful steps at the office, not quite steady.

"Congestive heart failure." It wasn't a question. "How far advanced?"

"Far enough that I don't care to waste my time," he replied, wheezing slightly. "Fundraisers, parties, all that nonsense. They wear me out, and what good do they do?"

"They keep you in office," Grace chided. "But I remember enough nursing that I know when he needs to rest. Norris wasn't feeling well, so he went up to his hotel room before anyone could ask questions."

"Why not just say so?" I asked.

"When I'm campaigning against a spirited young man promising strong tomorrows? Raise the question of my health, and I might as well hoist a white flag along with it."

"But . . . it's like you said. Why waste your time, if you know there's not much left?"

"I don't consider my time in office a waste," he said. "But it's hard. I've always had my eye on the next election, always hedged my bets, always played it safe. That time's over. I want one more term, just one. I want the chance to really fight for what I believe in. I want to leave a legacy."

"Well," I said, "it looks like you're going to get your chance, sir."

He dipped his chin. "Thanks to you."

"I don't know about that. But . . ." I watched the rise and fall of his chest, heard the rattling breath. I looked at Grace Fisher, her mouth tight with sorrow. "Don't waste it, okay?"

★　　★　　★

When I left Grace's office, Deputy Anderson was waiting for me in the hall, clutching his ever-present notepad along with the backpack I'd left in the cabin. "Deputy MacLean radioed over, ma'am. I'm supposed to drive you home and get your statement."

"Can I give my statement to Deputy MacLean? I had some questions for him."

"He said to tell you he has a stack of paperwork taller than you to finish, and he'll find you later."

I bit my lip, the pang of disappointment surprisingly sharp. Inside the backpack, my phone rang. I fished it out, wincing at the number of voice mails.

"Sorry," I said. "It's my sister. I accidentally left her at the search site. She's probably calling to . . . hold on."

I didn't bother with a greeting. "I'm sorry! We found Trey and we're—"

"Where are you?" she demanded, voice an octave too high.

"The hospital," I said. "Someone was supposed to fill you in."

"All I know is that they found the baby, and Steven was arrested. Whatever."

"*Whatever*? Steven's—"

She cut me off. "I don't care. Riley's missing."

I froze.

"Did you hear me? She's *gone*. Matt said Riley was in a snit all day, but he dropped her off at the chili fundraiser on his way to the hospital, and according to Mom, she disappeared. We've searched the church, we've checked the house from top to bottom, and we've called all her friends. Nobody's seen her. She's gone, Frankie. What if she was kidnapped too? What if Steven took her?"

For once, I could offer reassurance. "Steven's in custody. He didn't take Riley."

She drew in a shaky breath, tried unsuccessfully to mask her panic. "You don't know that! What if he's hidden her somewhere, same as he did with Trey?"

"I really don't think . . ."

"My daughter is *missing*," she said, her voice breaking. "You need to call Noah. Maybe they can get the searchers back out to Henderson's. He knows Riley, and he'll listen to you. Call him right now."

Noah listened to everyone. It was part of why Riley was so taken with him. Even in the middle of an investigation, he'd taken the time to talk to her, unfazed by her grumpy mood.

Matt said she'd been in a snit all day too.

She'd been in a snit a lot lately. I pictured Riley, standing in the doorway, listening to me talk about moving out, refusing my hug. Riley, faking sick, falling asleep in class, listless and surly every morning I'd come home from work.

Riley's snits were because of *me*. Or rather, my absence.

"I know where she is. It's not Steven, I swear. She's safe."

"What? Where? How do you know?"

"Instinct. Deputy Anderson's going to drive me to her right now." Travis stopped pretending like he wasn't eavesdropping and nodded eagerly. "I'll text you as soon as I've got her."

"A text?" she shrieked.

"Plus she'll call you herself," I said. "Give me fifteen minutes."

"Do you promise?" she demanded. "Frankie, where is my child?"

Rather than answer, I hung up the phone and turned to Travis. "How fast can you get me downtown?"

"Your statement . . ." he said, looking torn.

"Travis, do you really want to tell Noah MacLean that you couldn't help locate a missing child because you're worried about paperwork?"

"No, ma'am," he said, and we headed for the car.

THIRTY

"You can drop me off here," I said when we pulled up in front of the store. "Tell Noah I'll be around tomorrow if he wants to grab my statement then."

"I should come inside with you," Travis said. "Last time I was here, it was a crime scene."

"It's not a crime scene. Not until my sister gets here, anyway," I assured him and climbed out of the squad car.

It was easy enough to let myself in the back door, opening it slowly enough to avoid the usual squeak. The alarm had been deactivated—for once, that was a good sign.

The store was dark; only the light from the streetlamps outside pierced the gloom.

I stood in the silence until my eyes adjusted, worry niggling at me. Had I misjudged? Was Riley truly missing?

But as I shuffled past the back counter, I spotted her, curled on the floor in front of the stairwell, head pillowed on her backpack, one of the buffalo-check blankets from our display wrapped around her. The cat, looking bedraggled as I felt, sat nearby, washing its face.

Mindful of Charlie's panic, I sent a text promising we would call in a little bit. Then I knelt and jostled Riley's shoulder. "Hey, kiddo. Rise and shine."

She bolted upright, and the cat disappeared down one of the aisles.

"Aunt Frankie?"

"You sleepwalking these days? We'll have to start tying you to the bed."

She scowled at me. "I was running away, not sleepwalking."

"What a relief. I'd hate to see you trying to cross Center Street in your sleep." Admittedly, there wasn't that much traffic down Center Street even on a busy day. "What are you doing here?"

"Mom and Daddy were talking about you moving out because the house was too small for all of us. And you and Deputy Noah were saying that you were going to leave."

"You were eavesdropping?" She nodded. "You get that from your mom, you know. But that's not all you've been listening in on, is it?"

She looked away, gaze skittering around the darkened store.

"Did you know Grandma doesn't listen to her emergency scanner anymore? She says they're too careful about what they say over the radio, so there's no point in listening."

"That's not true," Riley protested. "They still . . ."

"They still tell you what calls are going to the hospital, don't they?"

She scowled.

"You've been listening to the scanner after everyone goes to bed, haven't you? That's why it's turned on in the mornings. And why you've been so sleepy."

Her eyes filled, shiny even in the dim light. "I don't do it every night."

"No," I agreed, smoothing her hair from her face, keeping my tone gentle. "Just on the nights I'm at work."

Which explained why she was only grumpy on the mornings after my shift.

Her tears spilled over. "I wanted to know what you were doing. I miss you."

"Oh, Riley." I wrapped my arms around her and squeezed, envisioning her skinny little form hunched over the radio, the volume turned low so she wouldn't wake the rest of the family, desperate to maintain a connection with me. "I miss you too. Coming home to you is the best part of the day. But you can't stay up all night, sweetie."

"I know," she said, her voice muffled against my shoulder. "That's why I decided to move in with you. The house will have room for Rowan when she comes home, and you wouldn't be lonely."

"You decided to do this without telling your parents or Grandma?"

"Mom was out with you, Daddy was with Rowan, and Grandma was busy handing out chili." She frowned. "Everyone has something to do except me. Everyone has someone to hang out with except me."

"I see."

"I don't take up that much space," she added. "I only brought one backpack, because you have a lot of stuff."

"Riley," I said, "it's true that I was thinking about moving in here. But not because of you."

She lifted a shoulder, chin wobbling. "Then why?"

"Because . . . you know how Rowan's crib used to be yours?"

She nodded.

"You grew out of it, didn't you? If you tried to sleep in there now, your feet would stick out through the bars, and your arms would be all squinched. You're too big for it. So you got the top bunk, and that fits a lot better, right?"

"You fit in the bottom bunk," she protested.

"I know, but living in the same house I did when I was a kid . . . it makes me feel like a kid. And I'm not one anymore. I've outgrown that house."

"This one's smaller," she said.

"It is. It shouldn't fit me, but I think it might."

She shook her head, vehement despite her drowsiness. "I want to move in with you."

"Yeah? How come?"

"Because you're fun. We can do stuff together. You can help me with my homework."

"Your mom and dad would miss you."

"No, they wouldn't. They have Rowan."

"Rowan's not you," I said. "She can't talk, she can't play soccer, she won't even be able to taste-test cookies for, like, a year. They need you around."

"So do you."

I sighed. "That's true. You'll have to visit a lot, which won't be a problem since you obviously feel comfortable walking here by yourself. And this way we can have actual sleepovers. With movies, and popcorn, and cookie dough."

"Mom says it's not safe to eat raw cookie dough."

"That's why we'll save it for the sleepover. My house, my rules."

She considered this, wiped her nose on her sleeve. "Can I stay tonight?"

I nearly blurted yes, then thought better of it. "Let's call your mom and ask. She's pretty worried."

"She probably didn't notice I was gone," Riley grumbled. I showed her my phone.

"See all those missed calls? She noticed. She's worried sick."

"She's going to be mad, isn't she?"

I helped her up, feeling a million years old. "Oh, yeah. No getting around that."

"Can't you call her?"

"I'm not the one who ran away," I said. "Get it over with, and then I've got an idea."

Glumly, she took the phone from my hand. While she wandered the store, her voice small and apologetic, I shucked off my coat and turned on the lights.

She handed me the phone, head bent.

"You knew she was there?" Charlie asked, her voice clogged with tears.

"I had a feeling. Can she stay over?"

"She ran away, Frankie. We shouldn't reward her with a sleepover."

"She's feeling neglected, which is partly my fault. This is more in the line of an apology, not a reward."

"I want her back here bright and early tomorrow," Charlie said with a sniffle.

"Why not make her open the store?" I suggested.

"Because she's eight."

"So? We did it when we were her age."

"With help," she reminded me.

"Well, I am going to be living right upstairs. Riley and I will open. You can come by and dispense justice after breakfast."

Charlie sighed. "I'm letting it slide. This time."

We hung up, and I turned to find Riley wiping her eyes—and nose—on her shirt sleeve again. "First things first," I said. "Tea. And a tissue."

We trooped upstairs, got provisions, and just as Riley was burrowing into the couch, I jerked a thumb at the door. "Come on, you."

"You said I could stay!"

"Yeah, but there's something we need to do."

Downstairs, I led her behind the counter. "Your mom let you work this machine yet?"

"Mom doesn't let me run any of the machines."

Somehow I managed not to roll my eyes. "This one is a little tricky, but you might as well start learning. Step one: get a key."

I pulled out the oversized brass key that opened the door to the stairwell. "Step two: get a blank. This one's big, so we need a specialty blank."

I walked her through the process, relishing the feel of her hand beneath mine as we cut the new key, breathing in the familiar scent of hot metal. When it was done, I held it up to the light, brushed off the brass shavings. "Looks good, right?"

She took it from me and mimicked the gesture, face solemn. Then she nodded approval.

"Try it out," I instructed her. While she fitted it in the lock and twisted, squeaking in triumph when it worked, I cut a length of ball chain.

"Excellent," I said when she returned, face flushed with pride. Carefully, I threaded the key onto the chain.

"What are you going to do with it?" she asked.

"Nothing." I held it out to her, the key swinging like a pendulum. "It's yours."

Eyes shining, she breathed, "Mine?"

"You're welcome here whenever you like," I said. "This way, even if I'm at the hospital overnight, you can still get inside. But—" She made a grab for the key, and I lifted it out of reach. "You have to promise that you always tell somebody at home. No more running away."

If the words sounded slightly hypocritical to my ears, so be it.

"Promise?" I asked.

"Promise," Riley said.

"Good. Now time for bed." I nudged her up the stairs. "You're opening tomorrow."

THIRTY-ONE

Riley passed out in the back bedroom almost immediately. I should have followed suit, but sleep proved elusive. Finally, I gave up and tiptoed into the kitchen for a fresh cup of tea and slightly stale doughnuts.

Where would Trey go now? I wondered. And how would his new family, whoever they were, explain this to him someday?

I looked around the tiny apartment, overflowing with everything I'd brought back from Chicago, despite my attempt to neatly arrange the boxes. The prospect of maneuvering around them for the next three months did not appeal to me. I could imagine all the bruises on my shins from knocking into boxes, the coffee I'd splash down my shirt when I tripped. I'd be as much of a disaster as Costello had suggested. Maybe it was time to find a home for everything, including myself.

No more running away, I'd told Riley. I should heed my own advice.

I'd managed to unearth a fresh set of sheets and a spaghetti strainer when my phone chimed with a text message.

Noah. *You awake?*

No, I typed back.

Light's on.

I have company. There. Let him wonder.

Riley's not company.

I sighed. No secrets in Stillwater. Although Noah, it seemed, was harboring some of his own.

The realization was enough to send me downstairs in my pajamas, throwing on the heavy fisherman's knit cardigan that had been my father's. I went up on tiptoe to peek out the back door. Noah was leaning against the porch railing, rumpled and gray with fatigue.

"Please tell me you didn't come here for my statement," I said, pulling him inside. "It's the middle of the night."

He lifted a shoulder, let it drop, and the weariness in the gesture made my heart ache.

"First thing in the morning, I'll go to the station. Charlie can cover the store. You need sleep."

He tugged on a lock of my hair. "That your professional opinion?"

I closed my hand over his. "Yes."

"Gotta finish it." He handed me a legal pad and a pen. "Get it all down, Frankie, everything that happened from the moment you left me at the scene. You and Charlie, why you split up, what you saw, everything Steven said, right up until I arrived."

With a sigh, I brought him upstairs, showed him Riley sleeping in the bedroom, and then pointed to the couch. "Will you nap while I do it?"

"No. But I'll take a cup of coffee."

"It would be criminal to give you caffeine now," I said. "At least rest your eyes."

He nodded, and within minutes his breathing had evened out. The words came faster as I moved deeper into the story, details returning in full force, my hand moving quickly over the page. I'd written plenty of notes and reports in the ER, but rarely did I have cause to tell an entire story. It was harder, this way, to compartmentalize. To lock away the fear and dread, to focus on the bare facts of what had happened. The emotions were interwoven with the words, impressions melding with events.

It was morning by the time I got to our trip through the woods. My hand slowed.

Steven had been about to tell me something. I'd asked why Kate hadn't simply gone to the police, and Steven's expression had turned amused. Coy, almost. He'd given Noah a look just before answering me.

He'd never answered, though. He'd tripped, and Noah had sent me ahead to the ambulance with Trey.

Now I wondered if he'd really tripped at all.

Noah had never been anything but forthright with me from the first day I met him. Maybe my impression was wrong. I'd been exhausted, it had been dark, my adrenaline spiking and my attention focused on Trey. It was possible I'd misinterpreted.

One way to find out.

I nudged Noah, and he came awake instantly, head snapping up and scanning the room. "Done?"

"Almost." I kept my voice low and casual, like I was idly reminiscing. "Do you remember me asking Steven about why Kate didn't turn him in? In the woods, on the way to the ambulance?"

He shifted, stretched, but there was a restlessness in the movement that made my stomach tighten. "I remember."

"Steven tripped, I think."

"Yeah."

"He did trip, didn't he? There must have been a tree root?"
Noah didn't reply, just watched me, still and quiet.

"He never answered my question," I pressed. "About why
Kate didn't go to the police."

"Didn't he?" Noah said, so off-handedly that my eyes
narrowed.

"No. He didn't. Which seems weird to me. What do you
think?"

He studied me, the shadows under his eyes deepening. "I
think it's fine. All we need in the statement is what happened
up to the point that I walked in. You don't need to worry
about anything after that." Noah slid the paper away from me,
scanned it. "That's good. I'll type it up at the station, have you
sign that one to make it official."

"What about Steven?"

"He confessed. We searched his house, found the proof
he'd taken off Josh—Kate's schedule and license plate, written
on the back of a campaign flyer. There's blood on the paper."

"The campaign hands out those brochures like candy," I
said. "Will it hold up in court?"

"Probably not. But it's politics, and in the court of public opinion . . . Steven's done. I'm guessing he'll try to cut a
deal." He stood, looked about as if he couldn't quite figure
out where he was.

"You did good," I reminded him. "You got justice for
Kate. If you hadn't come along when you did . . ."

"You had Steven under control," Noah said, and I wanted
to believe him.

So I did. About this, anyway.

"There are more, aren't there?"

He began to prowl the room. "More what?"

"More people involved." I'd started to think about it as I wrote my report. Steven hadn't committed his crimes in a vacuum. Other people must have participated. They'd tipped him off, eased his way, backed him in his run for Congress. "Like Ted Sullivan."

"As far as I can tell," Noah said, "Ted is an opportunistic sleazebag, but he wasn't involved in Kate's death."

"Okay, not Ted. But Kate didn't trust anyone to help her. She didn't go to a single person in the sheriff's department, the district attorney's office, or the state police. I assumed it was because she didn't think she could trust anyone. Now I'm wondering if she *knew* she couldn't. I think Kate realized that Steven wasn't the only person involved in whatever corruption she'd uncovered."

Noah stopped pacing as I continued. "Considering the level Steven was operating at, it seems likely there were plenty of people in other departments—the sheriff's department, for example—who were just as corrupt."

"Seems logical," he agreed, not quite looking at me.

"Seems dangerous," I said. "Especially if a member of that department began to suspect his colleagues were not on the up-and-up. He might start to feel like he can't trust people there."

Noah looked out the window, studying the blue sky dawning over Stillwater.

"He might even start to investigate on his own," I added.

"He might," Noah said. "That sort of investigation would be dangerous, particularly for the people around him. The ones he trusts. He might warn them off."

"They might not listen," I said, my throat suddenly dry. "Guess it's good it's all hypothetical, huh?"

"Guess so," he echoed.

I crossed the room to stand next to him, my shoulder brushing his arm. After a moment, I slipped my hand into his and squeezed.

"You're a good cop, Noah MacLean. A good man."

After a moment, he squeezed back. "I'm trying."

"I'm glad."

Trying to lighten the mood, I turned and waved my free hand at the cluttered apartment. "What do you think of my new digs?"

His eyebrows lifted. "Not bad. A little cluttered."

"A small price to pay for more privacy."

"Even with your roommate?"

"Even so." I paused. "It's good to be home, you know. I just couldn't live *at* home."

"Are you home, then? For good?"

A familiar fluttering began, directly behind my sternum. *For good* was another way of saying *forever*.

"For as long as I need to be," I said, trying to keep the fluttering under control. It was as close to the truth as I could come, as much of a promise as I could make to Noah or anyone else—including myself.

The corner of Noah's mouth curved upward, and he laced his fingers with mine. "Sounds like a start."

ACKNOWLEDGMENTS

Once again, I owe a tremendous debt of gratitude to my nursing experts: Katt Solano, who never lost patience while (repeatedly) explaining the basics of maternal-fetal medicine; Faye Collins, who generously answered eight million questions about how emergency rooms work; and my baby sister, Kris, who, in between saving lives and working on her doctorate, walked me through the finer points of hospital procedures in every department. (She also gave me the world's cutest nephew, because she's an overachiever.) Thank you, ladies, for your kindness, your knowledge, and the work you do every day. If there are medical mistakes in these pages, the fault is entirely mine.

Book people are the best people, and library people are the best kind of book people. Lauren Hilty is proof of that. She and the rest of the staff at the Grayslake Library cheered me on and made sure there was always a study room open. Andrea Larson and the rest of the Cook Library team welcomed me into their ranks and fed me cake; Marla Littlefield provided HR expertise; Aarin Olson explained the art of "accidental" fires.

I am forever grateful to Ryann Murphy, Melanie Bruce, Heather Marshall, Shannyn Schroeder, and Stacey Kade for their compassion and wisdom, and to Melonie Johnson and Clara Kensie for their constant encouragement and insight. Were it not for Lynne Hartzer, Loretta Nyhan, and Eliza Butler, this book wouldn't exist. Thank you, ladies, for being both an anchor and a beacon, and most of all a lifeline.

Thanks to Joanna Volpe, fearless leader and big dreamer, for all that you do—and for making me believe those big dreams too. I'm indebted to the entire team at New Leaf Literary and Media, including Kathleen Ortiz, Mia Roman, Pouya Shabazian, Devin Ross, Jackie Lindert, and especially Danielle Barthel, for always going above and beyond the call of duty. I am indebted to the team at Crooked Lane Books, including Dan Weiss, Matt Martz, Anne Brewer, Sarah Poppe, and Jenny Chen (who has the fastest response time of anyone in publishing), for giving Frankie such a good home. Thanks, too, to Dana Kaye and Julia Borcherts, wizards of publicity and all-around excellent people.

I am astonishingly lucky to have parents like mine: smart, good-hearted, supportive, and loving. What a tremendous example you've set—and how high a bar. Thank you for every single thing you do, for all of us. And thanks to Kris and JT, for lots of things—love, support, laughter—but especially for granting me unlimited nephew-snuggling privileges.

Finally, because I am the kind of girl who saves the best for last, I couldn't do this, or anything else, without the patience and encouragement of my family: my brilliant, beautiful children and Danny—best husband, best friend, best person I know. You are my heart and my home.